If It Kills Me

Phillip put his hand on Roz's shoulder. She rolled over enough to look into his brown eyes.

He couldn't have been more handsome. And this man was her intended husband.

A shiver ran through her and settled in her most private places. She couldn't tell if the feeling had any part of love in it. Definitely, it felt like lust. She wanted this man to husband her and she didn't want to wait much longer.

Why am I having these lusty thoughts? Not a good time to flake out. Not a good time at all.

After a few moments, she decided that maybe this feeling, these thoughts, were a result of all the fear, the danger, she'd gone through. Had she gotten fed up with being every evil person's toy to be pushed, mashed and shoved around? Maybe she was just angry.

She thought about it.

All of us ought to get mad.

I ought to be furious. They could murder me before sunset. Only right to get what little pleasure I can out of this situation.

She made sure she couldn't be seen over the rise. Then she took Phillip's hands in her own. "I love you, my heart."

"You, who were born to luxury. You, who were kidnapped and came to a land where life is hard. You get chased by thieves and looters."

Roz nodded.

"You tell me that you love me. You know I can't ever take you out of this misery by my own actions. And you love me?"

"I love you, Phillip." The heat inside her flared and her lips demanded kissing, serious kissing.

Other Works From The Pen Of
Mona Jean Reed

Reclaiming Little Marty—February, 2010
Snared—September, 2013

Wings

IF IT KILLS ME

Mona Jean Reed

A Wings ePress, Inc.

Suspense Novel

Wings ePress, Inc.

Edited by: Jeanne Smith
Copy Edited by: Joan Powell
Senior Editor: Jeanne Smith
Executive Editor: Marilyn Kapp
Cover Artist:

All rights reserved

Names, characters and incidents depicted in this book are products of the author's imagination or are used fictitiously. Any resemblance to actual events, locales, organizations, or persons, living or dead, is entirely coincidental and beyond the intent of the author or the publisher.

No part of this book may be reproduced or transmitted in any form or by any means, electronic or mechanical, including photocopying, recording, or by any information storage and retrieval system, without permission in writing from the publisher.

Wings ePress Books
http://www.wings-press.com

Copyright © Mona Jean Reed 2015
ISBN 978-1-61309-765-6

Published In the United States Of America

September 2015

Wings ePress Inc.
403 Wallace Court
Richmond, KY 40475

Dedication

To Pat Lindley, my sister, my friend.

One

In the Sudan, near the Nubian Desert, south of Egypt, Chaney, a blond-haired, blue-eyed white girl wearing a black burka, more appropriate for a Muslim lady, dropped to the dirt. The thirteen-year old screamed, kicked and hit the sand as if she were only two.

Roz intended to wait for this child to come to her senses, really, she did.

But Roz had no patience left.

"Get up."

Roz took one of Chaney's flailing fists and yanked the younger, smaller girl to her feet.

"Or get left."

"You're mean! Mean, mean, mean!" Chaney stamped her foot.

Roz muttered, "Yeah, I know." And walked away.

Chaney only stood for a minute or so. After that, she ran and caught up to Roz's side.

"I'm sorry; I didn't mean it—what I said."

Roz patted Chaney's shoulder. "You're tired, and we're both way out of our comfort zones. Did you ever think that this is hard for me too?

Chaney's face, though hidden under the all-concealing burka, looked up. She slowly shook her head, but said nothing. Roz walked away and Chaney followed.

Neither girl said another word for a long time. Then Chaney whined, "I wish we didn't have to wear this garb." Chaney flapped her burka to cool herself. The cap that held her burka on her head fell off.

"We have to. You know that." Roz said.

Chaney stopped, put her clothes back in order and then ran to catch up. "You told me already. They find out we're whites, 'n then they'll beat us half to death…'n make us hos." She sniffed twice and walked even slower.

"Come on, hon, we need to walk a little faster."

"I'm hungry," Chaney said.

"I know, me too. But it won't hurt us. When you need encouraging, pinch your waist. Let that remind you." Roz sighed. Would this kid ever get it?

"I did that. Again and again, I did that. But I'm still hungry."

"Bet I have at least three inches of fat in that roll and so do you," Roz said. "We have to let our hunger make us walk faster."

"But I'm hungry."

"I've heard that you can eat termites." Roz knew her grin didn't show under her burka. "There aren't many termite mounds in this desert, but if our hunger gets bad enough, we can always look for one while we walk. We could tear it apart and eat those things."

For a moment Chaney stood still, then she followed, saying nothing.

If Roz could see the younger girl's face, she knew Chaney would have her mouth open in disbelief.

With a silent giggle, Roz added, "The army hired one of my college professors as a survival expert. He's eaten termites. Says they have a high protein grams count and a kind of sweet taste, like lobster."

"He's crazy!"

"You know what?"

"What?" Chaney stood with her elbows out and her fists on her hips; even in a burka, she looked the picture of anger about to make itself known.

"I thought he was crazy too." Roz giggled out loud and added, "Now let's walk…fast." She took the younger girl's hand and swung it. After a minute, Chaney skipped in time with her swinging hand and Roz slow-jogged by the side of the young teen.

"All we have to do is keep walking." Roz walked faster.

"But it's hot under all this cloth."

"We're somewhere close to the Nubian Desert. It's always hot here."

"'Cept at night." Chaney slowed down.

"You got that right. We have to walk as fast as we can so we can reach Cairo before this place kills us."

If I don't stop walking, maybe I won't have to fuss at her.

"Why is everybody so mean?" Chaney said with a whimper. Then she stopped walking.

Roz looked back. "Keep walking. That's all we have…" she yelped and backpedalled fast.

But the fat tan and brown snake twisted into its strike posture. It sounded like boiling water under pressure, about to explode.

Chaney darted in front of Roz. "Gonna kill me another snake!" She held a rock a foot across. With a loud grunt, she raised it high and threw it at the snake. The rock hit just back of the snake's head.

"I hate snakes; hate 'em." Chaney picked up another rock.

"It's already dead." Roz jumped away from the snake's flailing body. "Some of its nerves don't understand. That's all."

"You don't know," Chaney threw the rock anyway.

"Actually, I do." Roz said. "Lots of animals do that. Chickens, for instance. My mom learned how to kill a chicken for dinner by wringing its neck. It runs around for about a minute with its head off."

"Yuck. I wouldn't eat it."

Roz laughed. "I didn't. Dad didn't eat much either. Mom got mad at us. But she always bought our chicken meat at the store after that. Sold the ones she'd already raised to some farmer."

The snake stopped writhing so much, merely quivered a little and then stopped moving at all.

"See, it's dead. Not even moving," Roz said

"Told you I was gonna kill me another snake. Hate 'em. Snake almost killed my big brother. Hate 'em. Hate 'em."

Off to the left, something moved through the scruffy leafage. Roz grabbed Chaney's arm and ran with her in tow for a few steps and then stopped.

"Sorry. That was just some animal. If those men found us…" She panted a few breaths. "Well, you know…"

"Mama says I'm like Lonnie...Ms. Denton, the lady next door. She goes to bars 'n clubs and gets laid for money, Mama says." Chaney's voice quavered. "She says I'll wind up doing that."

"That's cra—absurd! You're not that kind of person," Roz sputtered. How could any woman abuse her own child with such nasty words? Disgusting. "Don't you let anybody, even your mother, make you think you're—like that—ever."

"'Course Mama was lit, and mad at me for asking Lonnie for some bread, 'cause Mama didn't come home all night and we got hungry." Chaney sighed. "Mama says all kinds of things when she's skunked. But I know I don't wanna be no ho."

"Well, you're not going to be a whore, no matter what your mama says. We got away from them."

Chaney nodded. "Yeah. We did it."

"We'll get home and you're going to be a good woman that some lucky man will love for the rest of his life. He'll think you're the most beautiful, the finest woman of your generation. And you're not going to disappoint him. Understand?"

"Don't wanna be whipped again, like that Carl did to me neither." Chaney sniffed and her shoulders trembled.

"We're doing good. We got away from Carl and his gang," Roz said.

"And we got away from Sheik Kelmet."

"That's right," Roz said. "We'll get home. Let's walk a little faster…please."

I'm a hero's daughter. He survived his beatings and rescued fifty-two people. I can at least do my best to rescue Chaney. If it kills me, I'll be brave, like my dad.

How many more days until we get to Cairo?" Chaney asked.

~ * ~

The shadows had not gotten much longer when Chaney asked, "How many more days 'til we get to Cairo?"

With a sigh, Roz said, "I think about forty-eight, but all I know for sure is that we'll keep putting one foot ahead of the other and we'll get there—when we get there."

"Not gonna be no ho…never." The black of her dusty burka developed darker spots near her face.

"Please do me a favor," Roz said.

"Okay." Chaney used that drawling tone that said she'd do what she had to, but she wouldn't be any more pleasant than she had to be while doing it.

"Please stop talking about ho's. In the first place the word is whore. In the second place, I'm getting really, really tired of hearing it. Okay?"

Chaney sniffed, loudly.

Roz could see that this child was about to have another of her "temper-fits."

"Let's not think about it." Roz patted the younger girl's shoulder, but carefully avoided her back. "Let's just walk, fast."

"How many more days 'til we get to Cairo?" Chaney said with a sob.

"About forty-eight, I think. If—"

"Yeah, you told me already," Chaney said with another sniff. "If we don't be lazy and, and…and if Sheik Kelmet don't find us."

Two

In the Sudan, near the Nubian desert, south of Egypt.

This scrub landscape never changed. Carl wished he could be somewhere else—anywhere else. "Face it, you're stuck here. Don't matter how much you wish you'd never left Miami."

He kicked his new horse. Carl had needed another horse after his stupid animal stepped on a snake and had to be shot. He still had trouble believing he'd walked into this unknown village and bought one. Only problem, this was one slow beast. He kicked this molasses-paced horse he bought, tried to make it plod faster.

"Hill-country Arabs don't usually let an unknown white man buy from them that easy," he told himself. "I'm lucky."

Could have something to do with wearing a white cloth and a rope halo on my head. I look like a red-bearded Bedouin. And I speak this language better than lots of natives. Yeah, that's why I had luck.

He could feel his blood pressure pounding, rising.

"Why wouldn't I speak like a native? My parents moved from the U.S.A. to Cairo's poorest native quarter when I was five." He gripped the reins as if they were a neck and he, the murderer, squeezed out a life.

"Mom, the 'great' artist, wanted to be close to the pyramids that 'drew her.' Dad never stopped her from doing anything she wanted."

He felt terribly depressed. An unmanly crying spell fell on him and he tried to choke down the feeling, but couldn't.

"Mom wanted it, so Dad helped her come to this death-trap called Africa. And both of them died before my tenth birthday."

Tears fell; he reached up; felt them, then as if denying they happened, he sniffed deeply and swiped them away.

"They left me shifting for myself." He kicked the unfortunate beast under him.

"That's my luck." He spat with a vengeance while passing the last hovel before he left the village.

"Wish there was a real God," he mumbled. "I'd tell Him exactly what I thought of someone who would let a woman like my mother birth a child."

~ * ~

Carl's new horse didn't notice his kicks. Finally he stopped wasting his energy and they plodded at the horse's chosen pace for at least a half hour.

"Luck. Some luck," he muttered and kicked his new mount again.

"They said you're a good horse. You're more valuable than most…and this stuff you're taking your time walking on is certified, one hundred percent pure cane sugar.

"Yeah, I saw how good you are. Gray muzzle and yellow, used-up teeth. You got maybe five more years, four of 'em useless." The horse got a kick.

"But I didn't gripe. I'd still be walking if I'd said one word of complaint.

"I have a streak of good luck coming and I'm gonna get it." Carl kicked his new mount again, extra hard.

~ * ~

Carl had ridden his slow beast for a half day before he decided that maybe this really was a good horse. You just had to know him.

"I'm gonna call you Harley." Carl laughed about that. A fast motorcycle Harley wasn't.

Still, Carl like the way Harley twisted his little Arabian ears around and listened when Carl talked.

Yeah, he decided, Harley was a good horse; he just wasn't very good at running.

At Harley's pace, Carl had to stop for the night before he reached Mesella, Sheik Kelmet's home village. But Carl didn't mind the sleeping arrangement too much. He did all the usual camp duties. When his needs and Harley the horse's had been dealt with, he grabbed his rifle and climbed aboard the horse's bare back.

Horses always slept light and Harley would fidget if anything prowled in the dark. Then his rifle would settle the critter who came too close. Besides, the warmth of the horse's body kept him warm enough so the scars from his mother's belt didn't ache from the cold.

Carl started moving with the dawn.

"Yeah, Harley, Kelmet's little town would grow on me if I let it. It would grow on you too. Pleasant, well-run for Arab digs, you know."

Harley plodded along and made no comment.

"I'm buying me an island in the Aegean Sea. After that, I have to convince Meribet that she wants to live there. Be hard, but I know my lady…she'll love it and so will I."

Harley shook his head and shivered his neck.

"Wouldn't expect you to understand. You see, living on an island that I own will be almost like living alone on my yacht like I used to. Out there in the ocean, I could see on all sides. Nobody bothered me or got on my blind side. That's what's known as safety. I could sleep sound on my boat; unless it was a hurricane…even most storms didn't wake me…

Carl had to pause because his head hurt. That ache meant his blood pressure was giving him worse trouble than usual. He breathed deep and gave all his joints orders to relax. They told him this exercise helped in the same way a pill does. He did it ten times just as they recommended.

Carl's headache went away eventually and he tried to stay relaxed.

Three

Roz and Chaney found an animal trail and used it to walk more quickly through the dead-looking grass, bare soil and scrubby bushes. Greener plant life grew about a hundred feet away next to the small creek they'd been following.

"See that tree way over there?" Roz said.

"Yeah?"

"I think it's about ten-thirty or eleven. We can walk that far before the afternoon is over, don't you think?" Roz said.

"'Course we can, if we run. That's a long way."

"The only other big tree that's closer is that one over there, next to the creek. We'd have to lose a whole afternoon. Have to be in this hot desert an extra half day."

"We better run. Don't wanna be in this burka thing longer than I have to." Chaney shuffled into a slow jog.

Roz did the same. "We'll make it. If we hike the standard twenty miles a day, tomorrow we'll only have about forty-four more days before we reach Cairo."

Four

The midday sun beamed down with what seemed to be extra ferocity. None of the grasses or other plants looked as if they had ever been green. From horizon to horizon, only the monotony of desert grays and browns filled Carl's vision.

"This heat will get me if I'm not careful." Carl didn't stop; he eased the canteen off the saddle horn and drank a good swig.

"If I could, I'd just forget about her. But after what she did, I can't." Carl's fists doubled. He'd like to hit something, or someone. "Everything be a lot easier if I could just find that blasted creek."

Harley's ears see-saw'd.

"Didn't I tell you already?"

Harley's ears see-saw'd again and he shook his head side-to-side.

"Oh, all right. I'll tell it again. Listen this time. George showed me this creek with diamonds. The part with the diamonds has black sand. There were lots of eensie diamonds and a few bigger ones. Then I found one I could barely close my fist around and as clear as a piece of glass. Put 'em all in my canteen. Had to shove extra hard to get the big one in. It broke the canteen's mouth, but I didn't care. Figured no one would think of looking there and they'd be safe and so would I."

Carl vegged out and mused on what he'd like to do to one Okie blonde. Time passed and then Harley made that flapping lip noise horses do at times.

"I could forget that blonde if I found the creek. Wouldn't have to beg that sheik for work.

"George knows where to find those diamonds, but he had people to see. Only right. The people that gambled on his internet site owed him lotsa money.

"I never did GPS like I shoulda because that app's hard to use on my new satellite phone.

"See, I had more diamonds than I'd need for three lifetimes and I'm not so dumb that I didn't know someone might kill me to get my diamonds, even George. He's a friend, but there's a limit to friendship…especially when that friend's got money on the brain. So I stuck a bunch of the eensie ones in my shirt pocket and pretended that's all I found. Didn't open myself up for getting my throat slit by hanging around the creek too long."

Harley shook his head and snorted.

"Stupid. I know," Carl said. "Never thought of that miserable blonde stealing my canteen and waltzing off into the heart of the desert.

"First I thought I'd just go back and get some more diamonds. But there's too many creeks. I can't find that one, snot-framed part of one creek that's got black sand and diamonds. It's all her fault."

Harley snorted.

"Awww. I can't ask George to go back and find it for me. That's worse than begging like I had to when I was a kid. And who knows…he might kill me if I asked again. Besides, maybe I got the only big ones there was."

Harley's head nodded up and down.

Carl laughed and patted the old fellow's neck.

"You're right, chum. Now we have to do things the old-fashioned way. I'll have to earn money by serving, just like I've always done. I hate it. But what can I do? Have to get enough money for a decent crew so's we can track her down, get those diamonds and wring her sassy blonde head clean off."

A hint of ache crawled up Carl's neck and he sighed. "Have to remember: Time takes care of things. Just be patient. Give time a chance to work…Time takes care of things…" He did his breathing exercise and then gently kicked Harley into a faster walk.

Five

Roz and Chaney had been running along their chosen trail for quite a while and now the short shadows gave notice of noon.

"I'm hungry," Chaney said as she jogged.

"I know…me too."

"I'm looking for flints while I run, like you told me. Why we looking for flints?" Chaney asked.

Patience.

"We need one to make a fire," Roz said. "And I think I can make a knife at least as good as a caveman's from a flint."

"I already know, your parents were survivalists and they taught you how," Chaney said. Sarcasm outlined every syllable.

"Nope, learned last year. For a few months I had a half-Apache boyfriend. His bloodline included an eighth Nez-Perce and a smidgen of Lakota Sioux. Luke Wayne Two Elk was oh-so-proud of his kinship to Sitting Bull."

"He taught you about flints?"

"A little." Roz didn't like the remembrance. Last year, she'd flipped her friend's boyfriend to the floor in the first ten seconds of their encounter. That's when she knew she was pretty good at self-defense, just as her instructor said. Luke had been watching and challenged her to a real karate match. He had taken advantage of the situation and pressed on her breasts. She ignored that; it could have been an accident, even though it didn't feel like it. Then he put his hand between her legs in a way no one could say was an accident. Her red anger exceeded her control. He spent a night in the hospital; the next day he broke off with her.

"Why didn't he teach you a lot?"

Roz wondered at herself for bringing the whole mess up. "Let's forget Luke."

"I wanna know. Why didn't he teach you a lot?"

"I'm a pushy woman and insisted or he wouldn't have taught me about flint knapping or anything else."

"Why?

"Because I'm a female. Don't you know us dumb broads, we're not supposed… Never mind. Let's just walk fast."

She refused to answer any more of Chaney's prying questions about her boyfriends.

After another hour of jogging, both girls ran out of strength. Chaney collapsed on the dirt in the blistering sun.

"Tree's too far…We can't make it." Chaney wheezed.

"We'll get there…We'll be tired…but safe." Roz stood bent over with her hands on her knees while she panted and tried to take deeper breaths.

Chaney nodded. She managed to rise to a kneeling position and bent her head over her knees, saying nothing, just panting.

When Roz could breathe more normally, she watched Chaney. Finally she judged that Chaney's breathing had also returned to normal, so she stood and said, "Guess we ought to go." She offered the younger girl a hand up.

"Gotta be safe." Chaney groaned and let Roz help her to stand.

They'd only been running for a little while when Roz said, "Let's try to make it to those boulders before we stop again. If we get that far, we'll be sure to reach the tree before sundown."

"—safe," Chaney whimpered and kept running.

They reached the first of the boulders and Chaney crumpled in the slight shadow at its side. But just before Roz sat, out of the corner of her eye, she noticed a horse and rider south of them. At that moment they were only a speck in the distance. Still…

"Better keep walking." She urged Chaney and lifted her up.

"But I'm—"

"Hurry. Move it."

"Don't be so bossy," Chaney fretted. "We gotta stop; I'm tired."

"We have company. Don't think he's paying us any attention…yet. But we better hide, just to be sure."

Roz broke off a handful of the dry grass stalks from a nearby clump. By using them like a whisk broom, she swept away their footsteps. At least, all that she could reach in those few seconds.

"What about the tree?"

"Rather take my chances with hyenas than men."

"Not gonna be no ho," Chaney said.

Chaney stopped behind the next boulder she came to.

"Let's get further away, much further," Roz said.

Chaney went around several more boulders.

"That one way over there, as far from the trail as we can," Roz said and as they went she swept away their footprints. The girls said nothing else, just hid behind their target boulder.

~ * ~

The man stopped and dismounted at the boulder closest to the trail.

"We ain't that far from Kelmet's little city," he rasped. "Yeah, I know, you need your rests because you got old written all over you."

With his head down, the horse balanced on three hooves. He cocked his left hind hoof at an angle and stood with his sides heaving.

In a bit, the man said, "You think you can make it all the way to Mesella now?"

~ * ~

Roz heard the sandpaper voice and English words: Carl: She knew that voice too well.

At first, she tried to become part of the boulder; just like Chaney. That man was a monster worse than anything she'd ever seen in a nightmare or even on TV.

Dear Jesus, please don't let him find us.

Above them an eagle screamed. Roz flinched at that.

But Chaney picked up a head-sized rock. She muttered, "Gonna kill me 'nother kind of snake."

But Roz grabbed her. "No," Roz whispered and wrestled the rock out of Chaney's arms. Then she placed it gently on the ground so it didn't make noise. "We have to be quiet."

Chaney tried to get the rock, but Roz wouldn't let her. "We won't be killers, like that animal," Roz hissed.

"But…"

"I mean it."

"He's worse than any snake." Chaney whispered.

"You've got enough bad stuff to overcome; you don't need slaughter on your conscience."

"Nearly beat me to death."

"I know, your back is still tender," Roz said.

"He'll kill us if he gets a chance."

"We're not murdering anyone. Now hush! He might have hearing as good as mine."

"But—"

Roz put her hand over Chaney's mouth, muzzling her. Chaney fought, but she had to do it silently.

At the trail, Carl said, "Come on, chum, you ain't that old." Soon, hooves pounded away from the boulders at a steady, but not a very rapid, pace.

A screech rang out above them and Roz looked up.

"I've got this itchy feeling," Roz said and stopped holding Chaney.

Chaney kicked at her. "Why didn't you let me knock his head clean off! We'll never get away." She flailed at Roz with both arms.

"Don't be stupid." Roz grabbed both Chaney's arms. "We don't kill people. If you didn't learn that from your mom, you're learning it from me. Murder is dead wrong, no matter what."

"Not done it. In the army they kill people. All the time, they kill people."

"Either take what I said as the truth or don't. But you've been told what's right."

Even if we wanted to, Dad said men are a lot harder to kill than an animal, even a snake.

"You're mean. I hate you!"

"No you don't. You're angry, that's all. Besides, we don't have to worry. God destroys evil people. Bible says He laughs at their plans."

"I don't care, you're mean."

"I had a Sunday School teacher whose favorite saying was 'If God says it once, we better listen. When He says the same thing twice, watch out.'"

"Don't mean anything to me." Chaney sat down next to the boulder.

"The Bible says, 'God laughs at the plans of evil people.' It says it not once but twice. He won't let that man get his way. God will make things that should have gone right, go wrong. And then God will laugh at him."

Chaney didn't say anything for a long minute, then she sighed. "And you're still mean."

"Whatever." A shriek sounded above the girls and Roz looked up. "We've been here and not moving for too long. See those buzzards up there, flying in a circle? They think we're dinner. We've got to get out of here before they decide to slice us up."

Chaney looked at the sky, but didn't move.

Roz made an exaggerated shiver. "If it kills me, I won't be bird food." She pulled Chaney to her feet.

"We still trying to make it to that tree?" Chaney said. "We better run."

"Excellent thought," Roz said.

Chaney took off with the longest strides she could manage. "I ain't never gonna be no ho."

A shrubby plant grew nearby. A piece of the bush looked useable as a broom. Roz wrestled it loose and swept the area. With satisfaction, she listened to the increasingly faint hoof beats.

Thank you, Jesus!

The yapping laughter of a herd of hyenas encouraged them to move their feet. But even with the hyenas urging them to hurry, Roz dragged that piece of brush to erase their steps.

They were still at least fifty yards from the tree when the sun's disk began sliding under the horizon. They sprinted the rest of the way.

"Okay, you first," Roz panted.

Still gasping for air, Chaney untied her sandals, slid the open heels over her wrists and arranged them on her arms as if they were bangle bracelets. Then she took off her burka and draped it around her neck.

With a quick walk around the tree, Chaney sized up the trunk's slant. Then she positioned herself on top of the way it leaned and gripped the trunk with her right hand as high as she could reach. She put her left bare foot on the trunk, gripped the bark with her left hand, positioned her right foot and reached her right hand up a little higher…

While Chaney climbed, Roz used her piece of bush to wipe out as much of their tracks as she could see in the coming dark and reminded herself to do a better job in the morning.

Roz began her climb when Chaney reached half-way up the trunk. The next chuckle from that hyena herd sounded much too close. Roz had only gotten a yard above the ground when she saw them, and with the hyenas' encouragement, she reached the first crotch of their tree in record time.

"Hurry, sun's afterglow all the light we have," Roz urged the younger girl.

Monkey-like, Chaney climbed up her chosen branch until it swayed widely in the slight breeze. On the way, she broke off a number of branches. Then she gave Roz her burka and fitted herself in the crotch between the two branches she'd chosen as her bed.

Roz helped her place the loose branches as if they were a blanket and used the burka to tie Chaney in place, Last of all Roz said, "Good night, sleep tight."

Chaney responded as she always did, "Don't let the bed bugs bite."

In the near dark, Roz felt for a place of her own and tied herself in for the night.

As always, the hyenas and assorted other hunters played their dissonant symphony and the girls slept.

Roz roused when a herd of some kind of antelope raced beneath their tree. Hyenas followed. But neither the antelope nor the hyenas could hurt her, so she promised herself that tomorrow would bring her at least twenty miles closer to Cairo

Six

Carl topped the last hill and the prosperous-looking village of Mesella spread itself below. There were even a few farms with crops in green rows. He liked seeing something green for a change.

"It's like I told you," Carl said. "Time's gonna take care of this mess, time and the good sheik down there. Time always takes care of things."

Harley twisted his ears.

"Yeah, I know, I still have a choice: Do I want to keep chasing that girl and kill her directly?"

Harley nodded his head a bit and plodded along.

"If I do that, I may spend the rest of my life following her. She's craftier than any three other women."

No one argued.

"What I need to do is get Kelmet's money to pay a crew to track her and when I get her, kill her soonest. If I take that option, I'll have to remember what I say and stay away from this sheik for the rest of my life.

"Of course I could just turn her over to Kelmet. Let her live the rest of her life in the comfort of the palace." He thought about it. "Nope, not gonna do that.

"Who taught her to cover her tracks? I've gone through her life looking for reasons and ways she learned that. No part of my investigation back in the U.S.A. gave even a hint.

"All I know is that by myself, I won't know whether I'm on her trail or not. Four times I thought I'd caught her and the trail came to nothing.

"I got no choice. I'll have to talk to Kelmet."

Admitting that he'd have to get help brought Carl's feelings of neediness to the surface. This time he couldn't immediately ignore them. An ache started in his neck, but he could and did ignore that. He passed a baby goat bleating its heart out. No shepherd looked after it, or even another goat. He'd been as alone as that little goat after his dad died.

"If there was a God, I'd tell Him what I thought of Someone who would kill parents and leave little kids hungry and cold…" He looked at the sky and snarled, "If there was a God, I'd tell Him He was worse'n any bully, even worse than Mom. That's what I'd do."

Harley got another kick but didn't plod any faster. Carl still ignored the headache.

He reached Kelmet's palace about half after two and once more, he thoroughly believed his own advice. Time really did take care of things.

He forced himself to hold his shoulders back and when he reached the palace entrance, he leaped off ol' Harley's back like a Cossack who had spent his life on horseback. Harley's reins went into the hands of a man who stood nearby.

"I won't be long, an hour max. Just give my horse some water and keep him close." He reached in his pocket and pulled out a coin, a large coin.

"*Shakran* (thank you,)" Carl said.

Then he strutted up the few steps, through the scalloped arch and into the interior plaza. No president ever strode up to take their oath of office with more aplomb than he.

That ridiculous little doorbell-gong of the sheik's waited and he struck it.

Nisak, the sheik's personal man of all work, came. As always, the black man dressed in jeans, a tee and the checkered Bedouin headgear.

"Yes?" the man looked down his nose like an English butler.

"I'm to see the sheik."

"I don't—"

But Carl didn't let him go further. "I will see Sheik Kelmet."

"My master never gave such an order to me."

Carl drew himself up to his maximum five feet nine inches, twisted his face into its most threatening look and said each word separately, in a barely audible rumble, "Kelmet. ben. Mesella. Wants. To. See. Me."

Nisak gulped, turned and disappeared into the building.

Carl put his chin out and sauntered across the sunny courtyard. He examined the tiled pool and its fountain as if it were of immense interest.

Kelmet came. He wore his full regalia: Sandals, white pants gathered at the ankle, white coat-like thwab that covered his beefy mass from neck to mid-calf, foot-wide white leather sash, massive dagger of gold inlaid with ivory. Its scabbard stuck out the bottom of the sash a good six inches.

The black robe of the desert topped his costume. He also wore the checkered Bedouin headpiece and he had threaded the black "halo" of his headpiece through a wide gold chain.

Carl noticed. He revised his thoughts and plans. That gold chain…This wasn't Sheik Kelmet ben Mesella. No, King Kelmet the First of Mesella stood before him. And that chain served as his crown.

Best treat him like royalty.

Carl bowed from the waist.

"I believe I know where your son's woman went."

"You believe. How certain are you?"

"We know now that no one stole your woman. She left on her own. That one is an uncommon woman in the extreme. I knew her to be unusual when we took her. At that time we didn't realize what a rare prize we had. Didn't know how dangerous she'd be, either.

Kelmet frowned and gestured for Carl to continue.

"I found that she can even climb trees to protect herself and her maid at night."

"How could you know that?"

"She's good. Nearly impossible to track. But once I traced her to a tree. Found lion tracks under it, and claw marks on the trunk and lower branches. Not many lions around here but apparently they're not as extinct as the experts think."

"Yes, I know." Kelmet leaned forward. "Two years ago, I shot one not a mile from my city. His skin now adorns my wall. But you say the lion did not attack her?"

"I climbed into that tree myself. Believe me; it took effort, even for a man. Ten feet above the highest claw marks, I saw the black threads, burka threads. Much higher than any lion could have reached.

"I concluded, as I said. She's good. The elements of this land aren't likely to kill her." Carl paused and let that statement sink in.

"Good." Kelmet nodded. "Then you think my investment is safe."

Carl shook his head. "It's more complicated than that."

"Tell me."

"We don't want her reaching the U. S. A. Don't want her letting their government know we bring you women. If you can't keep her, she's too dangerous to let live."

He coaxed his face into its sad look. "I'd be forced to eliminate her. On the financial side, we'd have to double our price to you sheiks for your next women. My men will charge me much more to get you the kind of women you want if they're pretty certain that getting caught will lead to a death sentence."

Kelmet frowned. "Death sentence, for getting slaves?" Then he laughed.

"She's not like the normal slaves we get you. We get normal slaves off the streets after they leave their family," Carl explained. "They don't have anybody watching their back. That means we can take street people and nobody cares. These women are different. They have family. Families make trouble."

Kelmet said nothing, only nodded.

"This one is also the best of the eleven that we brought you sheiks this year. I know this woman. I'm the one who found her in the first place."

"How so?"

"She'd finished half her college education."

"I know that. I saw the captain's report on each woman."

"Before we took her, I did the full exploration on her. She made extremely good grades."

"I have the Captain's reports. But it did not give the actual grades. Only that she made the Dean's list."

"All her grades were A's from her entry until we took her. Top of her classes. Set the curve every time, except once, and that time her professor said that she and a male student had the same perfect scores, but he could only give one the top position. He thought the boy would make better use of it."

Kelmet frowned; he seemed puzzled.

Carl cleared his throat. "You're wondering how I got the teachers to talk? Especially with the U.S.A. so concerned with privacy?"

Kelmet nodded; his eyes narrowed, calculating.

"I pretended to be a government agent. You've seen pictures: black suit, sunglasses, badge, the whole bit. It's a risky thing to impersonate an agent. Could get me a long sentence, but I did it for you."

"You have my gratitude."

"I interviewed all of her teachers; took a lot of my time. Twenty-two of 'em. That's how I know her grades. I wanted to make sure we got you what you wanted." He added. "She had also joined the O.U. track team. That team wins a lot more than half their meets, even in a bad year. Like I say, she's good."

"Do you think I would pay a half-million for nothing? I knew she had intelligence, she is tall and further, that she is athletic. Her physical ability is why I didn't reject her for her emaciated condition. I could fix that detail.

Carl had never heard this. "How so?"

"I forced her and that maid of hers to eat until they began to look a little more…prosperous."

"Oh, that's why they were eating so often. I thought they liked the food."

"I know my son; if I had brought him such a thin one, he would have laughed at my joke and would never put his seed in such a mass of bones. My son is 'picky'."

Carl nodded and kept his smile under control. Kelmet's son was gay at heart if not in actions; he'd bet money on it.

"I want a grandson who has brains, brawn and the height to command respect. My progeny will need all of it in the unstable world he must master."

"Your grandson will also have a mother whose virtue is better than most."

Kelmet nodded, but his posture said tension, like a spring under pressure.

"By the way, I found the remains of a number of snakes."

"Snakes often die," Kelmet said.

"These all had injuries, crushed skulls mostly. African people always run from snakes. Too many African snakes are both deadly and hard to kill."

Kelmet nodded.

"This lady kills snakes. She's good."

"It is as you say." Kelmet sat back and seemed more relaxed. "How many days ahead do you believe she is?"

"I estimate a week, perhaps a week and a half."

"You will capture her for me, won't you? It will be a great personal favor."

"I'd be honored, sir."

"And you will treat her gently for my grandson's sake. She is not to be beaten hard." Kelmet wasn't making a request.

Kelmet gestured for Nisak. The man bent his head to his master and then the servant left. He returned carrying a leather pouch. With a deep bow, he gave the pouch to the sheik; he put something else in Kelmet's hand as well.

"Anger does not become such as I. This is to make amends." Kelmet took Carl's hand and put something heavy, round and cold in it. "Perhaps there are times for men to carry like a donkey, but not for you, you did not deserve the punishment I gave you in my anger."

Carl glanced at four gold coins the diameter of a silver dollar and twice as thick. He'd never seen such coins, but he didn't let his eyes linger.

He made his face somber and with a slight frown, stared for a count of five at the bridge of the sheik's nose. (And therefore truthful, so the books say.) Then he looked away. "I've already forgotten that it happened." Carl put on a slight, well measured smile.

He hadn't forgotten, of course. Who could forget that much humiliation?

"Perhaps the men who guarded her tent were careless, but I know you were faithful in your guard duties," Kelmet said. "As you say, she's good. When she is found, I will make her happy with her circumstance and guard her extremely well.

"Good."

"If she escapes again, I, myself, will execute her. Provided that she has borne at least one male heir. If she has not, I will put her in chains and have her artificially inseminated at her time of ovulation; my finicky son will agree to the procedure, of course. She stays under guard until she gives birth to a male, an heir, and then she dies."

Carl slowly nodded his head, once.

"This is for your service." Kelmet held out the leather pouch. When Carl's hand cupped under it, Kelmet let it drop. It landed in Carl's hand with a clink.

"That which is in the pouch should be sufficient for your assistance. However, as a reward for faithful service, when you return my property to me, you will receive another bag twice as full."

"Uh sir, things happen sometimes. She's not likely to, but suppose she should die? I'd hate for you to think I didn't do my best to fulfill my commitment."

Kelmet swept down the sunny courtyard, with his robes making a royal statement, an Arab version of Louis XIV, the French "Sun King."

"If she dies, bring me her left small toe. It bears my mark as a tattoo." He strutted back. "If you bring only her toe, your reward for your diligence is another bag, a twin of the one in your hand." Kelmet tapped Carl's shoulder twice.

Carl wasn't exactly sure what Kelmet said while he prowled the courtyard. So he said, "Yes sir." He shouldn't have this regal person repeat himself. Kings are not known for their patience. Then Carl bowed, backed up about ten feet, bowed, turned and walked away.

As soon as he left Kelmet's presence, Carl looked at the thick gold coins in his hand. The portrait on the front of the coins belonged to Kelmet with the single word, Mesella, beneath it. No surprise there. He turned it over. That side bore an oil well with crossed rifles behind it. It read, in English, "Kingdom of Mesella, Allah Be Praised." There was a tiny Arabic subscript.

He'd been right; the man had all the signs of being another Napoleon. He wouldn't be content with kingship of his eensy Mesella Territory. Whatever that madman had in mind would be large enough to require English as the official language.

He'd need to make a decision. Did he want to deliver that Okie blonde to "his majesty" and be rewarded royally? Who knows, if he played things just right, he could be an advisor to the king, or at least in the Mesella cabinet. Wouldn't that be something?

Or did he want to carry out his original plan, to kill her in the slowest, most painful manner possible?

He debated the relative merits of his choices while he put the price of his service in the saddlebags and mounted Harley. He gave the horse a gentle kick to get him moving.

Then Nisak ran out and before Harley moved, the man grabbed Harley's reins.

"Sheik Kelmet has a small favor, an errand he would like you to run. It's on your way and won't take long. You will be well paid."

"This better be good."

"There is a village that you are certain to pass in a couple of weeks. Here's the map. Come with me."

Nisak walked ahead of him to the sheik's stable. "All you need to do is take the saddle and the black horse under it to the village. Give the horse and saddle to the headman, Sighit al Azibik.

"My master is particularly concerned with the saddle. It is of great value as a heritage piece both to my sheik and to his cousin, Sighit. When you have completed that small task, please invite those who have horses for sale, or who wish to buy to come to our trade fair and ask them to tell others of our fair. My master's cousin knows what to do."

"When?"

"Tell Sighit al Azibik the week of October twenty-five, just after the holy days."

"Okay, Nisak. You want me to do anything else?" He tried to be polite and keep sarcasm out of his voice.

"My master gives you this in payment for the favor." He handed Carl a small leather bag that looked like a lumpy sausage and so stuffed it didn't clink when he put it in Carl's hand.

Nisak helped him saddle the glossy black stallion. The scuffed English-style saddle didn't look like much, but Nisak handled it almost with reverence.

Carl mounted Harley, took the black's reins and rode out. The black didn't like it.

Carl jerked on the black's reins. "Black boy, you better be worth this trouble."

Probably that little saddle's stuffed with something that has more value than memories. I'll look tonight.

Seven

Just after sunrise, the two blondes removed themselves from the tree that had been their bed for the night. They walked through the endless scrub without incident all day. Chaney's killing another snake gave them their only excitement. They found another tree to sleep in for safety when night came.

They followed the same routine the next day. But that day, Chaney killed a different type of snake. Though neither girl knew for sure, they thought this one must be a cobra, a real cobra with a smallish hood just back of its head. And then, not more than an hour later, Chaney killed another snake, one of those slow-moving tan ones with the brown spots and stripes.

The following morning, Chaney killed yet another snake.

"Chaney, all African snakes will be on the endangered list before we reach Cairo," Roz said with a chuckle.

"I hate snakes!" A medium size brown snake with a dark stripe running the length of its body on each side lay without moving. It had made the mistake of not having its tail hidden under the rocks. Chaney kicked the lifeless husk.

A vulture with a featherless head and neck landed on a nearby house-sized boulder. "Hey, buzzard boy. Come and get it." Chaney kicked the dead snake again and walked away. She had to run a few steps to catch up with Roz.

Chaney's mom pickled her in alcohol and messed up her brain before she ever made it out of the birth canal. Chaney can't put two thoughts together and draw a meaningful conclusion.

I have to be a real Christian to her...teach her things, encourage her...be patient with her...

"We're making progress." Roz walked along the small cliff just above the creek. "Did you notice? Our creek is at least a foot wider today than it was the day before yesterday. That tells me that we're closer to the Nile."

Chaney took out her canteen and shook it. "Gonna need more water pretty soon."

"Surely it will be at least a few days before we've gotten to a wide enough part of the creek where the crocodiles are real monsters," Roz said. "I haven't seen one more than about four feet long, nose to tail, have you?"

"How we going to keep the crocs away while we fill our canteens?"

"We're not. We have to wait until we find a piece of creek without crocs."

"Do we have to?"

"You want to push a crocodile out of the way so you can get a drink?"

Act nice!

"We just have to wait." Roz said with all the sweetness she could muster. "We won't get too thirsty. Remember the time we went three days without water."

"In that black hole after they kidnapped us," Chaney sighed. "Guess we have to wait."

"We can do it," Roz said. Then she walked even faster. "Let's not think about being thirsty. Just walk fast."

Chaney skipped a few steps while saying, "So we can get to Cairo faster. It's about what, thirty-nine days?"

"Forty-one, I think."

They walked about five miles and then the creek started another of its changes of direction. That morning it had been flowing north and a little east as Roz thought it should. But now, with the morning half over, it had turned due east.

"This is going to be a problem." Roz said. "We have a choice. You can see that this loop of the creek goes way over that way and comes right back."

"It does?" Chaney frowned and squinted in the direction Roz pointed. Then she shook her head. "Can't see it."

"Your eyes…" Roz examined the frowning girl. "Are you nearsighted?"

"Don't know. Last year, teacher said I should get glasses. Mama got so mad she went to school and cussed her out." Chaney's shoulder hunched forward. "I shoulda kept my mouth shut."

"Don't worry about it. Look real good, right through here…if you weren't nearsighted, you would see that it goes north again after it makes this loop. Let's get closer to the water."

They slid down the six foot high bank and walked on the muddy sand. "Watch for crocs. This is dangerous," Roz said. "If we can figure out how to cross this creek—"

"—without getting et up," Chaney added, frowning hard.

Roz nodded. "We can save ourselves a whole afternoon's walk and—"

"I get it; we'll see Cairo a half day sooner." Chaney chewed her lower lip and frowned. When that didn't help, she sat on a driftwood log and frowned some more. "All we got to do is keep from getting et up." Her shoulders trembled.

"Two of these little switchback loops are worth a whole day's walk."

"I'm tired; can't we rest a while?"

With caution in every step, Roz walked to the edge of the creek and scanned the muddy water. There were no crocodile noses and eye ridges for at least fifty feet in both directions. She stared at the water. The bottom…she could see it! A couple of feet to the right, the water grew even less deep.

The switchback loop made the water to travel this area much slower than elsewhere. Slow water can't hold as much mud as fast water.

Roz picked up a stick and poked it into the water. Just as she thought, here, where the creek changed directions, the slower moving current had dropped enough mud and silt to make a bridge that came within an inch of the surface.

She used her stick to examine the mud. It might be quicksand. But the stick didn't go in very far. *Just wet mud, not quicksand.*

"Chaney, come on, now!"

But Chaney didn't move.

"Now, while the crocs are somewhere else."

"Okay," Chaney stood and took a couple of slow steps. "I'm coming."

Roz, thinking Chaney would be right behind her, lifted the skirt of her burka and splashed across in two long muddy leaps.

~ * ~

On the surface, Roz left splash rings that spread circles through the water in all directions. The splashing also rang through the water from surface to bottom, concentric peals of sound that humans couldn't understand.

A monster, eight feet long, felt the sound of that dinner chime through his skin. The crocs further north tended to be larger than he and his belly seldom reached a satisfactory fullness.

Most dissatisfied crocs followed the current, the way of least resistance; they went even farther north. But this creature went south. Did he know more, or perhaps his forebears had been a more obstinate strain of crocodile.

Without a sound or a ripple, his nose and eye ridges disappeared from the surface. His strong tail muscles pushed him through the slight underwater current. No hint of his progress appeared as a wave or a swell on the water's surface.

Eight

Chaney dragged herself to the creek's muddy edge. She looked up and down the creek and trembled. "Here I c-come," she said.

Then she did a little forward and back movement as if she were jumping into an already-moving jump-rope.

"Just do it. Get over here."

Chaney stopped and looked up and down the creek. "I've got a bad feeling about this. You're sure there's no crocs here?"

"I got across."

When Chaney still didn't come, Roz decided she'd have to go back and pull Chaney across. She strode forward, intending to drag the little twerp across.

Roz had already waded half-way across when Chaney drawled, "Okay," and splashed into the water.

The water erupted.

Chaney screamed.

On full adrenalin overload, Roz grabbed and yanked. Not yet aware that she had done it, Roz flipped the smaller girl at the shore. But Chaney's burka came loose from her body and floated down on the water. The croc came up directly under it and it draped itself over the scaly demon's head and back.

The croc gave a hissing roar and staged a 'death roll.'

Roz reached the dry land almost before Chaney did. The monster had gotten a single tooth in her left hand. The gash started just above her wrist and ran the length of her little finger. It pounded with every heartbeat and bled freely.

A dazed Chaney wore only the slip-like undergarment and her sandals. Her canteen floated in the water near the edge. Chaney screamed and then she collapsed and cried and screeched.

Roz put her wound in her mouth and sucked it closed while ignoring Chaney's squalling. At the same time she watched the crocodile that wore Chaney's burka.

She picked up Chaney's canteen and tossed it in her direction. No helping it, Roz would have to go after that burka. Couldn't have anyone seeing Chaney's blond hair. Somehow, she had to get that garb without tearing it and without getting herself killed.

"Why did you make me cross?" Chaney blubbered.

"Stay here."

"I hate you!"

Roz's hand throbbed but she couldn't worry about that right now. She tramped through the mud and followed the croc. It swam downstream and did another death roll, but failed to remove Chaney's burka from its eyes and snout.

She'd need a stick at least four feet long before the end of this fracas. There should be one somewhere in the litter on the bank…but the branches and sticks near her measured less than three feet. She kept looking.

In the water, the croc did yet another death roll.

"Keep it up." Roz advised the croc. "You'll get rid of that thing sooner or later—sooner I hope."

It took the croc four more death rolls and a hissing roar to remove the burka from its person. The instant the cloth lifted off, the croc disappeared.

But Roz still hadn't found a suitable stick with which to reach Chaney's garb. The cloth floated down the middle of the eight foot wide creek. A large air bubble held it up, so far.

A tangle of branches lay on the nearby mud and Roz tore the mass apart. The best branch she found measured just over three feet long. It had enough branchlets and dried leafage to be an extra wide, extra thick, broom.

"That'll have to do."

With the branch, Roz swept the water toward herself. The burka responded by moving a bit further downstream. She kept up with it while sweeping the water toward herself. At the same time, she watched for crocs.

Finally, the burka floated within three feet of the bank and Roz snagged it and dragged it onto the creek's muddy edge. Then she bent to pick up the sludge-filled cloth.

A six-foot croc, smaller than the other monster, but still huge, lunged at her with its hideous mouth open.

Roz yelped and pushed the branch with all its branchlets into the wide-open maw. Twigs snapped, crackled and broke while Roz backpedalled. Her foot twisted on a bit of woody trash and she fell against the nearly vertical bank that rose behind her.

The six-foot croc, his mouth filled with nasty wood instead of tasty flesh, did a death roll in the mud on top of the burka. Another roll brought him about three feet from Roz.

Reflexes kicking in, she drew her feet up next to her body and scooted further away. She meant to stand, to climb up the six foot bank. But her shaky knees wouldn't hold her up.

In stunned paralysis, Roz lay there until the croc finished his death rolls. Then he disappeared into the water instead of going after Roz.

The croc's tail gave a last mighty heave and he disappeared; then Roz's strength returned. "I won't take much more of this," Roz muttered. Her stomach hurt and she wanted to hit someone. "If that stupid, stupid, little girl had done right, none of this would have happened."

She stepped ankle deep in the sludge, grabbed the dirt-filled fabric and marched all the way back to Chaney.

Her throat so tight that breathing hurt, Roz wanted to cry, but she didn't. None of this would have happened if Chaney had done what she'd been told.

"Here." She handed Chaney the burka. "I suggest you put it on and keep your mouth shut. I've just had the insides scared out of me and I'm in a bad, bad mood."

She turned and walked away, fast. She climbed up, over the bank and out of the creek's area. Then she tramped through the dry dirt, past occasional dead grass clumps and lifeless bushes. She refused to look back. The mud drying between her toes didn't help her mood.

She didn't know which was worse: the heat from the sun or her intense…annoyance…Maybe if she ignored Chaney for a little while, she'd stop feeling so, so angry.

Lord Jesus, I don't know how much more I can take. Please, make me brave, like Dad. And patient… I need so much more patience.

Behind her, Chaney whimpered quietly.

Still angry, but trying mightily for patience, Roz walked faster. She meant to stay with their usual pattern of following the creek but keeping about fifty to a hundred feet away from it.

"It's cold. And it's torn." Chaney flapped the wet burka around, and it's all dirty.

"You want to go back to the creek and wash it? Ready to give that croc another chance at you?"

Chaney squalled.

"I'm sorry, I shouldn't have said that. Just…be quiet for a while, will you? I need a time out."

"You're mean…mean…mean!" Chaney yelled… "And ugg-ly!"

At that moment, a grasshopper flitted onto Roz's crocodile-tooth-wounded hand and when she flapped her hand to get it off, it jumped up under her burka-clad arm, scratched its way onto her shoulder and before she could do anything, it had wriggled its way onto her chin. She flapped the face covering part of the burka, tried to push that insect down, make it fall out. But the grasshopper crawled upwards onto her lips. It seemed determined to force its way into her mouth, her throat.

Roz couldn't move.

Again she found herself in the waking nightmare that started at six years old. She still felt that huge butterfly net full of grasshoppers as it swished down on her head. She still heard those boys laughing at her.

The pain of grasshopper legs on her eyeballs was not yesterday's remembered agony; it seemed to happen now and her terror seemed eternal. She opened her mouth in a scream that only God heard. Her voice refused to work.

Painful tears streamed down her face. She felt hordes of grasshoppers in her mouth, her throat. Her stomach twisted and she gagged.

Next to an ant hill, she collapsed and lay there. Her whole body shook. Heartbreaking sobs of betrayal filled her and she couldn't stop.

When she came to herself, Chaney stood nearby, sweeping ants away from her.

Still sobbing, Roz stood up. Her muscles and joints groaned and barely supported her. It shouldn't have been such an effort.

She vowed once more not to let her waking nightmare chain her to the past. "I'm sorry, didn't mean to have a fit like that," she mumbled.

Roz made her legs walk, forced herself to be "normal." If she kept it up, this "nightmare thing" would go away, always did.

"Now you know how I feel. It's cold." Chaney whined and held her burka away from her body.

"I'm sorry you're cold, but it will dry and when it's dry, you can get most of the mud out by flapping it around." Roz's left hand still ached and she sucked on her wound to ease the pain.

"And it's not torn very bad at all," Roz said. "Besides, as long as it's wet, you've got your own private air conditioner. Maybe we should wet our burkas on purpose."

"I'm gonna be out of water pretty soon," Chaney said.

Roz shook her own canteen. "Me too."

"We're not that far from the creek now," Chaney said. "Let's go back."

"Good thought, but let's walk a little more. Let me put a little space around…what went on back there."

Nine

That evening Carl found a group of large boulders to shelter him from the blowing wind and dust that had come up that afternoon and built his evening fire. He tied down both horses, gave them water and gathered what fodder he could find. The last thing: he relieved the black of his saddle. Now he could do what he'd been itching to do all day.

In the fading sunset, he examined the saddle from all angles. He found no obvious holes or chinks where a foreign object might be stashed. But something waited for him in that saddle somewhere.

With his eyes closed, he went over the saddle with just his hands. Surely he'd find a seam, a slight tear, something. He found nothing. He picked it up and hefted it in his arms. The saddle didn't weigh much; therefore the treasure couldn't be gold.

He saw it then, that slightly too wide seam where the cantle meets the seat. He grinned at that. Sure enough, the seam wasn't even sown together. He teased the two pieces of leather apart just a little. The old paper hardly showed in the firelight. Using his little finger, he pulled it little by little toward the slight hole he'd made. Finally, a tiny corner poked beyond the leather and, using the nails of his index finger and thumb, he teased that paper out.

When he held the paper, he realized it wasn't paper at all… it was skin—parchment. It had to be very old. His mouth felt dry and he licked his lips. He had a treasure map. He knew he did. He only needed to find the location of the treasure.

With shaking hands, he opened the parchment. Arabic script covered it. No map features, not so much as a river or a rock. Certainly no X marking the place of the treasure.

A lion would have been proud of his growl. He crumpled the parchment, threw it down and stomped on it.

He didn't know what it was but it wasn't a treasure map…he knew that much. He kicked it just as his satellite phone rang. The sound surprised him so much that it rang twice more before he thought to answer it.

He pulled it off his hip, and Meribet greeted him with a sob.

"I need you," Meribet sobbed. "Help me, please help me."

"What's wrong?"

After another couple of sobs, Meribet said, "Dad's buying a restaurant. He wants me to run a restaurant."

"What's so awful about that? There's lots of people who own restaurants. Lots more run them."

"But not me. I don't want to run an eatery."

"Just tell your dad you don't know how to do restaurants. He'll get someone else."

"No, he won't." She cried loudly. "He's already said so."

"Oh, I see." Carl chuckled. "Bet I know what the deal is."

"What?" She sobbed without control.

When her sobs softened, he said, "Sweetness, I love you. You know that don't you? And you trust me?"

She sobbed an affirmation.

"In his way your dad loves you. He loves you enough to trust you and he don't trust easy. Deal is, he needs a restaurant to run money through."

"Why?" Meribet sniffed.

"It's so nosy feds can't tell where his money to buy and run restaurants and other things came from. He's given you a really responsible job. You're going to be laundering some of his money."

"But I don't want to. Besides, I'm not a short order cook, or even a chef."

"Just ask him to find you something else. He dotes on you. Maybe he'd buy you a clothing factory instead. I know you like fashion."

She sniffed twice before saying, "I love you. You were right. I need you here, with me."

"I'll be home as soon as I can."

His phone gave the series of beeps that meant out of charge.

"Sweetness, my phone is almost out of charge. Gonna have to go."

"No!" Meribet sobbed. "I need you and I want you here with me."

"I love you and I'll fly home as soon—" He knew Meribet didn't hear the rest, "—as I can."

He couldn't think of a curse strong enough. That little generator thing, it lay at the bottom of his pack. He'd have to spend two hours working the crank and then maybe he could do a ten minute call.

If he hadn't been so intent on that Okie blonde, he'd have asked the sheik to let him charge his phone.

"It's that blonde's fault. Now Meribet will run around doing who knows what because she's unhappy." He kicked a stone near his campfire.

"And she'll blame me…she'll think I don't love her and that's not right. I do love her." He circled his campsite while explaining his circumstances to the wind.

"I'd do anything for her. I really, really love her!" He kicked another rock. "I do." He kicked rocks and yelled at the stars until his normally husky voice grew hoarse. Finally, he calmed down.

"Have to call her tonight. If she's asleep, I'll have to wake her. Even if it's three oclock in the A.M." He fished through his pack for the generator.

Then out of the corner of his eye he saw that parchment fly off in a sudden burst of wind. As if he didn't have enough trouble.

He ran after it while cursing every curse he'd ever heard. But in the night, he couldn't see. He had to run back, get his flashlight and rifle. It took him a good ten minutes to chase that paper—parchment down. That night he invented some new curses; all of them intended bad times and turmoil for one female Okie.

Ten

Roz and Chaney needed to refill their canteens. They left the animal trail that had helped them avoid a constant detour around this dead-looking plant or that big rock and headed for the creek. Now they walked on the part of the bank that stood well above the water line at flood stage. But along this part of the creek, they had to deal with thick vines and ever so many seedling trees and a few older ones.

"I'm drinking my last sip," Chaney said.

"I know, but we're not going to elbow any of those crocs out of the way so we can get a drink. Even my dad wouldn't do that. Please have a little patience...please?"

They passed two snakes, but Chaney didn't see them. Roz didn't bring it up.

"This seems like the kind of jungle that Tarzan would live in," Roz said. She kept her eyes scanning, her ears open. Who knew what critter had already set up an ambush? Her skin felt ready to scream in pain as claws and teeth pierced it.

"Yeah." Chaney looked in all directions. "Why did it get so jungle-y all of a sudden?"

"All I know is that being here is giving me an absolute awful case of itches. I want out of here as quick as we can. Walk faster."

Finally, they came to a place where a large number of buzzards sat in the trees that bordered the creek. Those birds waited for something. At first Roz couldn't understand why they were there.

Then the wind shifted. Roz looked at the creek about fifty yards ahead and gagged.

In the creek, all the crocs took turns getting their jaws into some part of a large, stinky-dead antelope or wildebeest, or…something. Each croc in turn death-rolled out a mouthful. They almost seemed mannerly about taking turns.

After a shudder, Roz said, "Okay, this may not look very good—"

"—smells awful." Chaney held her nose.

"Thing is, the crocs are all over there. Give me your canteen and yell if you see any tricky buggers that swim toward me—any that aren't staying with the other crocs."

"Why would they do that?"

"They might decide they'd rather have blonde for lunch."

Roz quietly slid down the bank and onto the muddy water's edge. She tried not to make any quick movements that could attract these dinosaur kin.

She filled both canteens, and slinked back to the lower edge of the steep bank. Then she tore up that hill as if one of those critters were right behind her.

Roz handed Chaney her canteen and paused to let her body catch up with her edgy mind. She still felt a hot breath on her back as if a huge croc were right behind her.

Ridiculous! I'm okay. I know God will take care of our problems. I have to have faith, that's all.

"Okay, let's walk." Roz tried to sound optimistic, but her insides wouldn't settle down and she walked faster.

"Do you have to run?" Chaney complained.

"We need to be out of this jungle. There's bad things in there that we can't see, and I've got the itches sooo bad. Besides, we won't be twenty miles closer to Cairo by sunset if we don't hoof it."

"Bet we've already done ten miles today."

They didn't say much for a while. Then Chaney said, "When can we find something to eat?"

"See this?" Roz pinched her waist. "I'll bet I've still got at least a couple inches of fat stored right there. You do too."

Chaney pinched her own waist. "Yeah." She sighed.

"Might have been more last week, but we're still gross with fat."

"Thanks to Sheik Kelmet who likes his women fat." Chaney sniffed. "Why did he have to be so mean?"

"I don't think we'll be desperate to eat for at least another two, maybe three weeks."

"But I'm hungry."

"I know; I am too. If we find a way, we'll eat. I'm looking for a flint as we walk. Remember? We started looking for flint when we found those rusted pieces of metal."

"The thing that keeps hitting my ankle," Chaney complained.

"I've got one tied in the hem of my burka too, remember."

"So?"

Roz tried not to sound as exasperated at Chaney's lack of understanding as she felt. "With that metal, we got half our need met. When we find a flint, we can have fire anytime we want it."

"Then we won't be so cold at night, won't have to climb trees to keep the critters away."

"But more important, we have to cook our food; wild animals don't have farmers to keep them safe so they get parasites, bad parasites that doctors still don't know how to get rid of."

"We got good doctors."

"You want to take a chance on eating an insect egg that turns into a maggot in your stomach?"

"You're making me sick."

"I hope so. Those maggots like to work themselves out of your stomach and into your blood vessels."

"Ugh!"

"They finish their travels in your eyes or your brain. I had to study about them in my ecology class. That's just one kind of parasite, there are lots of others."

Chaney sniffed. "Tell me again…I'll know it's flint because…?"

"If you see a dark brown or black stone that has a kind of harder look to it than this beige sandstone. Maybe even shiny or glassy looking, give it to me and we'll go from there. Okay?"

"But…I'm hungry and I—" Chaney's expression suddenly changed. She had *that* look.

Chaney picked up a large beige rock that lay almost in front of her. Then she ran after a disappearing gray snake about four feet long. With a grunt, she let the rock fly. It hit the snake midway between its head and its tail. The snake flailed terribly.

Roz also picked up a head-sized stone and launched it. The crunch of delicate bones made her shudder, but it had to be done. Even a snake shouldn't suffer like that.

The snake trembled and eventually quit moving.

"There." Chaney dusted her hands. "I heard you can eat rattlesnake. Why can't we eat this snake?"

"Would you carry it until we find our flints? Please?"

"Yuck. Gonna have enough trouble eating it. Don't wanna carry it."

"I'll butcher it, but you can do your part by carrying it."

"Yuck, double yuck," Chaney said.

"We eat that, or we'll have to eat bugs or nothing at all."

"Yuck, phooey!"

"Sorry, hon, we're fresh out of McDonalds. Let's walk faster. There's hamburgers waiting for you in Cairo."

"How much longer before we get to the Nile?"

About an hour later, Roz noticed Chaney still carried the dead snake. The girl really wanted to eat—that spare tire around her waist had nothing to do with what her stomach told her.

"Come on. I want to reach that tree," Roz said.

"It's still early."

"Won't be by the time we walk way over there."

"Okay," Chaney drawled and complained the whole distance to the tree.

Roz finally quit trying to encourage her and just walked, fast. After what seemed a small eternity, they reached the tree and bedded for the night.

The morning came and the girls kept walking.

"Chaney, let's move it," Roz said.

Chaney's feet dragged as if she'd already run a marathon.

Since there really wasn't an immediate reason to hurry so much, Roz said nothing else. Just put her energy into reaching those next boulders that were still at least ten miles away. Looking back at Chaney dragging along would only make her more impatient and on edge, so she decided not to look.

Before she checked on Chaney again, the boulders turned much less pale with distance and closer to the true beige color the rocks would be when they reached them.

At last, Roz and Chaney approached the mountain of rocks near the tree where they meant to spend the night.

Rocks of all sorts lay in a haphazard pile. Roz began to sort through the mass.

"Surely we can find a couple of flint rocks here somewhere. These rocks look like something a flood dragged together. Maybe some flints got caught in it, so let's look real careful."

They'd been looking for flints for a while when they heard men's voices from the direction of the creek.

Chaney turned her head, listening, then looked to Roz.

"It could be our 'masters' still looking for us," Roz whispered. "We better hide—hide and hope."

A stricken look came over Chaney's face. She dropped the snake. "Over there?" The younger girl pointed to the most distant and the most massive of the rocks. Chaney didn't wait; she mumbled something and ran.

Roz grabbed the dead snake and tucked it under her left arm. A nearby clump of dried grass yielded a whisk broom to make their escape complete. She swept away their footprints, but pale dust hung over the sand.

Please Lord Jesus, God, let it be enough.

She hobbled backwards and swept away the footprints while disappearing into the boulders

"Hurry! Don't want to be no ho." Chaney dropped behind the distant boulder. Her whole body trembled. "Not for nobody."

Roz knelt behind the boulders facing Chaney.

"We'll be okay. We just have to be real still until they leave," Roz whispered. "Picture us walking into the embassy in Cairo."

Chaney murmured something.

"It's all right," Roz whispered.

She patted Chaney's shaking shoulders. Then she realized she still held the dead snake in her left hand. Carefully she pushed it on top of the boulders with only the undamaged part showing.

They won't come close to snakes, surely they won't come close.

Roz heard them talking plainly now. She snuggled her burka-clad body closer to the boulder. Just like Chaney, she tried to dig herself into the ground. What had started as trembling became violent shaking.

Think of Dad. Be brave. Stop shivering.

On the other side of their pile of rocks, someone made a remark and all the men laughed.

She might never know enough Arabic to understand their crude jokes. But she understood this language well enough to know what they'd like to do to two blonde females.

They said something about diamonds. She didn't understand that at all.

The voice of one of them had a rasping growl to it. Had to be Carl. Why couldn't he leave her alone? She knew he'd had a grudge ever since she'd accidentally knocked him out. The slave-ship's crew made jokes about it and called their first mate 'glass jaw' and 'pansy' when they thought he couldn't hear. Was that the sin of the century? Why couldn't he just drop it?

Was it because she'd told the captain that he intended to rape one of the blondes and indirectly got him fired? Even that wasn't the end of the world. There were better jobs than being the lead bad-guy on a ship that brought concubines and slaves to African sheiks and ruler-types.

At least Chaney couldn't understand enough Arabic to follow any of what these men said. If Chaney knew, she'd turn pure rabbit and run; get both of them hurt bad.

The sun had faded from its mid-day fury, but Roz felt a chill. At first she assumed that the horror of her situation had gotten to her.

Then she saw movement at the edge of her vision. A twin of the dead snake she'd put on top of the rock slithered into view. She held herself absolutely still.

But Chaney moved away in extreme slow motion.

While she tried to imitate a statue, Roz whispered, "Don't move!"

Chaney still crawled away.

"Chaney, be still."

"You be still. Snakes must think you taste good," Chaney said in a whispered hiss. "You move; he'll bite. I hate snakes."

"Those men are still out there," Roz whispered.

"Gonna kill me a snake."

"I won't move. Snake won't strike if I don't move," Roz pleaded.

"I won't give you up to that snake."

"He hasn't even coiled. Be quiet until those men go away."

"You're all I've got."

"Be still!"

Chaney crawled backwards.

Roz knew she mustn't move.

"Chaney!"

Eleven

Chaney still crawled backwards.

"Stay put!" Roz hissed. "The men will be gone in a few minutes. That snake can stare at me all he wants; I won't move a muscle. I promise."

Helpless, Roz lay still. Chaney retreated until she curled up at the edge of the group of boulders that sheltered them.

"Chaney!"

Chaney peeked her black burka'd head around the last of the boulders. A large rock lay about three feet away.

Chaney stayed low, scooted to it and quicker than Roz would have thought, darted back within the shelter of their boulders.

Careful to stay hidden below the top of the boulders, she pushed and rolled her prize toward Roz.

"They didn't see me. I waited until their backs were turned," Chaney whispered.

"Okay, you did good. Now, please, please be still until those men leave."

Chaney eased herself up so she could see over the top of the boulders. "They're gone. Now I can kill that ugly thing."

"I can still smell them," Roz whispered. "They're not gone; I know it. Wait a few more minutes."

But Chaney hefted the rock and stood.

"Don't do it!"

Just as she'd done with the other snakes, Chaney lifted the rock to her shoulder.

"Don't! Not yet!"

Chaney took two quick steps toward the snake, stood on tiptoes and tossed the rock with an impressive grunt. The usual meaty thud wrote the end to that snake.

Roz knew she'd failed and now she'd die and so would Chaney.

Lord Jesus, I'll be seeing you soon. Please don't let this hurt too much.

Moments later the gunshot-like crack of a bullwhip sounded from the other side of their boulders. The lifeless snake flopped across her neck at the same time as that blow.

Run. We should run!

Roz meant to grab Chaney and try for freedom. But her body wouldn't obey and the cold snake's body writhed across her back. Why couldn't she move?

Boots stomped toward them; Roz saw Carl through the eye-hole of her burka.

His whip cracked again. Chaney squealed and the murmur of her running feet died away. But Roz lay on the baking sand.

"I can't, I can't."

Other feet tramped toward her.

The whip exploded and a torch blazed across her left shoulder. She screamed. Again the whip bit and again she screamed.

"Get up," the raspy voice said.

She knew it would be better if she obeyed. She tried; she really tried to stand. And failed.

Again the whip cracked.

She couldn't move.

From her left shoulder, something heavy crawled down her arm.

What does it matter if I bleed? They'll kill me and Chaney too.

"Jesus, I'm sorry; I've made a mess of this. I'm so sorry," she moaned.

Then she felt that urge—a wanting that seemed to resonate from all of her insides, and yet it came from outside. Almost a voice—not that she actually heard it, but it was as "there" as a voice would be.

Tell him how to be saved.

She knew that inner voice, God's direction. But what good would it do this time?

A big hand gripped her bloodied shoulder. It hurt terribly. She stood to ease the pain.

Carl took her burka in both hands and ripped it apart across her face. The cap slid off her head.

"You wanna give me my diamonds or shall I take 'em out of your hide?"

Roz blinked. "Diamonds?"

Tell him! Let him hear about Jesus.

Carl shook her.

The yards of fabric, freed from the cap, threatened to fall from her shoulders. "I don't know anything about diamonds." She held the cloth on her chest. "But, but…I know about something more precious, more valuable…God will give you salvation.

He slapped her and she felt his hand tremble. "Take your clothes off."

Roz couldn't think; what should she do?

He grabbed her and with a growl, he shook her even harder. When she said nothing; did nothing, he ripped the burka from neck to hem.

His hand shook when he grabbed the fabric. But his trembling didn't stop him; he gripped the black fabric and pulled until she fell. Her garment remained in Carl's hand. She wore only her slip-like undergarment.

"N-No matter what you've done, God still loves you and…"

He shook the burka. Then he went over each seam. After that he felt the hem.

"…God, He wants you with Him for all of eternity."

"Take it off." He demanded.

His face, it's so red, is that a blush?

Not knowing what to do, she did nothing.

He backhanded her. "Take it off."

This man kills people. Lord Jesus, I can't…

He had a peculiar look on his face and he panted.

Tell him!

She'd better obey…

"Didn't you hear? God loves you and wants you to live with Him forever."

The peculiar look on Carl's face turned into a grimace.

"Gimme that." He reached for her undergarment, but he flinched and stopped short of touching her. Instead, he slid that big revolver out of the holster. It quivered visibly. "Maybe I'll shoot right now. You wanta keep breathing a while? Gimme."

She lifted her only covering. While covering herself with her hand, she gave it to him.

He held it up; both his hands quivered. The cloth had only a seam on each side and a hole for the head. He squeezed it all over.

When even a blind person could tell that there were no diamonds, he slapped her hard.

"Where'd you hide them?"

Her head spinning, she said. "I-I didn't."

He glared at her and again his face turned even redder.

Roz wrestled up her courage; God told her to do this. She'd better do it.

"Jesus d-died on the cross so you wouldn't have to. Don't you understand? Jesus p-paid for every sin—every crime, even the murder I saw."

He panted as if he'd been running.

"If you'll let him, Jesus will make you as clean as though you never did any of it. Least as far as God is concerned."

Carl said words she couldn't understand, raised his shaking fist to hit her and she put her arms up to deflect the blow.

But nothing happened, and his hands shook as if he had developed Parkinson's. Then he turned and yelled at someone.

Her undergarment and her burka lay within reach. Without taking her eyes from Carl, she crawled into the slip and gathered the torn burka's cloth around herself.

"Stay alive, stay alive," she whispered and closed her eyes tight.

Carl whistled and then yelled again. Another man came. Carl said, "I was going to kill her, but life as a common slave will be bad enough for now. Let her God get her out of that."

"Right," the man said.

"Sheik Kelmet said I could do whatever I wanted with this piece of garbage. Can you think of a suitable, uh, punishment, something she won't die from?"

"I know just the thing. You'll enjoy it." The man laughed.

"Can't stay," Carl said. "I have to pick up my horses; do my errand for 'his majesty,' the sheik. Then I got to uh, rescue someone."

The other man grunted, and Roz looked at him more closely. He stood at least six feet tall, skeleton thin and had a tribal scar of three waves on his cheek.

"If she escapes, Kazir, I swear I'll kill you. You're to tell me who buys her, understand? Who gets her and where they live. I'll be back in three weeks, four tops. Then I'll…" Carl walked away fast. He never stopped talking.

"Yes, sir!" Kazir, the tribal man, took control of Roz's shoulder; it hurt and she gritted her teeth; only a slight moan escaped.

"Over here," Kazir yelled to someone. Another man came.

"Take this trash to camp. George knows what to do with her. Think you can manage that?"

"Yessuh," the man said.

That voice. Roz knew that voice.

Twelve

Wondering, Roz saw a tall silhouette against the orange of sunset. He flashed a gleaming white smile.

"James?" she whispered.

He propelled her away from Carl and the tribal man. "Move!" His hand on her bicep hurt, but he seemed intent on getting away, not on causing pain. "Fix your clothes."

Roz tried to run through the sand and scruffy weeds, while making her ruined burka cover her and at the same time keep up with James, her strange guardian angel.

Nothing held her torn garment together. She finally wrapped the ruins of her burka around her shoulders twice and knotted it at the neck so that it became a sort of poncho. Her clothing stayed together in a modest if not very comfortable manner.'

When they were about fifty feet from Carl, James looked back. Then he barked in a voice that needed no microphone, "You just don't listen too good. I thought you'd know how to be safe. The other blond idiots might not know, but I thought you had smarts."

She stumbled on a clump of brittle grass and fell in the sand.

James yelled at her, "You thought you'd get away from me? Forget it." He pulled her upright and after taking a quick look behind him, resumed his grip on her bicep.

He dragged her along while they walked up a sandy hill or maybe a dune. After they lurched and slid down the other side, he whispered, "We get ahead far 'nuff, we'll talk. We gots a long walk."

Hope welled up. Maybe, maybe she wasn't dead yet. She did her best to walk faster.

James' grip on her shoulder grew less painful. That gleaming white smile lit his ebony face. He looked behind them once more and breathed a sigh.

"Okay miss, you want to be free. I knows it. I did too."

"But you weren't a slave—were you?"

"They don't call it by that name but a slave is still a slave."

"I don't understand. A slave is a slave is a slave," Roz said.

"That's what I thought. I used to play poker and I made a right smart livin' at it. Kept three families in groceries and paid their rent. They was just poor folks with no way out. Weren't even my relatives or nothing.

"If'n I did that much, I thought God sorta looked the other way because I had plenty left over for me. Not that He'd say gamblin's okay, 'course.

"Then something happened and for weeks I jest couldn't get no good luck no how. They bought me for my debt. Until now, I never could pay 'em off," he said.

"But you got free; how?" Roz asked.

"Bought myself off'n that slave ship. Been saving my pay and not gambling for a couple years. Been prayin' a lot, too. I told God I won't never gamble no more. This here's my job now."

"A job?"

"All I got to do is join with these men from here to the Aseewanee dam, do their cooking and any other jobs they tells me to, and if they don't kill me, I'm a free human bein' on my way home."

"Kill you?"

"Yeah, I kinda don't get along with some people."

"Oh, like your twin?"

"Yeah, like George."

"On that slave ship, he seemed to like his work."

"That's for a fact. I gots to do this right. If I do, I'll even have a little money in my jeans when I gets home. I means to do what I promised. No more gamblin.' I'll enroll in business school and get to be a bookkeeper. That's what I told God. And that's what I means to do."

James looked over his shoulder. "Walk faster." He dragged her along. "Bought myself off'n that ship with what I saved and a diamond I found on the shore while we been layin' over."

"Diamonds? There's diamonds here? In the Sudan? So that's what he meant."

James laughed. "Don't you be tellin'. I found a few and I be keepin' it quiet."

"I won't breathe a word."

"Ol' Carl found a passel of 'em. Kept 'em in his canteen, the one you stole."

"But I didn't—"

"He's mad; he'd kill you except he's got something else going. Be careful, still might kill you if you give him a reason."

"Diamonds?" Roz shook her head.

"Course, if you could give all them diamonds back, it might be different."

"But I don't have any diamonds."

Then she remembered the pebbles in one of the canteens. "Oh wait. There were some little rocks in one of the canteens I stole."

"What'd you do with 'em?"

"I dumped the rocks in the creek."

"Rocks!" James roared with laughter. "Them were raw diamonds."

"We needed the water lot more than rocks or even diamonds… Never thought about diamonds."

James said nothing for several strides. "Don't suppose you could tell me where you tossed 'em?"

"It's where we first climbed out of the creek. There's a cliff almost twenty feet tall."

Then she realized, "You're thinking of trying to find them, aren't you?"

"Thinkin' on it."

"Maybe you could buy us and we'd take you where I dumped them. Maybe between the three of us, we could find some of them… the bigger ones at least."

"You really think you could find 'em?"

"We wouldn't ask anything except to be taken to the American Embassy in Cairo. You'd have all those diamonds. You could go home in style."

"All I'd have to do is keep you alive and get you to Cairo."

"That's all we'd ask. And we'd be so grateful."

"I'll do it. Least ways, I'll try to get them to sell you to me. But I gots to tell you, I'll have to talk harder than I ever talked. My measly few diamonds won't be enough unless there's a cert-e-fried miracle."

"But you'll try?"

"Can't use them other diamonds that you threw out 'cause we don't have 'em yet. Gonna be a marvel, gettin' you free."

Ahead, tents stood near the creek bank and at least a dozen men milled about.

"Uh-oh," James said and increased his speed until he dragged Roz along. "We gotta impress the boss. See him up there?"

On the sunset-lighted hill above them, Carl, riding a gray and white horse and holding the reins of a black, looked down on them.

"Gots to be rough, only way. Screamin' be good, if you wants."

She screamed and whimpered as he instructed.

Another scream sounded ahead of them. Chaney. Roz had heard those screams often enough. Why must the kid scream so loud? And so often?

Who knew why? Chaney wouldn't change; maybe she couldn't. Maybe it's part of what being born to an alcoholic is about.

Have to live with it—if I get a chance to live.

Ahead, men stood as if lined up, waiting. Like those vultures killing time until the crocs left.

"Scream real good," James said.

Roz screamed and writhed. She howled, screamed and whimpered. She made it a good act, really convincing.

James didn't say another word. He just handed her over to another man. This one looked like James except for his gray-colored, rotten teeth. This was James' twin, George, a man who might be even more cruel than Carl.

She collapsed with her face in the dirt before this monster. This time she wasn't acting.

Thirteen

Minutes passed. Roz realized that she still lived and raised her head ever so little. Her neck stayed on her shoulders.

Encouraged, she raised up enough to see the ogre's boot heels. The hot sand seemed soft compared to the torture she'd endure if James didn't come through.

Her small momentary comfort grew less as Chaney's screaming grew louder. Would that girl never stop screeching? Someone lit torches. And after that, a sound of tapping began. Soon Chaney's screaming grew until it filled the whole outdoors. Roz lifted her head to see between the ogre's boots.

Chaney lay in the dirt on her back with her ankles tied to a wooden pole.

Two men held the pole and a third man wielded a flexible rod. The rod tapped Chaney's feet many times every minute.

Roz put her forehead on the sand. She'd read about this torture in a spy novel. One of the most painful, non-fatal punishments known. When they got through with Chaney, she'd think her whole body had been beaten, not just her feet.

Then it would be Roz's turn. It would be days before she could walk at all and for a long time after that, she wouldn't want to walk very far. Even the thought of escape wouldn't be possible.

The beating went as Roz predicted. She tried not to scream. Tried to be an example of how a truly free person behaves when treated as a slave. Tried to be as brave as her dad had been when he'd been tortured.

Long before Roz passed out, she heard screams. She never knew that her own throat made those sounds.

She came to while being dragged across the hard-packed dirt by her left arm. Someone picked her up and tossed her into the back of a pickup. Chaney screamed and settled into a constant crying. The pickup took off and Roz's consciousness faded and returned, faded and returned with each pothole and rock they crossed. The truck stopped and someone ordered them out, and she crawled from the truck. When her feet touched the soil, consciousness couldn't stand up to the intense pain. Someone grabbed her arm and dragged her away.

She heard James say something, and the dragging stopped.

The man who dragged her cursed James. She knew that voice better than she'd like...George had her.

"But you said I could have her if'n I paid for her," James said.

George laughed at him.

"And here's her price and the little one's too."

She looked up. James held something, offered it to his twin brother.

She didn't breathe. James held her lifeline out of here! Maybe, maybe...After all, they were brothers. Brothers cut each other slack, sometimes.

But George cursed his twin and batted the offered goods away.

"Stupid," George growled. "Can't even tell when you're gettin' the wrong end of a joke...niggah."

With a roar, James slammed into his brother with both fists. He hit him three blows before George could get a single blow on him. But a man as tall as the twins walked up behind James.

James landed one in George's middle.

"Break it up," the tall man ordered.

Both twins ignored him. George got in a blow.

Roz knew that tall man...Carl called him Kazir and gave him orders.

"I said, break it up." The voice held ice, only ice.

James didn't listen any better than George. He hit his brother twice more.

Kazir brought a club down on James's head. James collapsed with his face maybe a foot from Roz. He looked totally at peace…and totally out.

Poor James…

…Poor Roz and poor Chaney. If we're going to Cairo, we've still got it to do.

"Get on with it." Kazir stood with his legs apart and one hand on his hip and the other holding that club. He dared George to disregard his order.

Roz tried to stand, but couldn't make it to her knees.

"Stupid." George pushed her down with his boot and then picked her up by her left ankle. With her face in the dirt, he dragged her along. It hurt. She tried to keep her head up, out of the dirt. But the heartbeat that throbbed through her left foot made the world go dark again. This time she welcomed the dense blackness. Pain didn't register there.

Returning consciousness became the sound of a rusty gate opening. George's flashlight kept going dark and he shook it to make the batteries work, if only dimly. She felt herself being pushed inside by George's boot. With a groan, she tried to crawl further away.

"Slut," George said and spat.

Roz only inched far enough from the gate to let it close and avoid another kick. Even that movement took all her strength. But her hearing remained healthy—as healthy as Chaney's voice.

She'd had her fill of Chaney's bawling.

"Chaney, shut up!" she said with a moan.

Chaney kept on screaming, of course. She screamed until Roz either became unconscious again or perhaps she slept.

All Roz knew for sure was that the sun set hours ago and she still lived. Cold, in pain and in a place that smelled like a sewer, but still alive.

Her condition didn't matter; she intended to keep her vow to escape and take Chaney with her. An opportunity, all that mattered. God would provide, she didn't doubt that He would make a way for them. For now, she had no choice but to be a good slave in whatever way her master wanted her to be.

Kelmet: did he still own her? If not, who owned her, now that she had done the unthinkable and run away?

Fourteen

After Carl finished the evening's camp chores, he sat at the fire twirling the handle on his miniature generator. The moon glowered at him and he stopped and looked at his shaking hands. His insides quivered just like his hands. Neither had anything to do with the cold of the desert night.

He'd meant to kill the Okie when he caught her. Why hadn't he done it?

"It was that God talk. That's what. Her talking about Something I know don't exist."

He thought about it strongly enough to stop working with his generator.

After that pause, he worked the generator so hard he could hear it growl. "I'll kill that Okie so slow…" He twisted that little handle for a long time.

"I'll kill her real…real, slow."

After he recharged his phone, he had to figure out the right time of day to call Meribet and soothe her. His watch said eight o'clock p.m. there on the east side of Africa. What's the difference in hours to the west side of the U.S.A? Had to figure that out.

He'd marry Meribet, put her on his island as its queen and make sure her dad never got another chance to see her. Only way to get any sort of revenge on a man as powerful as Gregorio A. Carnelli.

Besides, he really, really did love beautiful Meribet of the shining black hair.

Because he felt restless, Carl checked on his horses again, made sure that crazed black stallion wouldn't break loose and that both the black and Harley had fodder to eat. He sat down, though he still felt uneasy, shaky...and cold, much colder than usual. He moved closer to the small circle of firelight. The night grew silent, not even a hyena yap to break it.

And then the hairs on his arms rose. He knew; he knew Something watched him. Something that, if it wanted, could grab him and sling him around like a rat in a terrier's mouth.

He refused to think that thought. This wasn't like him at all. Meribet, his loving, lovely Meribet. He'd get comfort and strength out of Meribet's voice.

He called. He woke her; it was the middle of the night. Meribet was fine; he said he was fine and they hung up. He wasn't fine. He could hardly breathe.

"This is stupid."

A night's sleep and time, a little time will take care of it. Fully loaded rifle in hand, he jumped on Harley's bare back and prepared to doze the night away.

~ * ~

The night passed and at earliest dawn he woke, Something remained out there, invisible and horrible.

After his morning's camp chores, he still felt this terrible—thing, watching him.

He paced awhile. His hands still trembled and his chest and stomach quivered.

"She did this to me. There ain't nothing out there, and there ain't no boogy-man God. They explained that to me in my philosophy classes."

Saying those words didn't stop his trembling. "That's stuff from cave man times. Modern people know better." He drew in a deep breath and shouted, "There ain't no God!"

This fear of "Something" had been a constant in his life until he got on the back of his first race horse. On a fast horse, he could outdistance any threat, and freedom from fear lasted a long time, weeks, sometimes a month, after a race. As a jockey, he'd put all his dreads behind him. When he grew too tall to be a jockey, his fright came back and he thought he'd always have to live with that impending doom and collapsed spine. He'd have to bow to every SOB who said, "Boo!"

"I oughta get my nerve back."

His gut pulled in as if preparing for a punch. "She won't get away with it."

He'd go back and fill that Okie full of holes. As he put his foot in the stirrup he hesitated. "I can't... she'll say something and I'll be worse off than I am now."

There was a way. It would take a little time, but it always cured this ailment of his and out here, he wouldn't have to worry about the cleanup.

A wadi cut the rolling landscape a few miles away. He stashed the black in that twelve-foot-deep canyon.

There was a village not more than ten miles back and to take care of the horses' needs, he'd had to trek to a well that was a couple of miles away from the town. It was the nearest water for three different villages.

He took the first woman who came to the well by herself.

She screamed and he muzzled her with duct-tape. He taped her wrists together and threw her over the saddle. It only took a couple of minutes max. When he slid into the saddle, he already felt better...even his blood pressure felt better. Harley took off at his usual amble. Carl hauled his prize to the wadi where he'd already corralled the black.

He staked her down using branches cut from a scrub tree. He cut them using the largest blade on his multi-bladed pocket knife. The tape worked just fine to fix her to the stakes. He should have thought to bring rope.

At first, he just watched her squirm...when she stopped writhing, he touched her with the point of the tiniest blade and listened to her muffled screams. It was as if the fear left him and entered her. He felt as if, Something had moved further from him. This was good, real good.

But then he examined his victim and saw more anger than fear in her eyes. Well, pain does a good job of taking away anger. He knelt and opened his pocket knife to his cutting blade. He had taken special pains with the sharpening of that blade. And now Carl held it an inch or so from her eyes. She choked, screamed and twisted, just as he knew she would. He let the cold metal glide down her nose, her lips, her neck and there, at her collar, he let the blade slice through her dress all the way down to the hem. Sometimes he had to wait at this point, because they tended to faint. But not this one; she still had anger in her eyes.

Carl knew he'd have to take longer than usual with her. Where should he start? He wanted to keep her alert, not let her faint too often, not let her die on him too soon. A toe? Yeah, a toe. He stabbed the point of the knife into her left smallest toe just deep enough to draw a little blood. She screamed and writhed. He ran the point up a little higher. He liked making tattoo-like designs on his victims while they lived. Artistry was in his blood from his mother's side.

She wriggled so much he couldn't draw on her as he wanted. He pulled up her left leg stake and held her foot in his hand. She squirmed mightily. First, he'd give her permanent sandals. He dragged his knife across her instep from small toe to large. The cut was just deep enough to make little beads, like rubies. She fainted then.

With a giggle, he cut the tape holding her right leg. Facing away from her body, he straddled her and lifting that right leg, he stroked her foot; marveled at it, so delicate…he would add his own creative touches to it as soon as she came back to consciousness.

Pain!

Pain shooting upward from between his legs!

He crumpled into a ball and held himself. No room in his brain for anything but agony. He couldn't even breathe.

Dimly, he saw her yank on her left arm's stake with her right arm. He couldn't process what he saw. He didn't see right; no woman did this.

She stood up while pulling the tape from her mouth. The instant she could, she cursed him with curses he didn't want to understand. Then she grabbed a piece of half-burned tree branch and she hit him. He went down on her second blow and by her fifth, he bawled as if he were still ten years old.

Mercifully she stopped with her twelfth blow. Harley stood munching on some bit of green. That, that, female marched over to his horse, grabbed Harley's reins, and swung up onto his bare back.

"Hayah!" she yelled and rode Harley toward him, tried to make Harley stomp him.

Was it Harley's good will or his own tremendous jump that prevented his being trampled?

She rode off, more bare in front than if she wore a bikini and riding *his* horse.

He passed out.

When he woke, he knew he hadn't been out long. The shadows had barely changed.

He heard a sound that at any other time he would have said was a hyena. He knew better; Something laughed at him.

A quick look around showed no resources. She'd untied the black and run him off. She rode Harley. Oh sure, he had a saddle but no horse. He had a canteen, but only filled with water…no diamonds. Oh yeah, he had a few matches and a bit of food. What were those few things against what he faced?

On finding no solutions, Carl sat down on a rock. "Oh well, time will straighten all this out. Always does."

After sitting and staring at his ruined camp for a while, Carl climbed out of the wadi. Maybe he could make things come together. He always managed somehow.

His left forearm and right shoulder had already turned purple. His head hurt terribly and he felt his face. He had at least two bruises on his face, no, three. The reason his head hurt surely had something to do with the knots he felt. He didn't want anyone to see him like this.

No choice, he had to stay out here, without so much as a horse for a couple of weeks.

"I'll have to gather lots more firewood, make a big fire every night to keep the beasties away. Yeah, and I'll go to the well and fill my canteen when no one's there. Sure, I can do that long enough for my bruises to fade some. Then I have to see about getting another horse."

And he knew Something watched him.

He shook his fist. "Whatever You are, You got a fight on Your hands. You ain't gettin' me cheap."

~ * ~

Two days later, near sundown, he visited the well. Harley stood about fifty yards away, peacefully chowing on a patch of brush. Good ol' Harley allowed Carl to grab his reins.

He used what he knew of searching to find the black. He found him. The stallion had outrun a lion or something, but just barely. His right butt and thigh bore claw marks deep enough to brand him. This would not make Sighit al Azibik happy; it couldn't be helped.

Fifteen

At dawn, Roz found that she had been tossed into a mud-brick enclosure. The walls measured about eight, maybe nine feet tall, with razor wire on top. They ought to be just about escape-proof even by a healthy person.

A number of other people lay or sat within this place. All of them looked as dispirited or ill and as ragged and dirty as any human beings she'd ever seen. Who were these people?

Worse than her surroundings, she found that the pain in her feet registered as extreme. She couldn't stand at all. Almost as bad: Chaney cried constantly.

By the third day after her beating, she'd noticed that the people in this enclosure changed often. That thin man who had the wavy tribal scar carved in his left cheek would come in and pick out several people.

He would touch them with his coiled whip and those people would be forced out of this…this cattle pen for humans. Later, other people would be forced in. Often they'd been beaten in some way.

Roz didn't know what went on here. The other people stayed away from the two blondes and she didn't know enough of the customs to make friends, though she tried a few times. They either refused to talk to her, or worse, they kicked or hit her.

No one helped. Just crawling to the trough that contained water and algae became the goal of life. The morning of the fourth day, she managed to walk to the trough. But her feet felt broken and she only did it once. Her croc-bitten hand throbbed just like her feet and infection made it red, pus-filled.

She tried to stay close to the trough, but the other people kicked her if she stayed real close for more than a minute. Once a day, most days, someone threw food over the wall, but the quickest ate it before she could crawl that far.

On the fifth day, she had a chance to get some information. They threw in a man who had been foot-beaten as she had been. He'd found a place near the wall and though he was as black as the rest, no one wanted to be near him.

She crawled to his side and said in her slow, but polite Arabic. "Hello."

A puzzled expression overlaid the pain on the man's face. "You're white."

"That's right and I'm also a slave."

"What did you do?" he asked.

"I tried to escape. I'm lucky I'm not dead," Roz said. "Now will you please tell me what is this place? What do they do here?"

"You don't know, do you?"

Roz wanted to growl at this dumb donkey, but as politely as she knew how, she said, "If I knew, I wouldn't ask. What do they do here?"

"Lady, you're in a sales yard."

"Sales yard?"

"They'll keep us here until they have a buyer or until the next auction."

"You mean they'll sell us like they sold slaves in my country two centuries ago."

"Gonna sell us, yep."

The enormity of what they did there flooded over her.

Roz had known she and Chaney weren't the first or only slaves in this country.

But somehow it seemed more than horrible that they sold human beings as if they were used cars. Chaney, herself and all these people weren't counted as human, just things to use and throw away.

Roz crawled away from the foot-beaten man.

For years she'd tried with all the gusto she had to make life work. But everything kept being taken from her.

First her friends, because of her dad's moving from one army post to another. But she learned to do without close friends. She still missed having a real pal to share her secrets with, but she'd become comfortable with it.

Then her mother died.

Now her dad, even her little brother, Bobby, all of them, had been taken from her. Would she ever see them again?

She had worked, no, labored, hard on being the best at her schooling. Her education had also been ripped away. Who would use a slave's education? Slaves don't need education.

They'd sell her and put her to working at something that would kill her slowly, painfully, like in a mine a hundred, two hundred feet underground. She'd never have the chance or the nerve to escape again.

Defeat. Total, overwhelming defeat flooded over her. She needed to find a quiet place and finish dying inside. But since they'd herded a number of people into this place earlier that day, every corner had its own set of humans. Only one place had no one.

She minced on painful feet to the portion of the mud-brick wall where the sun shone its warmest. No one wanted to be there. She sat with her back against the wall. Later someone stumbled over her legs. They cursed her and kicked her, but she said nothing, did nothing. She wanted to die and dead people don't react. So she bent her knees and put her feet against her hips and ignored them.

Roz couldn't totally ignore the heat and sunlight. She arranged her hair so that it formed a mat on top and a thatch that covered her face and most of her arms. She kept her arms crossed across her chest and out of harm's way. Her feet stayed under the shelter of her burka.

She couldn't see Chaney, but Chaney had to learn to fend for herself sometime and now worked better than later.

About sundown, Chaney crawled to Roz. "Why are you here where it's so hot?"

Roz drew her feet up further. She put her elbows on her knees and her hands on her forehead. "Where should I be?"

"You might want to be a little bit cooler. And you might try being with me," Chaney said.

"Why? You're better off without me. I'm so sorry. I should have left you with our first master. You'd have been better off."

"You think I want to be a ho?" Chaney sobbed and fresh tears made more trails down her dirty cheeks. "You think I want you hurting if I can help it? That what you think?" She squalled loud cries that must have been heard at the farthest part of this sun-dried town.

"Shh, shh." Roz scooted next to her. "It's all right, it's all right," she repeated until Chaney sobbed her way down to a more reasonable wail and stopped holding Roz so tight.

"Hon, there's not a chance we'll be sold to the same person. I'm so sorry I don't know what to do."

While sobbing and hiccupping, Chaney grabbed Roz again, held her tight and cried, and cried.

Roz did the one thing she wished her mother could do for her. She held the girl and rocked her slightly. All the while she murmured, "It's all right. It's all right."

Roz put her face against Chaney's head. Tears welled up and fell into the tangled mass of Chaney's sun-bleached hair.

"It's all right," she repeated.

But it wasn't all right. No chance that it would ever be all right again for either of them. Chaney, the child, couldn't understand.

"Dear God, I can't fix this." Then she grabbed Chaney, held her tight and cried.

And cried.

Sixteen

Carl followed the trail. The map told him exactly how many miles he needed to travel north and then west. Carl believed in maps. They were one of the good things out here in this vague landmass that had not so much as a sign to help a man make his way.

For the last hour, the black hadn't fought him and that helped. Helped a lot.

About noon he stopped. Something didn't feel right. Mostly, he'd gotten through those nightmare feelings he had for a while; he knew his feelings weren't that shaky "God" nonsense bothering him again. He dismounted and fished through his saddlebags. It took a bit of time, but now that he had his compass in his hand, he felt a lot better.

"Come on, Harley," he said and mounted up.

Carl hadn't needed to correct the black for a long time and with Carl relaxed, the black chose that moment to show off his truly evil nature. Before he could stiffen his arm and prevent him, the black's head snaked over and took a hunk out of Harley's side.

Harley screamed and slammed his head into the black's neck and then took a bite from the black's shoulder. He reared up with another scream and then he bucked, Carl wasn't prepared. He found himself sitting on the hardest dirt imaginable. He still held the black's reins and the black didn't like that at all.

Quick before the black trampled him, Carl jumped to his feet and pulled hard. The black responded with a series of jumps and hops, but settled, sorta. Harley kept making those neigh-screams that said he was one outraged beast.

Carl slowly walked toward his horse. "Hey there, Harley. Maybe they weren't lying when those village men said you was special."

Harley screamed again and pawed the air.

"Aww, let's not go there. I'll be more careful and keep this black cuss off you. You must of been a fiery spirit when you were a colt. Maybe I need to get you some ladies, so's we can have a bunch of little Harleys. Whatcha say, fellow?"

He almost reached Harley's reins, but the black reached out, teeth first, and Harley shied away. A few curse words later, Carl looked for a rock or bush on which to tie this infernal black stallion. He found a scrubby little bush that had the right degree of strength and wrapped the black's reins around it.

"Com'ere, ol' fella. It's all right, that black cuss ain't gonna get you again."

Harley nickered at Carl and came in a slow walk.

"Yeah, Harley is a good horse," Carl told his mount as he got on board.

He grabbed the black's reins and jerked on those reins until the stallion stopped fighting. Then he continued down the trail in the direction the map said.

"Maybe I could get back to the racing game as something better than a jockey if I had some little Harleys. Yeah, I could go partners with Paulos. We been friends a long time and I know he wants to get in that game." Carl chatted at Harley. "But we still gotta get this black creep here to his village. Let's try to travel a little faster, Okay?"

Harley didn't respond, of course.

Seventeen

About three weeks later, too many people had been packed into the human cattle-pen that held Roz and Chaney. They had to sleep sitting, leaning against another body. The smell of unwashed bodies and human waste made Roz wonder if she'd developed asthma.

She remembered her first day on that slave ship. She'd been terrified, almost numb, and they made her clean up who knew how many bushels of human dung. They'd made most of the ship below decks into the area where they chained the thousand or so people who would become common slaves. Now, as then, ammonia closed down her lungs, made every breath cost too much. Surely the Lord would see that she got through this tough time. She survived that ship; she would live through this.

The tribal man with the whip entered, but he didn't drive any more people into the pen. Instead, he used his coiled whip to touch several people and pointed to the gate. Two of those he touched shuffled toward that opening and the third, a man, broke into tears.

The crying man said words Roz didn't understand. Then he ambled toward the gate all the while looking back at the man with the whip.

The fourth man also shuffled toward the gate, but another man and a girl of about ten backed away. The man with the whip let the coils drop and raised his arm in preparation for making that weapon work.

People screamed and backed away from the place where the blows would fall. Most of the crowd headed for Roz's sun-baked bit of wall. Roz saw her danger and stood. But they surrounded her before she could move away.

The many bodies pushed on her until she couldn't breathe. Elbows and outstretched arms struck her. People crowded in still closer. One more push would collapse her ribs.

The whip exploded.

The shrieking crowd packed around her even tighter. She couldn't breathe. Her face and shoulders prickled and then her knees stopped carrying her weight. Her last thought as the world turned yet darker: *stay alive...*

Utter blackness settled on her.

Roz's next thoughts seemed disjointed...partial... Nothing made sense. She lay in the dirt and every joint hurt. Even ordering her arms to push her mouth and nose from the dirt took several minutes. It took some time to figure out the loud, pushy voice she'd been hearing for a while. They did auctions of slaves here. Must be the auctioneer.

A long time later, Roz climbed to a sitting position. When she could think more clearly, she looked around. There were fewer people in this pen. She didn't have to take a head count to know that. The people's murmuring told her of their upset.

Where did Chaney go? Maybe on the other side of the knot of people as far from the gate as they could get?

Then Roz heard the screams...Chaney's screams from the other side of the mud brick wall. Too late. She wouldn't even get to say goodbye.

Roz couldn't give Chaney last minute advice and encouragement. Chaney had to survive on her own. She listened to the child's screams and then to someone's threats and curses. Finally Chaney's screams became a quiet sobbing and she heard the loud pushy voice she'd heard at times all day.

After that, Chaney's sobs grew more distant. Chaney and her new owner would be miles away by nightfall. She wished it could have been different. She'd miss Chaney; even miss her screeching and complaining at every little thing.

While wheezing in the ammonia-scented air, Roz leaned back on her too sunny spot against the wall. Exhausted, she had no energy left.

Should she just give up? She wanted to; she really did. If she just gave up; if she could die and get it over with. But she couldn't make her dad's little ditty stop running through her head.

Stay alive, above all else, stay alive.

Then the old refrain her dad had instilled in her became her new song—a slave's song, a wary song of anger without a means of expression, a song of surviving—a song of escape.

Like any slave, none of the horrors would mean anything. She'd do what she had to do to stay alive. Slaves have to be good survivors.

"Dad, I'll get through this alive," she whispered. "Somehow, I'll get home. If it kills me, I'll get home."

The man with the whip threw the gate open again. He touched three people with his coiled whip and pointed to the gate. Obediently, they shuffled in the direction he told them to go.

Two more touches of the whip and two more people left to be sold. Then he walked directly to Roz and touched her with that brutal giver of pain.

She drew in a shocked breath. She didn't think, just started walking as the other people had done.

She reached the entrance gate and looked back.

Why am I looking back? I've got nothing here; things can't get any worse.

At the gate, another man waited. She looked at the ground, not at him. This person lived and believed in cruelty or he wouldn't be here.

He mumbled, "Move right," and she did.

At least the air is fresher out here.

A man stood on a crude mud-brick platform. He spoke rapidly and loudly to a group of about forty men who had gathered around. She recognized that sing-song voice. This had to be the auctioneer she'd been hearing all day.

Except for an occasional word like strong, healthy and various numbers, she couldn't follow that man's stylized Arabic. The auctioneer pointed to another man who also stood on the platform.

Why am I looking at him? It means nothing. I don't have to watch someone being sold. At least I have that choice.

Roz looked at the ground, better to see the ground than this, this…

More words from the auctioneer. He told the man who was being sold to, to what?

Startled, she looked up.

The slave shook his head, and the tribal man stomped up on the platform and tore all the slave's clothes loose. Head bowed, the man on the platform stood jaybird naked.

Would they make her take her clothes off?

Too soon her turn came. She stepped on the platform and walked to the center.

"Dear Lord Jesus, help me. If You can—no, if You <u>will</u>, please help me."

Tears fell but she made no sound. She focused on the platform's clay floor, refused to see the buyers, her buyers. The auctioneer started the bidding. She heard catcalls and hoots. She had enough Arabic to know that he told them she would be a good concubine.

Then the auctioneer added that her new owner would have to keep her on a leash. That brought laughter, more hoots and surely unprintable curse words.

Lord Jesus, please help me. Silence answered her. *Please! Help me.* Often in the past when things got bad, she'd felt a kind of soft whisper somewhere deep in her soul that told her He was there; He would help her get through the bad thing.

But now, she felt a void as deep and as empty as space. It seemed that even Jesus had deserted her. Yet she knew that couldn't be. He promised never to leave His own. She didn't understand but she still had faith. She knew He wouldn't leave her and…

I'm still a hero's daughter.

She made herself look at the clay floor.

La-la-la-la-la-Don't listen, La-la-la-la-la- ignore the whole thing. La-la-la-la- Won't listen. La-la-la-la-la- Don't listen La-la-la-la-la ...

The tribal man stomped over, slapped her, gave her a choice...undress herself or he would do it for her.

More whoops and laughter followed.

Slowly, she removed the torn burka and the undergarment. Heat that could only be a blush covered her from her toes upward. The auctioneer asked for bids starting with twenty.

"Twenty," she heard a voice. The only insulation she could have from now on was to shut herself away, to not know, to not hear, to not care about what went on outside of herself.

La-la-la-la-la Let them bid La-la-la-la-la. I won't listen. I won't hear. Let them bid. I won't listen La-la-la-la-la-la-la-la-la-la...

She refused to look at the men gathered about. It wouldn't matter.

Nothing would matter except that someday, somehow, she would escape—unless they killed her first.

She wished she could have gotten Chaney free.

"Twenty-five," The auctioneer exploded into rapid, probably profane, Arabic. He repeated twenty-five many times. When someone said twenty-five, he raised the price to thirty-five and again bullied his audience.

I don't have to hear this. La-la-la-la-la

The auctioneer kept on bullying, tried to get one of the men to offer thirty-five. Then sherd a breathless thirty-five echo from some distance away. She didn't look up, why should she?

"Sold!" brayed the auctioneer.

She picked up her clothing and wrapped it around herself. Her new owner would claim her soon enough. She didn't need to see him now, had no desire to do so.

She whispered, "It's done. Lord, please be with me."

The auctioneer said something to her. She didn't understand him, didn't want to. Then the tribal man prodded her across the platform and down the step. "Wait here," he said.

She stood on the spot where he'd told her to stand.

Nothing mattered.

Whoever owned her would tell her what to do and she'd do it. Right up to the minute she decided she could safely get away. That desire to escape would be her only emotion. Had to be. Only safe way. If it killed her, she'd escape someday.

Eighteen

A hand touched Roz and she jumped. With the slow reflexes of a person ancient beyond words, Roz pulled her gaze from the dirt. Chaney stood before her.

"My master bought you too," Chaney said in English.

Then Chaney turned to the lean black man behind her. He wore a red plaid shirt with the sleeves cut away and a toga-like affair, also a plaid but a different plaid, this one mostly a faded navy. He'd tied it in a knot on one shoulder and underneath, he wore knee length khaki shorts. A battered felt hat perched at a jaunty angle on top of his wooly rust-red hair.

"You him too," Chaney approximated the Arabic.

The bony man raised an eyebrow and stroked his rust-colored beard.

Wondering at this apparition, Roz asked in Arabic, "Why?"

"Two sons, two sons." He held up two fingers. "Need two wives." He gestured with the chest-high walking stick he carried, pointing first to Chaney and then to Roz. He spoke slowly; obviously thinking she knew no more Arabic than Chaney.

"*Minfadlak* (Thank you.)" She bowed, hoping that would please him.

"We go." He handed a pair of gourd-canteens to each girl. The canteens had wide thongs tied to them. They fit around a person's neck, causing little strain.

The bony man shrugged his shoulders to shift the pack on his back, turned east and gestured for them to walk ahead of him. They both did so. A slave must be obedient. They'd learned that lesson well enough.

Yet, were they slaves? He'd said wives. Roz shivered.

Let this unknown man become my father-in-law?

Roz shook her head only a tiny bit. She couldn't change this. A slave must be obedient. She put all her energy into walking.

Let someone else choose my husband?

Despite her still tender feet, Roz's walk approached a stomp. She said nothing, but tried to think of a way out of this mess. At least he didn't want to kill her.

Thank You for that favor, Lord.

Nineteen

His whip in a neat coil, Kazir snapped it into the loop that held it at his waist. The auction had been a great success.

Kazir unlocked the door to the room he rented in his cousin Mufa's compound. Once inside, he locked it again. In the middle of the room hung the light socket; his only connection to electricity. He'd fitted that socket with a double bulb holder. One of the holders contained a plug for an electrical cord so he could recharge his phone. The other socket contained a bare light bulb. He felt for the pull chain and yanked it.

Then he went to the chest that contained all his possessions. After unlocking the chest, he felt deep inside the mass of clothing, guns and other items.

He'd hidden his treasured satellite phone there. No one here must know he had one. They'd steal it; even Mufa would steal it. Kazir had a newer, smaller, better one than Mufa had.

He punched Carl's number.

Carl had been looking forward to an evening of rest for his sore arms. The black stallion had been single-minded about his dislike of Harley. In the worst way, Carl wanted a good place for the night. Then his phone rang.

"It is as you said," Kazir said. "The two white females brought a good price."

"I get the impression that there's more," Carl said, and yanked the black's reins.

"Come, as you promised, make those females more miserable. My ears still ring from their screaming. One of those stupid Christians bought them."

"That's good!"

"They said it's the one who lives on the hill about fifteen kilometers from town. The brainless one doesn't know the females will be taken from him in a few days. Only right to take from the cursed infidels."

Carl laughed. "I'll be there in three days."

The black stallion reached toward Harley with his lips back and teeth exposed. Carl muttered and yanked on the bridle.

"Yeah, be about three days. As soon as I get this infernal horse to his new owner."

"I could bring the whites to you, for a price," Kazir said.

"Not this time; I know her; she'd be out of your hands and running again before you could blink."

"I know how to keep females," Kazir said.

"She's not getting away this time. All I need is for you to tell me where she is."

"Make you a special deal. I've got five full sets of irons. No one has ever escaped from one set. I'll lock each of these females in two sets. No woman gets away from me."

"Naw, you don't understand. I'd like the pleasure of seeing her first fear and one way or two, I'm gonna get the satisfaction of pounding the last breath out of her."

"I'll make the stupid female think she has nothing to worry about. Then you can see her fear."

"You still don't get it. She won't want to get away from a Christian. She's as good as locked up. This is the best way. Don't do anything until I get there." The black reached toward Harley again and Carl yanked hard.

Both men were silent for a moment, then Carl added, "See you in three days."

After closing off the call, Carl laughed out loud. Things were going his way just as he'd always known they would.

"Just give time a chance."

Harley's head made an exaggerated up and down motion.

"Oh yeah, old fellow. Time always works things out. It couldn't have turned out better. We get rid of this black monster, I'll go to Mufa's town, take care of that ugly blonde problem and then I can go to Khartoum to catch my plane. An extra couple of days, and I can say that's done. I won't let it take forever like I meant to. I don't really need that. Not if it means getting to Meribet sooner.

"Oh yeah. Just give time a chance."

Twenty

Roz's insides seemed a copy of this prickly, inhospitable landscape—and the heat, especially the heat. As Roz walked ahead of the strange man who bought them, she tried to make sense of her feelings.

One, she definitely felt gratitude. They were to be brides for his sons, not slaves.

Two, she had so much anger at this man's nerve, his gall,.. To think that she, Roz Duncan, would be turned over to a man as his property. She'd have no opportunity to choose her supposed husband. If her feet had been more "normal," she might have escaped right that minute. She felt angry enough to walk the whole of the Sahara and never feel the heat.

Three, fear threatened to overwhelm her. What if her husband liked to beat up on women? She'd heard all sorts of tales about Middle Eastern men. She was strong; she had enough karate/self-defense savvy to take down black belts, sometimes. But on a day-in, day-out basis, throwing her husband to the ground regularly had nothing to recommend it—even if she could do it.

And yet, this man had rescued them from a harem, or, or a brothel. She couldn't reasonably do anything outrageous. God wouldn't like it.

All through the afternoon, Roz worried and fumed—fumed and worried.

~ * ~

They had walked only a few hours. Yet Roz's sore feet burned as if blistered.

Finally they stopped for the evening. Chaney's feet also hurt. The kid didn't cry, not yet. But Roz knew the signs; it wouldn't be long.

Their master started gathering the ever-present thorny brush.

"Get this thing," he instructed.

Burning feet or not, both gathered as much of the brush as they could.

"Ow!" Chaney yelped again and again. "Ow! That hurts. Ow!"

When Roz had been in her teens, she found that anger almost never helps you get your way. It definitely wouldn't work now so she kept her mouth shut and did what she'd been told. She tried not to get stuck more than she had to and let it go at that. Together the two girls managed to drag a large pile to their master's side.

He took it and set about building a fence about eight feet in diameter and almost the same in height. He left an opening and a small pile of brush near that opening.

Then he motioned for them to follow him. A limb had fallen from one of the acacia trees that grew nearby.

"This, get this." He picked up the limb and pointed to other sticks and limbs.

Both girls looked for more fallen sticks and branches.

A herd of desert-dwelling elephants must have been in the area within the last six months. Had to be, from the quantity of sticks and small logs lying on the ground.

Roz and Chaney had no trouble getting an armload each. They took their loads into the brush fortress. Their master said, "More, need more."

When they took the third load back to the fortress, he said, "Good."

He motioned to them to bring their last loads of sticks into the brush fort. Then he used the remaining brush to close the entrance. Both girls collapsed and massaged their sore feet.

From somewhere in the depths of his pack, he produced a cork-stoppered glass bottle of matches and built a tiny fire.

"Fire, good fire."

He seemed in a pleasant mood, as if he were well pleased with what he'd done.

Both girls kept massaging their feet.

Then he sat down. "Name of me." He pointed to his chest. "Dan-e-el." He pointed to Roz. "Name of you."

"My name is Rozelle, but everybody calls me Roz and—" she chatted in English.

Then she remembered and said in Arabic, "I am named Roz."

He pointed to Chaney next.

"Name: Chaney," She pointed to herself.

"You learn my God."

With that he took a small stick and drew a straight line in the dirt, then drew another line, not quite so long. The middle of the second line crossed the first at right angles.

"You know this sign?" He rubbed his chin with its strange red beard.

Roz nodded and her stomach tensed. Did that drawing of the cross mean he was a Christian—or did it mean he hated Christians? Not knowing made her chest hurt.

Dear Lord Jesus, did you send a Christian to rescue us?

"This sign of my God. He is great God. Has power over everything."

Roz wanted to jump and shout. Here in this brutal land, her Lord hadn't forsaken her.

She blurted, in English, "He's my God, too."

Then she remembered herself and said in Arabic, "His name is Jehovah and His son is Esus, my Lord, who died on the cross to save us from our—bad doing—What we did to hurt—" She shrugged her shoulders.

"*Faasid nashaat* (sins)," The man said. "You Christian?"

Roz searched her not quite adequate Arabic. "Yes. I..." she pointed to her head with her right hand and to her heart with her left.

"*Yer sad-diy* (believe)," the man supplied for her. He beamed with good will.

Her insides sang and she nodded. "Believe that when Esus died on the cross, he died for my sins, and on the third day, he," she shrugged, "up from the ground."

She shook her head. She knew no words to express resurrection in Arabic. She patted the soil then she waved her hands as if she were flying and pointed up.

"*Hayy marra ukhra* (was resurrected)." The man's smile mirrored her father's smile. Remarkable!

"But God resurrected Jesus and now He lives in heaven. I believe that I'll be resurrected too and I'll live with Him forever because I believe in Esus and what he did on the cross saved me from my sins."

Joy filled her. Joy of being able to speak enough Arabic to get her meaning across, even if badly. But she had a greater joy. In Christ Jesus, this man and she had kinship—they were brother and sister.

He clapped his hands. "I did good to buy you."

"Chaney, tell him you are a Christian," Roz said in English.

Chaney didn't even attempt Arabic. "I've been to Sunday School some."

Roz wished Chaney could have said she was a real Christian.

"Chaney, say 'I love Jesus' in Arabic. Remember, they call Him Esus."

Chaney put her hand on her heart and patted it while saying, "Esus."

With another beaming smile, Daniel said, "Is good. Very good. Sleep now." With that he took his toga-like garment off, spread it on the ground, then wrapped it around himself.

We're supposed to sleep, just like this, in the dirt, like we did in the sales yard?

She looked at their puny brier-patch fortress and hoped that all the hyenas and who knew what else found plenty to eat tonight. But she dismissed those thoughts. She mustn't spend her night worrying; she had to rest.

"I'm cold," Chaney said.

"Me too. Not a lot we can do about it." Roz picked up two large pebbles and tossed them over their fort and then she patted the sandy soil.

"If we curl up as close to the fire as we can without getting burned," Roz said. "We won't be comfortable, but I don't think we'll freeze."

Chaney put her head on the ground and then put her hands under her head for a pillow. "I won't ever get to sleep. I'm too cold."

But before Roz could settle into sleep, the girl began a soft whistle. Snoring, Chaney-style.

Roz wondered if she'd ever see her dad or her brother again. She bit her pointing finger and some tears escaped, but she made no sound.

At some point, Roz slept and knew nothing more until the darkest hour of the new day. A sound like a person sniffling with a bad cold startled her awake. A novel she'd read said that if awakened in a potentially dangerous situation, the best thing is to pretend sleep. This gives you time to plan your best moves and surprise your enemy.

Without moving, she opened her eyes a little. The fire had burned so low that only embers remained. But the moon's light let her see very well. Through a thin place in the brush shelter, she could make out a foot—a foot, not a hoof. It moved and she saw its tail. It had a tuft of hair at the end—not the brushy tail of a hyena,

Though she didn't move, her frightened heart exchanged places with her lungs.

What should she do? Scream? No. Wake their master? Probably. But he slept on the other side of the fire.

If she called him, she'd wake Chaney. Mustn't wake Chaney. If the squirt started screaming, who knew what that animal would do? The snuffling sound grew louder by the second and their unstable fortress shivered. That beast meant to tear it down.

Roz had to do something. What could she do? Still not moving, she searched through her pitiful store of knowledge.

Throw rocks?
No.
Stare at the beast and point at it until it went away?
Worked with a snarling dog.
Not likely. Not at all.
Fire?
That'll do.

Their collection of sticks and small logs lay near her head. Still lying down, she raised her right arm in slow motion. Her fingers felt for a stick or two to fuel their blaze—something small that wouldn't crush the fire's remaining embers.

The creature's noisy breathing stopped. Slowly Roz dropped the handful of twigs into the embers. Within seconds they blazed up.

The animal reacted with a guttural cough and a soft growl. It probably wouldn't bother them if she made a bigger fire.

Still frightened, Roz sat up slowly, picked up a few larger sticks and put them on the fire. She waited for the larger sticks to catch and blaze.

Nothing else she could do, except pray that the beast wouldn't decide to knock down their defense before she got the fire going. She prayed and she kept praying.

Again, the brush fortress shivered. Without thought, Roz leaped to her feet and grabbed the largest hunk of firewood in the pile.

The piece of firewood fit her hand like the handle of a hammer; the larger end looked enough like a club to be one.

Roz encouraged herself by thinking of the young King David of Israel. He had killed at least a lion and a bear when he was just a boy.

Maybe, with God's help, I can convince this beast to go away.

Please Jesus, let it be so.

She squatted and rocked from side-to- side, like a tennis player ready to leap in any direction when her opponent slammed a serve at her.

Could be that if the Lord directed her hands, and if this creature wasn't starving, she could convince it to leave with a solid blow on the nose. She thought about it and stopped panting in terror.

I won't be afraid.

Her eyes closed to slits, she exposed her teeth in a snarl like the carving of an ancient demon she remembered seeing at a museum. Two could play the attack game if it came to that.

With that in mind, she made a sound much like air escaping from a tire hose and slapped her club into her other hand.

They said dog noses are super-sensitive to blows and many other animals were nose sensitive as well.

Stay alive!

Then the sticks she'd put on their campfire caught the flame and the light flared. With that, the animal rumbled a curse and disappeared into the darkness.

A feeling of relief strong enough to make her dizzy flooded over Roz. She sat down, hard.

The master sat up. "You handled that beast wisely. I could not have done it better myself."

"Thank you, sir." He couldn't see her shaking hands.

He added several more sticks to the blaze. "That might have been a lion. Haven't seen one since I was about ten, but still…"

At the thought of having been *that* close to a lion, all the air left Roz's lungs. She thought she might faint.

"I hope you will be able to handle my wife that well."

"Sir?"

"She will not be happy to see you."

With a sinking feeling, she said, "We are brides for your sons. That is what you said." When he said nothing, she prodded with, "It is, isn't it?"

"Of course you will be brides. But my wife and I meant to buy a donkey with the money that bought you. And you have no dowry. My wife will not like what I did. But we will discuss it tomorrow. Sleep now."

Why couldn't he keep his bad news to himself until morning?

Twenty-one

Do what you have to. Stay alive.
Eventually Roz slept.

In the morning, the farmer, Daniel, gave each girl a sip of water and a bit of stale pancake-like bread and took the same for himself. Then he told Roz to cover her head and she adjusted the remains of her burka to accommodate her master's wishes.

He told them to start walking and they did. He walked behind them at a brisk pace, not a run, but certainly not a stroll. By his fast walk, he pushed them forward faster than their bruised feet would have allowed otherwise.

"Does he have to walk so fast?" Chaney complained.

"I've read that some people can keep up that pace for hours."

"I don't have to like it," Chaney said. Then she sat right there on the trail and massaged her feet. "Did he really say we're going to be his sons' wives?"

"That's what he said. That's better than being in a mine two hundred feet in the ground. I think it is, at least."

The farmer didn't come closer. He stood and waited. Some minutes later, he said. "We go." Then he moved toward the two.

"Come on," Roz said and pulled Chaney to her feet. "We have to do this."

"But I'm—"

"I'm tired too. And I'm sure our new owner isn't terribly rested."

"I'm tired of everybody pushing me around. Not gonna be no ho. Mama said being married is like being one man's ho."

"I'm not going to listen. So hush, will you?"

"You're mean." Chaney took off at a much faster pace.

During their third rest that day, Chaney whispered, "I bet we can run faster than he can. We don't have to be no ho of any kind, not even married ho. Let's run, now!"

Roz shook her head. "No! If we get lost out here, we'll die. Got to find the creek first."

"You're scared."

"You betcha. And my feet still hurt. Can't escape now. We have to do what we have to. Gotta stay alive."

Deliberately, Roz stood up and moved away from Chaney. The little snip needed to cool down big time.

Besides, if she were to be a bride, then surely she wouldn't be treated too badly. She could wait; maybe the family went to a town sometimes. Maybe they could escape from the town easier than from here.

After they'd rested a short time, the man stood and urged them on. "Must be home. Must bring my boys their wives."

"Will we be there soon?" Roz asked.

"We make four shelters, walk four days." He paused and then said, "Might be five."

Twenty-two

Because of the pain in his arms, Carl treated himself. He paid a man who lived just outside the town to keep the black for a few hours. Then he rode Ol' Harley into the town Mufa ran.

Harley perked up at being in a town. He seemed to be a sociable sort of critter and even pranced when there were other horses around.

The streets reeked as streets generally did in these crumbling Arab towns with their broken mud-brick buildings and their disintegrating plaster overlays. Carl took shallow breaths to avoid being overwhelmed by the ammonia and warm fetid smells from the open sewer that ran down the middle of the street.

"I ain't gonna wait forever." Harley got a kick into faster gear. "Be starting that Okie's treatment this very night."

"Let's see, Kazir's room sat in Mufa's compound. If I remember right, that's at the west end of town."

When he reached the mud brick wall of Mufa's place, he jumped off Harley and strode up to the gate. First he'd have to have one of Mufa's servants let him in.

The doorbell amounted to a rope and a cow-bell sort of thing that clanged about fifty feet away. Sooner or later, a servant would come. He felt that "someone watching" feeling and looked all around, but as always, saw nothing unusual. He'd like to hit someone.

There were days when "old world charm" failed to enchant him—days like today. Why did everything take so long?

Eventually, an elderly man with a limp came to the gate.

"I'm here to see Kazir; is he in?" Carl said in his most polite voice. Politeness to servant-types never failed to perk them up some, get them moving.

The man said nothing, just opened the door with a bow. When Carl walked his horse through, the man attended to a locking mechanism...or something.

Carl tied Harley to a post inside the mud-brick fence and gave the old horse an affectionate pat on the neck.

After that, Mufa's servant led the way down a worn path in the dirt. The grounds were nothing but dirt with a few rocks. Only a single palm reared its head. No other plant life grew and no fountain or other decoration flaunted itself inside the mud-brick fence.

A box-like affair fifteen feet long and almost as wide stood about fifty feet away from the main house, Kazir's room.

The limping man bowed and pointed, then he left without ever having said a single word.

Carl thought this servant a bit odd, but he shrugged, went to the door and knocked.

Kazir opened the door perhaps an inch. Then he opened it just enough to let his thin body slip through. He dropped his pistol into its holster as he came.

"You came sooner than I thought you would," Kazir said.

"Let's get on with it. Quicker I get that Okie gal flattened, the better I'll like it.

"Then let's go." Kazir led the way to a shed, unlocked the super-size lock, went inside and came out straddling a powered mountain bike...the frame of a regular bike, including pedals and chain, but in addition it sported a gas-powered engine about eight, maybe nine inches across, and about four inches thick. A round tank had been clipped beneath the strut that connected the handlebar and front wheel assembly to the seat and rear wheel assembly.

"That's your transportation?"

"Gets me around and takes almost no gas." Kazir rolled his machine down the path toward the front gate.

Carl followed; still astounded that Kazir would use something that needed a modern product, like gas.

"You can get gas out here?"

"Get regular monthly delivery, most months. My standing order is ten gallon. I usually sell most of it. Like I say, my bike, it does not need much."

Carl snorted at the thought of monthly gas delivery. But he had more serious business than petrol deliveries. "Show me who bought that whore. I wanta get started." He unhitched Harley, opened the gate and let Kazir walk his bike through.

Then Carl walked through with Harley and pulled the doorbell cord several times. At the repeated clank, that same man eventually came limping to the gate and Carl mounted Harley.

"Let's go," Carl said.

Kazir kick-started his bike and took off. But Harley bucked an old-horse's arthritic buck twice and needed Carl to guide him much more than usual. They crossed the village and climbed into the gentle hills on the east side of town.

About fifteen minutes later, they came to a round, thatched roof building of the type that belongs in the rain-forest, not there in the desert. No livestock roamed inside its broken fences.

Thinking curses, Carl brought Harley into the open space in front of what remained of the house. He shook his head and eased his feet to the ground. He already knew, he knew, no one lived here.

The hut's opening that would have held a door or at least a curtain had been demolished; a truck could have driven through the hole. The roof sagged. At the next windstorm, the whole shack would fall.

Still thinking curses, and knowing he'd have to find her again, Carl walked around the house. He did his best to get a sense of which direction he should take in his search.

A full set of farming hand tools: rakes, shovels and a couple of hoe-like adzes, had been thrown against the wall on the far side of the house away from the door opening.

That meant something. The people who lived here left in such a hurry that they didn't take their tools. Or, it could be that the people who lived here were killed.

If the people were killed, there would be signs. Carl looked around. Scavengers weren't known for neatness. Always left a bone or two.

At first he saw nothing, but finally, already nearly hidden by the blowing sand, he found a partially eaten left half of a pelvis. It furnished good marrow and suet for the ant population that covered it. That bone gave enough proof; he didn't need to look for more. The Christians had died.

But if they were killed, who took the Okie? He knew she had too much smarts to let herself get killed.

A scythe with a broken handle lay on the ground and Carl stumbled over it. With another curse, he picked it up and slammed it in among the other farm tools.

The scythe's wooden handle sank into the trashy knot of farm tools. But its long curved blade swung around until it stuck straight out and caught Carl by surprise. He drew his hand through the blade. The blade had enough sharpness to leave a bright red line on the back of Carl's hand.

That injury seemed a final insult.

Carl cursed his abusive mom, he cursed his weakling dad, he cursed life. He cursed God, even though he knew there wasn't one.

Kazir rolled up beside him. An amazed expression filled his face. "Looks like one of my brothers got here first. They must have taken her. Have to find out who. I'll get on it as soon as we get back to town."

But Carl cursed in rhythm to the fury banging in his skull. He never heard Kazir's so logical words.

Carl ignored the pounding that foretold a blood pressure explosion. How many more days would he have to track that Okie blonde? How many more days with Meribet had that slut stolen from him? How pained Meribet must be. She needed him, needed him bad.

He examined the ground, but found no manure of any kind—not horse, goat, or cow, no chicken either. The place seemed clean, almost sterile.

Without a word, Kazir fell in line just behind Carl.

Carl knew why he didn't see any manure. Dung beetles had already stored it underground as the little round balls that would feed their young. Beetles don't work that fast. No animal had lived here for at least a couple weeks.

"You said the sale took place four days ago?"

"Called you near sundown, same day."

"Liar. Nobody been here in a couple weeks, more likely three." Carl's eyes squeezed down and he faced Kazir. "You're going to tell me what you did with her. You're going to—"

"—I didn't do nothing. I just run the sales."

"You're going to tell me now."

Kazir backed up and Carl stayed in his face.

"Greedy fool. Where'd you hide her? If you think I'll pay you twice."

"I-I didn't—"

Carl's hands seemed to live without his control. He shook the man until they both fell and Carl roared, "Where is she?" Carl banged his friend's head against the sand.

Kazir wrestled Carl's arms away and stood up. "I didn't take—"

But Kazir's getting up only made Carl angrier.

"You pukein' idiot." He slugged his one-time friend.

Kazir took the blow and rolled away. He backpedaled. "I didn't do nothing. We know Christians lived here; she should be—"

Carl hit him again and Kazir fell.

Immediately, Kazir picked himself out of the dirt, turned and ran out of the compound into the dry scrub that lay beyond.

"Moron, not gonna chase you on foot," Carl growled and marched to Harley. He mounted up and unsnapped his whip.

Harley, as usual, seemed to know what Carl wanted and with very little guidance cantered after the fleeing man. A break in the ragged fencing let the horse through without a problem.

Kazir looked over his shoulder and Carl's whip slashed his tribal-marked cheek.

He screamed, then turned and ran back into the compound, headed toward his bike. The whip hit him again across his back as he neared the remains of the house.

Once more, Carl whipped the man who had been his friend, but this time the whip wrapped around Kazir's arm and didn't come loose. Kazir grabbed it and pulled.

Carl hadn't expected such a move. The whip flew from his hand and lay on the ground.

Carl jumped off Harley and ran at Kazir, intent on pounding him into the ground.

"I didn't take her!" Kazir bawled.

Carl said nothing, just came at Kazir full tilt.

Kazir turned and ran. Still in total retreat, he looked over his shoulder. He never saw the scythe that caught him mid-chest.

Carl saw the expression on his friend's face and suddenly, he ceased being angry. The rusted blade turned a brighter red as it protruded from Kazir's thin back. The man sagged and the blade let him go. He folded onto the dirt.

Anger fading, Carl minced forward as if silence would help his friend. He knelt and swept the dirt from Kazir's face.

"Aw, why'd you have to go and do a fool thing like that?" Carl cried great floods of tears. "Didn't you know I wouldn't really hurt you? Why'd you have to run?"

An eagle screamed overhead.

Still kneeling on the dirt, Carl wept without caring. Kazir had been as close to a buddy as he'd ever want and now his friend was gone.

When that eagle screamed a second time, Carl realized someone might blame him for this. There were no police worthy of the name for a thousand miles, but Kazir had family. Mufa, for instance. Mufa controlled a personal army. That gang helped him run the little hell-hole of a town that held his compound. Best not to anger the man. Best not to be found with Kazir's body.

On thinking about it, Carl decided it would be best if no one found Kazir. He picked up his friend and shoved him inside what remained of the house—put him out of sight.

He grabbed a shovel and an adze from the pile of tools and boarded Harley. He chose a spot in the scrub about two hundred feet from the fence and started digging.

The soil had more sand in it than some and the digging went fast. Carl made the grave a generous six foot deep trough with sloping sides so he wouldn't be trapped if the sides caved. He'd made that mistake once and almost died. None of the dozen or so graves he'd dug since had straight sides.

When the grave suited him, he got on Harley and went back. First he had to get the bike, couldn't leave it for someone to find. Couldn't have it pointing to Kazir's nearby grave.

With Harley following, he peddled the bike to the grave, tossed it in and stomped it down. Then he added enough dirt to smooth out the bottom of the grave.

After that Carl went back for his friend. By then, Kazir's blood had congealed some and he managed to wrestle the corpse onto the horse without any visible blood on himself or his beast.

Harley didn't like this duty and made that fact clear by his snorting, prancing and hopping. But Harley was a good horse.

When Kazir lay in the lowest part of the trough-grave, Carl stood over him with tears streaming down. "Sorry about this, old friend."

He gave a deep sigh and said, "You know me…I hate long goodbyes." Then he picked up the shovel.

With all the force and passion at his command, Carl scooped dirt until at least a foot of soil covered Kazir and no part of him could be seen. He slowed down after that. Periodically he compacted the soil by beating it with the back of the shovel.

"Pity this happened, my friend. I had some interesting deals in mind." He sighed, and stopped long enough to slow his breathing. "There's an end to everything, ain't there? That's time for you. Be an end to time someday."

After that, Carl filled the grave until the dirt made a mound only a half foot or so higher than the surrounding sand. Then he hammered the mound with the shovel until it leveled out with the rest of the dirt. Satisfied, he carefully made a hole in the middle and replaced the scrub bush that had held that position before he dug.

"So long, Kazir. I'd see you in hell except you and me both know there ain't none."

Carl mounted Harley. "Have to get a crew together and find her…somehow." He took one more look at his friend's grave, sobbed a couple more tears and rode away at Harley's best speed. He wanted in the worst way to be away from this cursed "farm." Someone dogged his every move, but he'd kind of gotten used to that. Now, he felt like it stood just behind his shoulder blades.

He still had to pick up the black and deliver him before he could even begin looking for that blasted Okie…"Shoulda killed her when I had her…That God-talk she did…Scary…Shoulda put a bullet right in her blamed, stupid, open mouth."

Twenty-three

The man and the two blondes walked for four days: four days of sore feet and four brush fortresses. Chaney only killed two snakes. Then, about mid-morning on the fifth day, they came to a valley.

"This my land. My house there."

With pride, Daniel pointed to a flat-topped dwelling at the bottom of a rocky rise so far in the distance that it appeared pale and gray.

A large vegetable garden with neat rows of plants stood at the base of the hill. There were short plants that she didn't know and two kinds of taller plants. Roz recognized those, even from so far away, as okra and pole beans on tripod supports.

The man had said he made his living as a farmer, but Roz had hoped for something, anything, better than this.

According to the sparse plants, this sandy soil hadn't seen any fertilizer, even manure, for at least a hundred years. There were so many pale boulders that the land resembled buttery popcorn spilled across a huge bleached oak table. Any school kid in her part of Oklahoma knew more about agriculture than to try to farm this desolation.

But worse, how could they escape? She saw no sign that water ever flowed in this near-desert. She sighed. Just have to be an obedient slave or bride or whatever I am. Until I can run away. Patience, got to have patience.

"Now, we find if you worth price," Daniel said. "You must be good. Must obey wife. Must learn everything she teach."

"Yes, we will obey. We will learn." Roz said, and punched Chaney into nodding.

"You must be strong, strong."

"We will be strong, strong."

Then Roz had a thought. "Sir, how to say—" She made a cradle of her arms. "Mama, mama." She said in English and tried to imitate motherliness by patting the face of the imaginary infant.

"*Ahmm.*" Daniel said.

Roz nodded. "*Ahmm*, Mama."

He paused. "We go now." He set off walking even faster than usual and made them walk in front of him.

Roz barely kept ahead of him. He wanted to appear positive about what he had done and she hurried Chaney along. They had to act as docile as a pet dog, not give any indication of their coming escape.

"Habbie," he called when they were still at least a hundred yards away. "I'm home."

A thin, dark-skinned woman only slightly taller than Chaney came out of the house. She hesitated a moment, then stood with her hands on her hips.

"Habbie is not happy," Daniel said. "You must do well indeed if we have peace in my house. Do well!"

Roz gave Chaney's arm a tug to urge her to move faster. This would not be fun.

When they were a short distance from the bare area around the house, Habbie marched out to meet them. She still had her hands on her hips and a scowl on her round face.

"Where is our donkey?" she demanded.

"But dear, we were wondering where we would find Christian brides for our sons. I found them Christian brides." He turned to the girls. "Take off the burka."

Roz removed the torn burka from her head and wrestled with it to keep herself modest. She motioned Chaney to pull the front of the burka over her head into that cape-like form that would show her face and hair.

Habbie looked at the girls, then walked around them.

With a snort of impatience, she stood in front of Daniel. "I suppose these weak white things are going to till our fields?"

"But dear, our sons."

"Of course, they're going to take some of the load our boys are carrying. And of course, they have splendid dowries so our sons can buy their own farms."

"Dear, how many of our men are so fortunate as to have brides that our neighbors would want in their harem?"

"And that's another thing. How long do you think it's going to be before our neighbors see these weak white things and take them from us? They took our donkey. They'll take these women too."

Roz didn't know anything she could do to improve the situation. So she did nothing.

"They'll get strong, all right. Tomorrow, they both spend a half day helping you and the boys prepare our fields."

Habbie turned back and paced around the two girls with a frown on her face. "The rest of the day they learn to be wives. I doubt these white things know what a wife is."

"But dear, they will learn. And they are Christians, as we are."

"Today, we dye their skin and find clothes and head scarves. No one must know these are not of our people. Our sons' wives will be stolen if they know."

She turned to Roz and Chaney. "Wives…hummph!"

Daniel took Habbie's hands, kissed them, then said something Roz didn't understand and Habbie replied with a smile on her face. Then Daniel walked away.

With another scowl, Habbie said, "Go in there." She pointed to the house.

With one hand keeping the remains of her burka in place, Roz grabbed Chaney's arm and walked through the door of the flat-roofed house. Inside, her eyes adjusted to the dim light coming through the two small windows near the ceiling. A couple of small tables, a roll of carpet, two chests and three shelves furnished the house. The whole family must sleep in this one tiny room.

Habbie followed the two girls inside. Immediately she went to the chest near one of the windows. After digging around, she said with a cry of triumph, "I knew I had them. Put these on."

She handed each girl a wide black scarf. "You can embroider them later. Unless you want to be a harem slave the rest of your lives, never let your blond head show," Habbie said. "Never."

Habbie dug into her chest again. She came up with two sack-like black dresses with long sleeves and also some undergarments. "Put these on. Can't have you naked. Won't have you wearing Muslim clothes. Put those burkas in this chest. We'll reuse the cloth later.

"Yes, ma'am," Roz said. Both girls did exactly as Habbie said.

"Now, we dye your skin." She rummaged among various cans and jars. "Can't have that white showing, won't be safe," she repeated.

Habbie looked at and discarded various tins, bottles and jars. At last she said, "Henna should work until we can find a kresneb bush. Kresneb bark has a good brown color. Henna dyes Daniel's hair and beard. Dyes skin too."

She took the small glass jar of dried leaves outside to a fire pit. A large pot occupied most of the fire pit's space.

Roz watched from the doorway while Habbie moved the large pot over, put the small pot in place and added more wood to the fire.

After that, Habbie went to the water bucket outside the door. A dipper full of water went into the little pot followed by a few dry leaves from the jar.

She stirred it enthusiastically. When it boiled, she returned to the house where Roz and Chaney waited.

"Walk around the inside of the house twenty times," she told Roz.

Wondering why, Roz obeyed.

When she finished, Habbie went outside and stirred the small pot. Then she said, "Again, twenty times.

Roz said nothing, Habbie used her walking around the house as a timer and did as she'd been told.

Habbie said, "Good." Then she went outside to retrieve the pot.

A man riding a rangy gray horse and leading a sleek black one rode up just as Habbie removed the pot from the fire with a rag that lay on a nearby boulder.

The man dismounted and tied the black to a large rock. He tied the old horse to the largest log in the log-pile. Then he approached Habbie.

When Roz saw him, she backed away from the door. In silence, she put her hand on Chaney's mouth and dragged the protesting girl into the darkest corner.

"That's Carl," Roz whispered.

Carl told Habbie, "Ma'am, I'm looking for escaped slaves."

Inside, in their dark corner, at first Roz closed her eyes and prayed hard.

"We don't have any slaves, escaped or otherwise," Habbie growled. Her voice grew louder and Roz knew she must be walking toward the house.

"That man kills people," Roz whispered. "Stay here. Habbie's going to need help." She left the shivering Chaney and slipped toward the door.

"I trailed them here." Carl said. His voice accused Habbie.

"Slaves and slavers come through here all the time. Could have come through and used our spring when I went to the field with lunch for my men," Habbie said.

Roz crept to the door. She started shaking and couldn't stop.

Lord Jesus, help us.

"Woman, all I want from you is information about my property, two slaves. That's all I want. They stole a canteen that had all my diamonds in it." He let his left thumb rest on the beat-up holster that held a large revolver.

"After I make them slaves give me my diamonds, I'll give you a diamond, a reward for your help." He caressed the gun handle.

Habbie stammered, "G-Go ask my husband, he might have seen them. He's working our field over there. You'll see him when he starts the next r-row. Our sons are with him."

"I asked you," Carl growled.

"I did see a three p-people walking on that ridge just after sunrise. I don't know anything else." Habbie sounded innocent and terribly scared.

"You better be telling the truth," he snapped.

"I-I'm not, not, lying," she stammered. "We don't b-believe in lies."

With a snarl, Carl stomped back to his horses, mounted the old one and by grabbing the black's reins up near his chin, he forced that extreme spirit to follow.

Just inside the door, Roz pasted herself to the wall. Why would he chase them? It was crazy. He was crazy. If he'd wanted them, why hadn't he kept them instead of sending them to the slave auction?

She didn't know. She only knew that if he'd followed them this far, he probably wouldn't stop.

She whispered, "If it kills me, I'll get through this. Jesus, please help us."

The silence held for a few seconds. Then…

"May the devils of Mohammed dislike your face," Habbie snarled. Still outside, she walked to the corner of the house, cleared her throat and spat.

Twenty-four

Carl mounted up, but the black chose that moment to chew on poor Harley. He had to stop and get a better grip on the black. Then he heard that woman curse him and spit at him; at him! She despised him that much!

He knew, he absolutely knew the mama lied. They had his slaves and they were hiding them.

When he got through with that Okie, he'd have some fun with those yokels who thought they could get away with taking what belonged to him.

He reached the top of the next hill and his phone rang. Had to be Meribet, had to be.

Got to get this Okie dead so I can marry my gal.

Meribet's sobs greeted him.

"Mama's not acting right." Meribet cried big time.

"Sweetness, if your mama's giving you problems, just walk out on her. You don't owe that floozy anything. Your dad did the parent stuff, not her."

"But she woulda. Dad said he'd kill her if she tried to see me before I turned eighteen. He told me so himself after she said it to me. Said he didn't like her being so religious. He thought it was cute when they dated, but now he's acting like he's afraid of her. Like maybe she could pray down fire, or something."

"Your dad frightened by a little five foot three Walmart cashier?" He chuckled.

"But he is. I say her name and he gets quiet and turns pale. He's scared of her."

"Naw, not possible. I know him. He's not even anxious. Can't be." But his insides told him, *If someone like Gregorio Angel Carnelli is afraid of a Christian...*

"I'm afraid of her too, but not like him. I'm afraid she'll ruin my credit."

"How could she do that?"

"I loaned her my credit cards right after I moved in with her. She needed some new clothes. They don't pay her very well, you know. And she sent big offerings to all the Christian missions."

"I'll be home as soon as I can."

"Hurry. I haven't bought anything in two months, not even a lipstick. I can't afford to."

"I'll hurry," he said. "But you gotta ratchet up your spunk. You can do it. You're a gutsy gal with a lot of backbone. That's one of the reasons I love you."

Meribet sniffed and said, "I need you!"

"I'll be there soon's I can, and then we'll get married. Nobody can bother you after that."

"I love you too." Meribet's words were a combination coo and purr.

"But sweetness, it's going to take a little time, probably a month."

At the word month, Meribet's shriek deafened him.

Twenty-five

Habbie stayed outdoors for so long that Roz worried.

"You stay back there, it's safer," Roz told Chaney."

Chaney nodded and tried to squeeze herself into the wall.

With all possible caution, Roz poked her head out, but just barely. Habbie watched something toward the east.

Finally, Habbie walked through the door. "He's gone, at least for now. Daughters, he will not hurt you. I will see to that."

Habbie's hand trembled when she set the small pot of boiled henna leaves on the two foot square table near the door.

"Thank you, Mama." Roz said.

A smile softened Habbie's business-like words. "This dye is red, not brown, but if we get enough on you, your hands and feet will not be white any more.

"We can say that your coming is a cause for celebration. Muslim women often paint designs on their hands and arms with henna. They'll think we're doing the same kind of thing and approve."

Then, Habbie used a stick to dip a rag in the dye and after cooling it by waving it about, she told Chaney, "You first."

Chaney put her hands out and Habbie swiped the dye up and down Chaney's left hand and forearm.

"It's orange!" Chaney objected and pulled her arm away.

"It's better than white." Roz pushed Chaney's right arm out so Habbie could finish. "Unless you want to be a whore and live in a harem," Roz said.

Those were magic words. Chaney put her right arm out and spread her fingers wide.

Then Habbie said, "Now you."

After Roz's hands and forearms were suitably dyed, Habbie handed the rag to Roz.

"Now your feet. You do hers and she does yours."

Roz knelt and swabbed Chaney's feet as she had been told.

"Be sure to color between your toes," Habbie instructed.

Roz glanced up to see Habbie making motions with her hands and body. Boys do that when cheering for one of the fighters in a playground brawl.

She cares. She has no reason to care, but she does.

To know someone cared brought a knot to Roz's throat. She'd been thrown into a sea of evil. Yet maybe it wasn't as bad as she thought.

Roz knew that God had done it. He must have reasons for not stopping evil right now. But if His people cooperated, as this man and his wife had done, maybe He makes the evil easier to bear.

When the henna dried on Roz's and Chaney's hands, forearms, and feet, Habbie said, "Wear your scarves to hide your face and hair. Always look down so that no one can see your blue eyes. Never look up; never be uncovered except inside this house."

"Yes ma'am," both girls said.

"The men will be home soon. You will meet your husbands. Your marriage will be in three weeks," Habbie said.

"What? Why can't she just speak English? I didn't get it." Chaney shook Roz's arm.

"We'll be married in three weeks." Roz said the Arabic words slowly. That way, Chaney could understand and Habbie wouldn't be offended.

"Three weeks?" Chaney blurted in English with dismay obvious in every syllable. Then she covered her mouth with her hands, as if realizing her impoliteness.

But Habbie didn't seem to take offense. "We make one trip a month to our church. It is too far," she said.

Roz said, "Where is your church?"

But Habbie said, "We must prepare food for our men."

With their scarves in place, they followed Habbie to the fire pit.

"You, bring firewood." She spoke slowly and pointed Chaney to the pile of logs and sticks that lay by the south corner of the house.

"You, take the bucket, bring water from the spring over there." She pointed Roz to a greener area about a block away at the base of the nearest hill. Then Habbie picked up the big pot and carried it to an empty pail that sat nearby. She bent over and with a strained grunt, poured most of the water from the pot into the pail.

Then Habbie lugged the large pot back to the fire pit. But she didn't put the dry pot on the hot coals.

Roz picked up the covered bucket and a dipper gourd that sat on a table just outside the door to the house and marched toward the greenest area.

With the scarf covering most of her face, Roz could see little. They put blinders on nervous racehorses. The horses got used to it; she could too. Blinders had to be better than all those jealous women competing for just one man. That's what she'd have in a harem. She shuddered.

Lord, You put Daniel in that town. You gave him the idea of buying us. I can't escape; I have to get used to living here, don't I?

She still questioned God about the marriage part. But faith meant she trusted God. She'd always said she had faith. "I guess I get to see if my faith is what my mouth says it is."

She'd have to get used to this place, these people, live with these people, learn to live on this land...for now. This family deserved that much.

She looked at the ground around her. She had no farming experience, but even she could tell that this unfertile ground wouldn't grow much. It would take a real agriculture expert to make a difference. And she had no idea of what that expert might recommend.

Obviously, these people knew only a little more than she did. But they had a willingness to work. She'd have to work as hard as they did.

As she marched toward the greener area, a pack of small gray grasshoppers flicked themselves away from her. But the hair on her arms stood at attention.

Surely I can be around grasshoppers without going into some kind of hysterical backlash. I won't go through that again. I won't!

A puff of wind caused a single grasshopper to hit her cheek near her mouth. A second one flew inside her scarf and trapped itself in her hair. It wriggled mightily.

Then, in her mind she was only six. A boy she might have loved in a few years slammed that butterfly net full of grasshoppers over her head.

This time for a moment she managed to block the intense nightmare and the pain in her eyes. But she blocked the need to scream for help, for Mama, only with the greatest effort.

She felt insects in her mouth…the intensity of the betrayal. Mama didn't come…Insect legs scratched her throat…Gagging…So much pain in her eyes.

"Mama!"

Nearly blinded, she'd stumbled to her home across the street from the park. Mama hadn't come to help her because Mama lay unconscious. She'd collapsed by the door. Heart attack, the doctor said.

Roz learned at the age of six that no one, not even Mama, would always be able to protect her. At six she began to learn its corollary…that you must protect yourself.

I have to grow up. I'm not six and I'm not helpless. If it kills me, I won't be helpless.

She grabbed the insect, pulled it from her hair, threw it down and stomped it.

Roz staggered the final steps to the spring. She wouldn't be overcome, not now, not ever. Once again, she swallowed down the nausea.

The spring turned out to be only a shallow depression in the carpet of dirt and scruffy plants.

Roz's mother had been very good at camp-craft. "We need to know how to live in the wilderness. Our settled world could blow up in our face," Mama told her at their camping trip only a week before her first heart attack.

As Mama had instructed all those years ago, first, Roz hung the dipper on the sturdiest branch of a nearby weed. Then she teetered at the edge of the spring and with great care she lowered the bucket so that only the top millimeter or so of water entered the bucket.

A lizard-like creature about six inches long stared back at her from beneath the foot and a half of water in the dark basin. Roz smiled at that. Mama told her that old-time hunters and prospectors said that only very good water would support such an animal.

Roz filled the bucket as full as she could without disturbing the salamander, or stirring up the muck and clouding the water. Then she retrieved the dipper and finished filling her bucket.

Roz lugged the full water bucket to the fire pit. Habbie motioned to her to pour water into the pot that contained the dried beans that had been soaking.

When the fresh water and beans boiled, Habbie added handfuls of wheat grains and lentils to the beans in the pot.

Habbie then gave Roz a hand-carved wooden spoon with a very long handle. "Now, stir, stir all the time. Stir until I tell you to stop. This is how we make *fuul*. *Fuul* is good food; you must make it every day for your husbands."

A few feet away stood the bucket where Habbie had poured the bean-soaking water. She took that water to the garden and poured it on her plants.

When she left, Chaney leaned over to Roz. "When we gonna leave? I'm not gonna be a ho, not gonna be no married ho neither."

"Just simmer, will you? And being married isn't the same as being a whore. In a good marriage, the man loves you and you love him."

"I don't like it."

"Besides, maybe we won't be married, so calm down. Please?"

"You're not that smart. And you're not my boss."

Habbie strolled back to the fire. "The fire needs more wood." She pointed to the wood pile and looked at Chaney. "Bring some logs."

From time to time, Habbie instructed Chaney, "Get more water from the bucket and put it in the pot."

Several times she told Roz, "Stir, all the time, stir." Later she ordered Roz, "Put more wood under the pot."

When Roz's dress and scarf had the consistency of a wet bath towel, Habbie added a handful of dried meat chips.

Eventually the beans softened and the lentils turned to mush. Then Habbie seasoned the *fuul* with salt, onions and dried herbs.

Twenty-six

With great care to keep the shale-like sandstone rocks from becoming an avalanche, Carl climbed a small hill to the east of the family's home. When he neared the top, he crawled the rest of the way. He dragged out his binoculars with a curse. The cheap things were the only ones he'd been able to buy at the village a good twenty miles from here. He should have had the foresight to buy some before he left Port Sudan.

Shoulda bought some more duct tape too; never know when I'll need it. Village people are all robbers and thieves. Hadda pay three times the price.

He watched the women, tried to look into the dark tunnels made by their scarves. He had to make sure these were his blondes, as he strongly suspected they were.

An eagle or vulture of some sort flew overhead and made that high-pitched cry as they do at times.

One of the women looked up. For a brief moment, she used her hand to hold the scarf away from her face. He nodded. The Okie would be curious about anything she didn't know.

With satisfaction, Carl cautiously backed down the hill. He could feel his blood pressure go down. In a few days, he'd be back to start the slow process of doing in one Okie female. But now he had this errand for 'his majesty.' In the valley, the horses waited for their trip to Kelmet's cousin's village.

Harley stretched his reins. A greener clump of weeds lay just beyond his mouth. The black also stretched his reins, but he wasn't after eating. His jaws were a little over a foot from Harley's shoulder.

Carl gritted his teeth. He'd at least like to kick that blamed black stallion.

Halfway down the hill, Carl stopped. His arms needed the rest. They hurt every time he moved them.

That black devil, Carl cursed it... He'd like to tie that animal down and kick it until his legs had no more strength. He'd do it, if it were his. If it were his, after he got tired of kicking that beast, he'd shoot it, each hind hoof first then after a wait, those delicate bones right above the hoof, then the hock, all the way up, last of all he'd shoot the jaw…if it were his.

But the black belonged to Kelmet; he'd been paid to take it to Kelmet's relative. He slid down the rest of that hill faster than he intended.

Carl mounted Harley and took the black's reins. As he'd learned to do, he choked the reins up close under the animal's chin. After Carl made a dozen or so quick pulls that caused the bit to pinch the animal's mouth, the black settled a little.

Every mile brought his anger at that Okie into sharper focus. She took him from his loving Meribet who needed him so bad. He'd show that blonde just exactly what she'd earned. It wouldn't be long now. Time would bring one stupid woman a final payday.

Twenty-seven

At mid-day the men came home. Daniel introduced them. "Phillip, this is your bride, Roz. Adam, this is Chaney, your bride." The two men nodded but said nothing. "Let's go inside," Daniel said.

Habbie stayed outside to stir the pot and keep the *fuul* from burning.

When the men, Roz and Chaney were inside, Daniel said. "Now girls, please remove your scarves. Give them to your future husbands."

After removing their scarves, Roz and Chaney waited while the two young men stood looking at them. They stared a long time.

Maybe these men don't like blondes.

Phillip's height, ebony skin and narrow, sensitive face made his son-ship to Daniel obvious. Except for his heavy, muscular shoulders, he had the wiry look of a champion long-distance runner.

Adam seemed of a different type, a little shorter, with bulkier muscles, a round face and not quite as dark as Phillip—more like his mother. He couldn't be more than a year older than Chaney. At the most Roz estimated that he might be fifteen.

Finally Phillip said, "This is my bride?" He hugged his father and then slapped him on the back. "Thank you so much. She's a treasure, just as you said."

Adam stared at Chaney as if she were the most amazing thing he'd ever seen."

"Are you going to stand there all day? Send them out. Our food is done," Habbie yelled from the fire pit.

Phillip handed Roz her scarf and their fingers touched for the briefest instant. He jumped and looked at her with a startled expression.

But Roz felt none of the electricity she'd read about in novels. Still, it wasn't unpleasant. Definitely not unpleasant.

If she stayed, Phillip would have to do. In this place she had no way to choose her husband.

Surrender to circumstances?

Since when have I given up and let someone else run my life? Hasn't happened before. Won't happen now.

I won't allow it. Roz Duncan and only Roz Duncan chooses the person she marries. That means I've got to leave here in less than three weeks— Chaney too. But how? This landscape offers no escape options.

Though she seethed inside, Roz said nothing; she took her scarf and tied it in place. Then she went outside to help with the meal. Habbie told Roz to bring a large flat bowl from its place on the shelf inside.

When she brought the bowl, Habbie ordered Roz to hold it while she ladled the *fuul* into it.

"Tell your sister to take the rug that sits in the corner and lay it down."

Chaney grumbled at getting second hand orders. "Why can't she tell me if she wants me to do something?"

"You've got to learn more of the language, silly. She's just trying to get things done fast."

"I don't have to like it." Chaney disappeared into the house and did as she'd been told.

When Habbie finished ladling the *fuul* into the bowl-like platter, she took it inside with the two girls following.

Habbie put the platter of *fuul* in the middle of the carpet and said, "The bread is on the shelf, there."

Roz put the bread on the rug where Habbie pointed.

When all the family, Roz and Chaney, were seated on the rug, Daniel said, "We praise thee, Lord Esus and ask Your blessings on our food."

The whole family said, "So let it be." Roz parroted them, "So let it be."

Dear Lord, get us out of here. Please get us out.

Twenty-eight

Roz followed the family's example and dipped pieces of bread into the community platter of *fuul*, much like eating chips and dip back home. Phillip stared at her.

Hunger brought such a massive appetite that no food had ever tasted as good as this *fuul*. She liked this! Another bite of bread and *fuul* went into her mouth.

Then she looked up; Phillip stared at her. Had he even moved his eyes from her in all these minutes?

She'd eaten four more bites when she remembered that she had to get away from there. She mustn't stay. She mustn't like this place too much. Above all, she mustn't be attracted to this man. The *fuul* and bread stopped tasting good.

Phillip ate very little and he kept staring at her.

After the meal, before the men went back to the field, she asked Daniel, "Am I allowed to talk to my future husband?"

"Of course," Daniel said.

"But only if another person can see you at all times," Habbie said.

She nodded. "Phillip, please don't stare at me. It makes me uncomfortable."

Phillip's deep color developed a burgundy tint. "I want to see the beauteous bride I never knew I'd have. Is that a sin?"

"Uh-oh." She realized she had spoken more openly than a Sudanese woman. "It is," she didn't know the word for embarrassing, "uh, unhappiness to be looked at all the time."

Never taking his eyes from her face, he said, "You are too beautiful. I will feast on you with my eyes, never doubt it."

Daniel cleared his throat. "Boys, we have work to do." He rose smoothly from the carpet and walked out. His sons followed him.

Roz didn't see Phillip, his father, or his brother until the sun had fallen below the horizon and only the orange afterglow of the day remained.

In the meantime, both girls got a lesson in grinding grain and in sweeping dirt floors.

A single oil lamp lit the simple evening meal. The lamp was a flat ceramic bowl with a spout in which a wick lay. Roz had seen similar ones in many Bible pictures.

All through supper, Phillip wouldn't look in her direction.

If it kills me, I'm going to escape. Why am I bothered about his looking or not looking at me? I won't... I mustn't care about this man.

When they finished supper, Habbie supervised putting the house to rights. It took a while to satisfy her. At last the few dishes had been cleaned and everything waited its role in the next day's work.

Roz wondered how she should act toward Phillip. To act interested in him would be dishonest. Yet she had to admit that this hardworking man had a lot more to recommend him than any of her silly boyfriends at home.

But outside she heard Chaney. "I not do it!"

"I, the husband, say my wife will follow tradition and walk two paces behind me."

"I not go, man make me slave," Chaney said in her halting Arabic.

"Aw, I just want a good marriage, and you're not making it easy."

Chaney wailed.

Habbie rushed outside. "Both of you, stop this now. It's bedtime. Go to sleep."

Chaney blubbered her way inside and grabbed Roz. "He's so mean!"

Not knowing what to do, Roz patted Chaney's shoulder. She said in Arabic, "There now, it will sort itself out."

"But he's mean!" Chaney whimpered.

"You and Adam need time to get used to each other. For now, do what Habbie said. Go to sleep."

But Chaney blurted, "He hurt my feelings. He doesn't want a wife; he wants a slave."

"It will be all right," Roz said.

Tears streamed down Chaney's face. "I won't be anybody's slave."

"Go to sleep," Roz ordered, and then she turned her back on Chaney and lay down. She made a point of ignoring the squirt's complaints.

Roz lay on the thin pallet in the space Habbie allotted her. She still wore her shapeless black dress. For a cover she had only the single thickness of cotton cloth Habbie had given her.

In the night, Roz froze and when the sun shone the next day, she knew she'd fry. What a country!

She supposed she could get used to it, if she had to. But she wanted to go home.

It would be a real pleasure to hear Bobby's little complaints. She'd even enjoy the sinking feeling of utter fear she always got when her dad bragged on her—she seemed to be the only one who thought she could fail. Roz didn't sleep well.

At sunrise, Habbie waked Roz and then patted her husband's shoulder and then Adam's.

"Wake your sister," Habbie told Roz.

Last of all, Habbie patted Phillip's shoulder and scooted backward.

Phillip responded by lashing out with a fist that hit Habbie in a glancing blow on her left calf. Both legs also kicked out. He seemed to think he was in a fight for his life. A couple more blows and he became truly awake.

Habbie said nothing, only looked at Roz and pointed to her son.

"I'm sorry, Mom," Phillip said.

Roz wondered at what she had just seen. For now, she folded her pallet and smoothed her dress into a more orderly arrangement. Then she woke Chaney, told her to hurry. After that, she put on her scarf and went outside.

Twenty-nine

Under Habbie's hands, the fire crackled into a worthwhile blaze.

"The water bucket is empty," Habbie said.

"I'll get more," Roz said. She picked up the water bucket, took it to the spring and in spite of her trouble with grasshoppers, lugged the heavy bucket back.

At Habbie's direction, she set the large pot in place in the fire pit and put some of the water in it.

"Jesus, Lord, please don't forget about us. We've got to leave and we'll need help—lots of help, all we can get."

When the water boiled, Habbie put a quantity of grain in the pot and said, "Stir." She handed Roz the long-handled wooden spoon. Roz took it and stirred the porridge.

"Bring more wood," Habbie told Chaney.

Chaney trotted to the wood pile, but then she backed away.

"Gonna kill me 'nother snake," Chaney growled and ran toward a head-sized rock that sat near the edge of the packed dirt around the house. Just as she'd done so many times, she picked up the rock and faced the snake that had coiled in front of the woodpile. With a grunt that could be heard in the next village, she let the rock fly. When the snake stopped moving, she kicked it out of the way, threw the rock toward the more wild area and brought the wood as she'd been told.

"You did well to kill that snake, but we don't want carrion eaters near our house. Please take it over there, near that rock." Habbie pointed to a boulder half the size of the house that stood about a block away. That is our garbage place."

By the time the men were ready to go to their work, the grain had softened. The family ate and talked.

Phillip kept his eyes down and wouldn't look at Roz while they ate.

"Today, you go to the field. Daniel bought you instead of the donkey we needed, so you must do the work of a donkey," Habbie said.

"At least until noon," Daniel said.

Roz nodded. She meant to do whatever she had to do. She'd see that Chaney followed directions as well.

When Chaney and I escape, we'll leave these people with no donkey and no money to buy one and no way to buy brides for their sons.

What can I do? I can't trade my life for the price of a donkey—can I?

She pondered that thought all the way to the field. Daniel and the two boys carried all the tools and enough water to see them through a hardworking day.

While they walked, Daniel said, "I'm sorry, I don't know anything else to do. Habbie is right; I should have bought the donkey and been happy with that."

"But then, we would have been in a harem, or worse," Roz said, "Thank you for buying us out of that unspeakable misery."

How can I desert this family? How can I even say 'thank you' and mean it? I'm going to escape. I have to—don't I?

When they reached the field, Phillip, Adam and their father laid their clothes at the edge of the field, except for a breechcloth.

When they bared themselves, Roz backed away. On the slavers' ship, she'd been handcuffed to pipes that were put there for the, the, "thing" they did.

Every day, one unlucky girl of the eleven blondes had to stand at the poles while wearing only a bikini bottom. The girl's arms stretched out, held there by the handcuffs on her wrists; her legs held apart by manacles attached to those same poles.

All those vile crewmen had been allowed to touch her, lick and squeeze her. Anything they wanted, provided they didn't penetrate or leave bruises. The captain demanded that the other ten girls watch this proceeding. It was their training, he said.

After the men got through with that day's expensive blonde, they could do anything—anything—to the cheap slaves chained in the holds. In her nightmares, Roz still heard their screams.

Roz's breakfast developed a life of its own and she swallowed often and breathed in shallow pants.

Once when she had been chained to those poles so she could be their toy of the day, she had thrown up. The rules were that if any of the men could make the girl upchuck, all the men got to touch, lick and squeeze her a second time. She never let her stomach rebel again…she wasn't going to this time either.

Yet, here in this place, just looking at these nearly naked men brought so much bile into her throat.

I'm not going to throw up. I won't; I won't.

A voice heard, yet not heard, came…God's voice.

You must forgive.

She rebelled only a few seconds. If God wanted it, then she'd better do it. She whispered the words:

I forgive those, those beasts in human skin. I forgive them. Dear God, I pray that all of them will hear your voice and repent of their sins. You forgave me; I forgive them.

Twice her stomach jumped, but each time she managed to swallow it back.

I'm not on that ship; this is different. I forgive them. Please Jesus, give all of those men your salvation. Give them good health and peace.

Still dazed, Roz barely heard Daniel. "We have only two adzes. Watch my boys work while they do a row, to see how it's done. Then you take their tools. I'll come behind all of you with the rake to smooth out the land, make it ready for planting."

Phillip started his row first. Adam waited to start his row until Phillip had made a couple dozen strokes, enough to safely allow his brother to swing his adze.

This man, Phillip, isn't like those on that ship. He's kind and sensitive—smart too. Can I be a wife? In school I learned that some women never recover from the kind of things that were done to us. Am I one of those?

No, I'm not. I won't be. I have forgiven those men and I'll continue to forgive them.

"I'll never be able to swing that thing, not like they do," Chaney said.

"Mama liked to grow tomatoes—after she got too sick, I tried to grow them for her. I've used a hoe, but not a tank-sized hoe like those adzes."

I won't be a cripple. I'll be a wife. I'll enjoy my husband. If it kills me, I will enjoy...

Something happened. Roz couldn't describe it...exactly. It felt like falling through a window as she had done when she was four years old. She'd climbed on the window sill and a big white dog ran through the yard. She watched him and leaned on the glass, not realizing it could break. Then suddenly the glass gave way. Crystals of breaking glass rainbowed around her. Because she was so young at the time, most of her scars weren't noticeable.

This time the rainbow didn't signal being cut. She'd been holding herself back from Phillip. Could she give herself permission to love him physically and emotionally?

"I can't do it," Chaney whined.

"You can do a lot more than you think you can. I've watched you."

"Not that. I can't, no way."

"We'll see in a bit. But right now look at our husbands. They're so strong—to say nothing about how coordinated they are. None of the boys I knew back home were as manly as these two men."

"I can't do that."

"You can certainly enjoy watching Phillip and Adam."

Phillip's shoulders don't need football pads to make them wide. And his lean hips—his thigh muscles knotting and releasing.

Deep inside Roz, lightning bloomed. It grew and its warmth spread greater pleasure with Phillip's every move. No boy she'd ever dated aroused her like this. She shifted her weight from her left hip to her right hip and momentarily her pleasure increased.

Lust. Pure lust, that's what I'm feeling...It's wonderful! Mama, why didn't you tell me this is what you had with Dad?

When the boys completed a row, Daniel said, "All right, girls, I'm sorry but Habbie's right. Boys, help them get started."

Both girls marched to the starting place. Roz tried to keep her breathing normal. She would start her row a few swings in advance of Chaney.

Phillip gave Roz his adze and put her hands where his had been. The sweat of his hands had warmed the wood and made it moist.

Phillip bent his body over hers and grasped her forearms. "Lift it over your head and swing down. There's a rhythm to it. It's easier after you find your pace and tempo."

The heat Roz felt had nothing to do with the already-too-warm morning. She'd better learn to do this quick, before marriage became an afterthought.

"Okay, let me try it," Roz said. She found the adze's down-stroke hard to control, but managed a slight bite into the dry soil.

"Again, try again. If you make the raising and the down-stroke all part of a whole, it's not so hard, at least, not for me."

Roz nodded her head and tried again. She didn't want Phillip that close again. Didn't want to find him so attractive. She certainly didn't want to want him like that...And yet...she felt disappointed that she mustn't have him "that close" again.

Roz did her best; Chaney grunted a lot and maybe she did her best as well.

When she finished the row, Roz knew she couldn't lift that, that torture instrument of an adze, not even one more time. Chaney had collapsed without a word about three yards before the row's end.

"Please," Roz gasped to Daniel, "Have to rest. Can't do more."

Phillip and Adam ran to the girls. "We thought so. Our mother can be a harsh woman sometimes. We'll take the next two rows, not one," Phillip said.

"It's my turn to check on Mama," Adam said. He trotted over the rise and disappeared without another word.

"What's that about?" Roz asked.

"Mother's alone. We don't like to be too far away, not these days," Phillip said.

"I don't understand," Roz said.

Phillip said, "We're Christians living among people who hate Christians."

"You're afraid someone will attack her?"

"Yes." Phillip picked up the adze and looked at the rise. Sure enough, Adam trotted back.

Adam didn't say a word, just picked up his adze, walked to the place Chaney stopped and started swinging. "She's all right; no one around."

"You rest, we'll do two rows," Phillip said. "Then you can try again."

Roz sat with Chaney, but she saw nothing except the gorgeous man who would be her husband.

When Phillip checked on Habbie, somehow she couldn't wait for him to return. Yet, attracted to this handsome hunk of man-flesh or not, she had to return to the U.S.A. It wouldn't be right to let her dad think she'd died.

It definitely wouldn't be right to let those men on the ship keep on kidnapping people.

I'll go home, somehow. If it kills...

Thirty

At lunchtime, they walked back to the house.

Before they reached the rise, Adam said something Roz didn't quite hear and Chaney took offense. Daniel told both of them to be quiet.

Roz walked faster, away from the rest. But Phillip gained on her and they walked together in silence.

Then Phillip said, "We can talk now, learn about each other. I don't want to marry a woman I don't know."

"I don't want to marry a man I don't know either." Always Roz had given her studies first place and had never gone out much.

I won't flirt with Phillip. Not very good at it anyway...but I can talk to him. No harm in talking.

"So tell me, my husband-to-be, what do you like, what do you dislike?"

Phillip laughed. "Are all your people so direct? We put many more words into our introductions."

"Oh dear, I suppose you think I'm a forward woman," Roz put up her right hand to cover her eyes. "I scolded you for staring at me, first thing. Now I make you think I'm too, too—"

"Delightfully different?"

Roz laughed. "I'm different okay, always have been."

Maybe I can provoke him into letting me go away by being disagreeable, arguing a lot. Chaney's got a good start on arguing. I can follow her lead.

She tensed her muscles as if preparing for a physical attack. "I'm not likely to change, you know that."

"I don't want you to change."

"That's good. I need the life I planned to have."

"In fact, as my bride, you may be the biggest answer to prayer I've ever had."

Roz had her next statement prepared, but those words stopped her. She frowned. "I don't understand."

"Years ago, I began praying that the Lord would give me something important to do," Phillip said.

"Something important?"

"I don't want to farm this desert the rest of my life," he said.

How could she be unpleasant to this impossibly handsome, improbably serious man? "I've seen a few farms that were much like this. Then they learned a better way to farm dry land."

"You know about farming?"

"Not much. I know that on dry land you don't disturb the soil very much and always plant cover crops if you have to plow. But there are people who've made it their life's work to figure out the best way to grow things on dry land."

"Where? Dad and I have looked for this kind of knowledge."

"We have schools that teach farming in the U. S. A. That's where those teachers are."

Phillip's dark face grew darker. "You people are selfish."

"Selfish?"

"So many people need to know these things. And your farming teachers sit in your U. S. A. You don't help us at all."

Roz turned on him. "Now hold it. My people have done more to raise the standard of living over this globe than any other people have ever done in the history of the world."

"But I—I mean—"

Roz faced him nose to nose. "We give our knowledge and help anywhere we can."

"But—"

"Your own government won't let us help you." She poked him in the chest with her index finger. "That's the reason we don't help here."

"But I—" Phillip backed up. "I mean, we—"

"They—your government—won't let us." She frowned at him. "But do you do anything about your government?"

"Well, I—we—but—"

"No. Of course you don't. You just sit around sucking your thumb and complaining that we're selfish."

"I guess—" He ducked his head.

"Anyway, you people wouldn't listen if we came over and told you everything we know. At least most of the people we've tried to help don't. They don't listen; just use us as an excuse for their bad planning and laziness."

Surprised at herself, Roz walked faster, much faster than Phillip. She'd ordered herself to argue, and it just came out. But he seemed so sweet, so innocent.

A tear slipped down her cheek and she wiped it away. She heard him behind her, walking slower, allowing the distance between them to increase.

How can I pick a fight with him so often he won't want me? One argument and I'm whipped. Yet, I have to go home. I have to.

When she reached the house, everyone else still walked down the hill. Habbie gave her a calculating look. "You have fought with my son."

Roz squeezed her eyes almost shut and made her mouth a thin line. "Yes, I fought with your son."

"Good. Teach him to respect you, respect your opinions. And you, respect your man but fight well." A slight grin softened her round features. "Get the platter. We have a meal to present."

The family ate with less enthusiasm than before. Then the men went back to the field while Roz and Chaney stayed to learn how to be Sudanese housewives.

Chaney began sweeping with her shoulders bowed.

Roz ground grain, but she had no more enthusiasm than Chaney.

"My daughters, this is not good!" Habbie shouted. "Did you not have mothers to teach you how to be women?"

Both girls looked at her. Chaney frowned. Maybe Roz also frowned.

Habbie put her pointing finger in Chaney's back and pushed. "You must stand up."

Chaney groaned and tried to straighten up. After a momentary attempt, she simply stood still while tears trailed down her cheeks.

"How will your husband ever learn to respect you if you cry all the time?"

"I d-don't cry all the time; I don't," Chaney said.

"You're right. When you're not crying; you're arguing with him. Arguments you can not win."

"But—." Chaney dropped her broom. "He not want wife—"

"This is not good." Habbie picked up Chaney's broom and put it back in her hands. "I must teach you things my mama taught me when I was five. Must teach you to be good wives."

Roz watched Habbie and Chaney go into the house.

She turned the millstone. A shower of pale dust fell from the outer edges.

How am I going to leave this place? Escaping would be wrong after all this family has gone through. But I can't stay. I just can't.

Thirty-one

The black stallion became wilder by the hour. He bucked and nipped at Harley until patient ol' Harley took to nipping at him. Even that didn't settle the black.

Carl took the black's reins and choked them up close under the animal's chin, as he'd done earlier. The quick pulls pinched the animal's mouth and the black settled a little. That lesson lasted perhaps an hour. Then again the black tried to nip at Harley.

Harley returned the favor.

By the end of the day, Carl's arms groaned from keeping the two animals away from each other. He staked the horses on opposite sides of his camp, got his camp kettle out of his saddlebag, poured each horse in turn some water from his canteen and then he lit a small fire. After the horses had slurped up their share, he took a handful of sandy soil and wiped the inside of the kettle. Then he wiped it out with a cloth and put some water in it. When the water boiled, he added small bits of jerky and a handful of rice. Then he took his knife and gathered what fodder he could find for the horses.

"This'll be over in a couple days," he told Harley while spreading the grass. "Just give time a chance to work." He gave his animal a consoling pat on the shoulder.

He approached the black. "You devil, I'll be glad to get your hide in someone else's hands." Then he threw the horse some weeds and grass.

After eating, since he had no one to take a turn at watching, Carl dragged himself and his rifle onto Harley's bare back. He'd doze, but be ready to shoot any critter that threatened. He knew how to stay alive in this predator-infested wilderness.

As Carl expected, he slept lightly through the night. Crazy dreams of being chased by ghostly creatures that resembled some of his past victims didn't help. At the first gray of sunrise, he dismounted, stretched, ate a couple bites of jerky, sipped at his canteen, walked around a little, gave both horses water, saddled both horses and slipped into Harley's saddle.

The village run by Kelmet's relative would be the end of the line for this black monstrosity. Carl so looked forward to reaching it.

"Be there in a day or so," he told Harley. "Just be patient. Time takes care of things like this. You know it does." Then he patted the old horse's neck and kicked him slightly to urge him into a more canter-like walk.

An hour later, he found a trail that seemed to go in the right direction and Harley, as he usually did, followed it without needing much direction. Carl relaxed a little. Especially he relaxed when the black didn't fight his control. But Carl's fist still held that bad boy's reins just below his chin.

When the animal continued to behave well, Carl relaxed a little more. He didn't exactly doze as he might have if it were just him and Harley. Still, he wasn't at his best when the trail disappeared.

In a tangle of rock and scrub, Harley plowed in as if he'd been there before and knew where he should go. But the black didn't like it. Even though Carl held his reins tight under his chin, the black bucked, stomped and jumped.

"Fool," Carl told the worked-up beast. "I'm gonna pull you down; don't care if your mouth bleeds the rest of your..." The horse reared, all but pulled Carl out of the saddle. "...suckin' life."

The black reared again and the reins slipped through Carl's fingers. He managed to catch the end of one, but not both. "Whoa!" He commanded and let go of Harley's reins to make good his attempt to restrain this black beast.

At that moment, Teeth first, Harley drilled in on the black's shoulder.

When the black reared up, Carl lost the reins.

Then Harley rose up in a matching fight-pose. Harley's saddle became a slope too slippery for any human to keep.

Carl fell…hard. Semi-conscious, Carl watched the two beasts scream at each other and paw the air. He breathed three times before he regained enough sense to know what had happened. He had to separate those two before they tore each other apart.

Still wobbly, he tried to get close without getting a hoof in the face. If he could grab their reins, he could get control. The two horses screamed curses at each other; they alternated between using their powerful heads as battering rams with teeth and trying to smash each other to non-existence with their hooves.

At his age, Harley couldn't keep up this non-stop aggression very long. The first time he backed away from the black, Carl grabbed one of his reins and under the influence of much adrenalin and even more anger, Carl leaped into the saddle, grabbed the other rein and brought Harley to a stop.

The black didn't stop. Teeth first, the black attacked again, but this time Carl held Harley steady. He did his best to grab either of the black's reins and failed. Fidgety, Harley stomped and reared. And the black attacked again. This time Carl kicked the black horse under its chin. The black stopped for perhaps the blink of an eye then he bolted out into the wide rock and brush-dotted plain. Carl cursed and kicked Harley into a lope.

An animal in good condition, like the black, could run for quite a distance. Carl cursed about that and kicked Harley again. He didn't want to chase that fool black horse through this heat. He would, though—had to.

The black seemed to become a distant ghost, but he kept running. Would the animal never tire?

The uneven ground ahead overflowed with large rocks and boulders. From the way Harley started picking his way through, it was probably filled with holes and burrows. Not good land for horses to run on. Carl knew what would happen minutes before it did, but he had no power to prevent it.

As he'd predicted, the fast-running black went down, a spectacular flip that couldn't help destroying the animal. The horse didn't even try to get up.

"Whoa, there," he told Harley. "Take your time and walk easy. We ain't gonna do any good now."

When they arrived, Carl dismounted slowly. The black horse lay on the ground with its left front leg lying at an impossible angle. It kept making that low-pitched whuffle-groan. Back in his jockey days, Carl had heard that sound several times. It said the horse had unbearable pain.

Carl refused to look in the black's eyes. He just shook his head and grabbed his rifle.

Afterwards, Carl kicked the dead animal and cursed. Why had he agreed to do this "little favor?" He knew why. He needed the money for Meribet's island. That's why.

He was stupid, that's why. It didn't matter that Kelmet paid him enough in gold coin to make moving around difficult for ol' Harley, not to mention dangerous for him. He was still stupid. He should have refused.

Then he felt that numbness around his mouth, in his right hand and that nausea in his stomach. His blood pressure intended to stroke him out. He needed to calm down, take it easy. He lay down right there on the sand and rocks. Did his breathing exercise ten times. Then he did them another ten times. After that, he took Harley with him and walked over to a tall shrub that offered a little shade. He tied Harley to it as an alarm system and lay down. He didn't exactly sleep, just dozed a little for about a half hour.

After he'd napped, Carl felt somewhat better. He dreaded the thought of going out like his mother. Dad said she'd stroked out and died in the middle of one of her tempers. He ought to get back to the states and protect Meribet, help her disappear out of her dad's *and* her mom's life. Then they'd go to the island he meant to buy before the month ended. If he lived on his island, he wouldn't have any more blood pressure problems— Wouldn't have that stroke nightmare yanking on the base of his skull.

But that was for later. Now he had work to do.

Buzzards don't waste time. The black stallion lay under a quivering, moving blanket of large, hungry birds with rending beaks and slashing talons. A couple of shots from his revolver left two dead vultures and sent the rest into the air. They soared up and that shrieking, flying circle said they wouldn't wait long for another serving of horse flesh.

He focused on removing that valuable saddle, not easy with the bloody carcass on it. When he finished, he mopped his face, cursed, and shot the next overgrown crow that settled near the horse's body.

While more birds gathered, he tied the saddle down on Harley's backside on top of his saddle bags. For the fun of it, he shot another buzzard and watched the disgusting carrion eaters scatter away from the gunshot.

Harley snorted and danced.

"Okay, I know, you don't like this one bit. Neither do I." Carl patted the old animal's neck and climbed into the saddle. "Let's go. We deliver this saddle and then we can get back on her trail. Maybe when we find her, I'll just shoot her and get it over with."

Harley shivered his neck and snorted.

"You're right, old chum. I'm gonna at least tie her in the sun. Ain't gonna waste this opportunity."

Harley twitched his ears and nodded his head up and down.

"Right. Let the ants have the Okie. Be like watching Mom die slow like I wish she had. Yeah, let time have its rewards."

They found the trail to the village and Harley settled into his best trail-following walk and Carl drifted into his usual trail-traveling doze.

Was he awake or was that laugh in his nightmare? He had no idea. All he knew was that it jerked him out of the rest he wanted and needed.

~ * ~

Before Carl settled for the night, he comforted his beast with an extra couple of pats. "We'll probably reach that village tomorrow before the day's heat sets in."

Harley acknowledged with an up and down nod.

Thirty-two

Habbie woke Roz and Chaney. The pair helped her prepare breakfast and then the girls went to the field with the men. The hard work of preparing the field didn't get easier with familiarity, but noon finally came.

After the noon meal, the men went back to the field. The girls stayed with Habbie for more lessons in running a Sudanese household. Both girls got lessons in making a crude broom. They each cut tough grasses and bound them to four foot long acacia limbs that served as broom handles.

Then Habbie handed Roz a sack of wheat grains and gave her more tips on making a millstone do its work. This lesson concerned not wasting her energy.

After that Habbie turned to Chaney. "Now, my child, you must learn the best way to sweep a floor that is made of dirt. It is an art that you must master." She picked up her broom and went into the house. Chaney picked up the one she'd made and followed her.

"Your strokes must not be so muscular that you remove the floor. Use a tender touch." Habbie demonstrated. "Do you see? The dust bunnies come loose, but the floor does not."

Chaney applied herself by frowning and biting her lower lip while tenderly stroking this delicate dirt floor. Then she looked up and screeched, "Snake!" The word didn't leave her mouth before she'd pushed Habbie out of danger.

The brown snake immediately coiled into its strike posture.

Chaney grabbed the little wooden table that held one of the two lamps this family owned. The table sailed through the air, but it never touched the fast moving snake. Spilled oil bathed the floor.

"I hate snakes." Chaney picked up the table and using it like an adze, she hit the snake. "Hate 'em! Hate, hate, hate."

Eventually Habbie gently patted her shoulder. "Child, it's quite dead now." The snake still quivered, but the major flailing had passed.

Roz, who ran inside at Chaney's first scream, took the remains of the table from the younger girl. "It's okay. The snake is dead."

"I hate snakes."

"Yes, I know. But now we have a mess to clean up," Roz said. "Let's start with taking the snake where you took the other one. Be best if we didn't attract carrion birds or hyenas, so it's got to be thrown far away from the house. You want me to do it, or do you want to?"

"I'll do it." Chaney seemed more subdued than usual.

"I'll see if I can put the table together. Habbie, do you have a hammer? No? I guess I can use a rock."

Chaney picked up the quivering snake and would have walked outside, but Habbie caught her and hugged her.

"Thank you, you've saved my life," Habbie said.

"I guess all that field work stands good for something." Chaney flexed her bicep. "I'm a lot stronger now,"

Again Habbie hugged her tight.

"It's all right. Glad to do it, ma'am." Chaney hugged Habbie, picked up the snake by its tail and swaggered out the door. She walked on the outer edges of her feet so that she looked as if she were bow-legged. The snake dragged behind her.

Roz had to bite her tongue at Chaney's imitation of an old west hero.

Two nails had to be hammered back into the table and the lamp needed to be refilled.

"Looks like an advantage of dirt floors is that they aren't so hard that most things break," Roz said. "But what will we do about the spilled oil? It's part of the dirt now."

"It will be fine until we resurface the floor. Don't worry about it," Habbie said.

When she returned, Chaney learned more about sweeping a dirt floor.

"You will make good wives, both of you," Habbie said. "My husband did well to get you. But we will only tell him that you're good at killing snakes. We won't praise him very much. Men get such big heads if they're praised often. It's one of their worst failings."

She grinned and went outside to stir the pot of fuul for their supper.

Chaney finished sweeping while Roz returned the millstone and pondered the ethics of escaping.

Life here is hard, but they treat me well. I don't want to leave, at least not by running away. Still, I can't stay.

I never thought I'd be married before I finished college. Never thought of being married to a man of another race. Yet I could love Phillip deeply if I let myself.

It isn't fair.

What is fairness anyway?

What about Dad? And Bobby?

The evening meal came at last. After the morning's work at turning the dirt with that huge adze, and the afternoon's excitement, and her labor with a heavy grindstone, the *fuul* should have tasted better than any food Roz could remember. She ate little and tasted nothing.

If I escape I'll tear this family apart. But I can't stay here—can I?

Thirty-three

With that white cloth and rope halo on his head to roughly imitate Muslim dress, Carl picketed Harley down and strode into the center of the village. A man hurried down the main road with the reins of two stellar-looking Arabian stallions in his fists.

Carl stopped the man and asked to meet Sighet al Azibik.

After his introduction to Azibik, he put up with the usual guest-greeting routine. He knew he'd have to stay in this village for the afternoon, maybe the night. In that case he might get some help. He knew these back-country Muslims. If they thought you were kin or friend, these village people were pushovers. Do whatever you "suggested."

When he had been thoroughly introduced, Azibik invited Carl to join the group at a meal. After the entire group, including Azibik's elderly father, had been seated on the floor, Azibik's women served them.

Carl used his best manners in carefully dipping into the spicy *fuul* with only his right hand. He used great care to plunge the pancake-like bread into the *fuul* but not so far that his bare fingers touched the *fuul* mixture. The other men were just as fastidious as he.

He looked at the small bowl of hot spice, the *shata*, many times before deciding to dip his bread into that concoction. He glanced at Azibik. The man seemed to be goading him. The last time he'd dared take *shata*, he'd had to do the unmannerly thing and ask for water.

Surely they didn't make the *shata* that hot here in this place.

It was that hot.

Though he thought he'd never draw another breath, Carl's smile achieved the needed degree of permanence. He took another bite of bread and *fuul*. Then a sip of the overly sweet tea. After that, he ate more bread and *fuul*.

Azibik, Azibik's father and uncle watched him. He had no choice. Again, he dipped his bread into the *shata*, put the liquid fire in his mouth and chewed. The temperature of the room mirrored the heat of the *shata*.

Carl swiped his sleeve across his sweaty forehead. While grinning his most sociable smile, he listened to Asibik's conversation. He knew Azibik and his entire family watched him after he ate the *shata*. They'd know by how he ate if he were really the kindred person he said he was.

Carl continued to lean toward Azibik and to grin, as if declaring his undying friendship. First, he gave Kelmet's invitation to come to Mesella for the trading fair of October seventeen. Then, at last, Carl could get down to his own message.

"My friend, if I could show you Christians on your own doorstep, would you be interested?

"There are a few."

"You know about them?" Carl said. "I'm surprised. I thought all good Muslims in this great country were opposed to living near Christians."

"They have their uses." The man took a sip of the tea in his tiny glass.

Carl also sipped the lukewarm tea. "As what? Vermin to exercise your dogs?" He laughed at his own joke.

"We let them get enough goods to make a raid worthwhile. Then we harvest them, take everything they have that we want. Takes much less energy than farming."

"Interesting." Carl nodded his head.

Better be extra careful around these land-dwelling sharks.

"Oh yes, it is great fun to raid them." Azibik took a sip of his tea. "We do it for sport and to learn more about using our few guns in a battle situation."

"Ah! Then I have something to offer you, my good friend." Carl sipped his tea as a way of saying he wasn't pushy.

"Speak, my friend, I will listen to what you say."

"I have declared these people as my personal enemies."

"As have I," said Azibik.

"I would like your help."

"You have it," the village leader said.

"I want the blond girls who were stolen from me. I'll pay better than twice what you get for other slaves, one hundred gold Krugers. I don't care what you do to the other Christians." Carl raised his lip on one side in a snarl.

Azibik stroked his beard. "Then you would have us capture your quarry for you."

Carl laughed his heartiest laugh. "You'll be paid well for your trouble. Of course, if you don't want the pay," Carl shrugged and put a morsel of *fuul*-laden bread in his mouth.

Gotta watch my blood pressure.

"I can get them myself. I thought you, my friend, would like the pleasure of this venture."

"But, I did not say we would not want to earn your money."

"Then you would be willing?"

"Oh yes, we are willing. But not for one hundred. We need twice that, for each of these women."

"Why, that's—that's—"

"That is what we require, my friend. Or you could see that we get the guns we need. Our village has never had reasonable firepower."

"I thought I saw several guns."

"Did you not also notice that the guns you saw were old? Of modern guns we have only my Kalashnikov and a Steyr AUG."

"You drive a hard bargain." He frowned and did little fiddling motions with his right hand fingers as if calculating, thinking hard.

Azibik said nothing, only watched without moving.

Carl sighed. "You need guns. All right, you'll get guns. If I give you six guns, then what will you charge to get my blondes?"

"The rate you stated will be acceptable."

"At one hundred, we have a deal—"

"—Acceptable, assuming none of my men are hurt," Azibik said. "If they are hurt in any way, even scratched, then you will need to pay us for our injuries."

Carl narrowed his eyes. "And your injuries will cost me what?"

"Say, another six guns or six rocket launchers for each injury."

"Guns I can get. Can't get launchers right now."

"Then ammunition for the guns, one large box for each gun." Azibik measured the air with his hands to indicate the size box he wanted.

Carl sat with a frown on his face and stroked his chin with its week's worth of red beard. He wanted Azibik to think he drove an extremely hard bargain.

"All right, but three guns, not six, and if any of your men are so stupid as to get themselves killed, it counts as no more than an injury."

"You are the one who drives the bargain hard, my friend. We will bring your quarry to you."

"It would be better if you would hold them for me. But no mistake, I want those girls."

"Then we will consider this transaction, all of it, done."

"I'll return in four weeks, perhaps five. At that time, I'll take delivery on my property."

Carl rose and gave his hand to be shaken.

Azibik also rose. He shook Carl's hand first, then the dozen or so other men shook his hand. Finally, Azibik shook his hand again.

"I'll get your guns and return, my friend," Carl said. "Thank you for your kind hospitality."

They said other pleasant words to each other and Carl left. Many of the men trailed him to his horse.

Carl mounted Harley and waved the company so long.

"Won't be hard to scare up a few guns and a little ammo. I know exactly where I need to go and who I need to see," Carl told his horse.

Harley's up and down nod rated a pat on the neck.

"Yeah, with my expertise with the lingo and customs, I'm gonna be the gun king here. I'll be good at it, ain't no doubt."

They traveled down the rutted path for at least an hour. Carl spent his time day-dreaming about Meribet.

"Have to give myself enough time to go back to the U.S.A and get Meribet. Bring her to my island. But first I gotta buy my island."

Best to stay out of Carnelli's sight. Meribet is the only Carnelli I ever want to hear of again.

His phone had the number for Karakanis Real Estate in Iraklion on Crete. Only real estate people he knew. They specialized in Aegean properties and he already knew Paulos, old man Karakanis' son. Paulos knew and loved horses just like he did. Paulos wanted to start a racing stable, but refused to leave real estate so long as his dad lived.

Paulos answered on the second ring.

"Paulos, I need your help."

"You always got my help. What you need me to do?"

"I want you to buy me one of your nice Aegean islands. Doesn't have to be huge…a couple, three miles across be fine.

"I know just the place," Paulos said. "It's a day trip from Athens. Seller will want a down payment, of course," Paulos said. "What you got?"

"I have an account in Alexandria. How much you think your seller will need to hold the property, minimum?

"Thirty percent."

"Okay, you get them to agree to two hundred thou, total. And we've got a deal. My bank be sending you a draft for sixty thou. Should be there by the end of the week."

"Gonna take some talking, but I think I can do it. We'll try our best at least."

Carl said goodbye just as the phone beeped its out-of-charge message.

A real pain, that hand crank generator.

"We got that done!" Carl slapped the old horse on the shoulder.

Harley responded by flapping air through his lips.

"You got that right. I'll miss the U.S.A. But a villa in the Aegean with Meribet as its mistress be just fine. I'll have a villa, a yacht and a top of the line Lamborghini automobile. Better get a Lamborghini for Meribet too. Even in Athens and Alexandria, they'll be saying I'm one powerful man. Maybe even in Rome."

Things hadn't gone this well for him since he first met Gregorio.

He'd love to gloat and let Cap know that success doesn't necessarily come with blinding white suits and polite English.

But no, he'd stay away from Cap.

Gregorio A. Carnelli held Cap's leash…Cap would do anything to get his master's approval.

Thirty-four

That evening Phillip asked Roz to sit with him on one of the boulders near the dying cooking fire. Habbie sat just inside the door. Both of the family's oil lamps lit her sewing.

"I shouldn't have taken offense. Shouldn't have accused your people of being selfish," Phillip said.

Slowly Roz said the Arabic words, "I shouldn't have been angry. By now I should expect everyone who isn't an American to be bitter and envious of us."

Phillip said nothing, only frowned.

"I still think that most people could do a lot better for themselves, but I shouldn't have burdened you with my opinion. I'm sorry."

"Friends then?" Phillip asked.

Nodding, she said, "Friends."

"Before we argued, I meant to tell you that you're the answer to all my prayers," Phillip said. "After we're married, would you consider our going to your country?"

"Go home?" He'd truly startled her. "Why? Why would you even need to ask?"

"I want to do something important. But I can't, not without the learning."

"You want an education?"

"I don't want to sit out here in this desert and as you put it, suck my thumb."

She ducked her head. "I didn't treat you fair, what I said."

"I know, but you're still right."

"I was?" She looked into his eyes. Did he mean it?

"If we can't live good lives here, then we should go somewhere else." Phillip said, and then hastily added, "But don't tell Dad I said that. He loves this land."

"My grandfather had the same passion. We never did get him off his farm, even after his third heart attack."

"Heart attack?"

"It's a bad sickness. He died while doing the work he loved. They found him lying over the steering wheel of his tractor. I was only five; I didn't really know him. We only had with him with us for sixty years and two months,"

"*Only* sixty? To live sixty years—that's a long time."

"Most Americans live seventy, seventy-five or more years. You should come to my land, your family too. Maybe we can prove we aren't selfish."

"I shouldn't have said that," he said.

"Maybe there's something we could be doing about your government that we aren't. Maybe, if we go back, I can start a letter-writing campaign to Congress or something."

What if Phillip is joking?

"You were serious about going to the U.S.A, weren't you?"

"I've never been more serious," he said.

"What do you want to do when you get there?"

"We need missionaries, lots of missionaries to come here, teach us about Esus, about our God. Tell us how to live. We've failed and we don't even know it."

"You want to be a missionary?"

"Would you mind being a missionary's wife?"

"If you're the man I'm thinking you might be. If you'll stick by me and treat me as your equal. I'd want nothing better than to follow my husband to the ends of the earth."

"No doubts?" he asked.

"No doubts about us. I should warn you, being an American missionary isn't easy. You'll need a lot of education, an awful lot."

"I've always wanted an education. Dad taught us to read a little, but he isn't educated, so he can't help much. He can't do ciphers at all."

"I can. Math basics aren't hard, just a lot of memorizing. If you want, I can teach you the basics."

"You'd do that for me?" With a grin, he jumped up, grabbed Roz and would have hugged her.

But Habbie gave a loud cough. Phillip sat down and put his hands in his lap. Clearing his throat, he said, "When can we start the learning?"

"How about now?" She picked up a stick. "I know you can count to ten because you count rows in the field."

"I count a lot more than ten rows," Phillip said.

"You need to know what the numbers you say with your mouth look like when you write them." She used the stick to make a mark in the dirt. "That's one."

Phillip picked up another stick and made an identical mark. "One."

"This is two."

Phillip grimaced and made a rough approximation of her neat figure in the dirt. "Two."

They wrote the numbers one through nine twice more before Habbie called them in for the night. The next evening they began again. This time Phillip made all nine numbers in the dirt with very little assistance.

"Okay, you've got the first basic. Now we can do a little math."

She reached over and picked up a small stick. Then she broke it. "First…one and one are two."

"One stick." He looked into her eyes. "We will be one flesh in two weeks and those who become one are not broken."

He hadn't spoken to her like this before. Her lungs wanted to do hiccups, pushups or something. An awkward joy enveloped her.

He touched her hand with his fingertips and this time Roz definitely felt a spark. Startled, she looked into his marvelous brown eyes. "I think I'm beginning—"

Just then Habbie cleared her throat and Phillip jerked his hand away.

"We'd better continue with our lesson." Roz drew a deep breath. "One and one equal two. So two and one equals what?" She picked up another stick and put all three sticks on the ground.

Phillip pointed to each as he counted them, "One, two, three. Two and one equals three."

"Okay, you've made progress. Now write the numbers just as you said them."

"Would your parents approve of me?" Phillip asked.

"My mom has died. Heart trouble just like her dad, only worse. My dad appreciates hard work."

"I'm a hard worker. Always have been."

"I've watched you. I know. You'd be just like a son to him once he gets to know you."

"What could I work hard at when I live in the U.S.A.?"

"You said you wanted us to come back to your Sudan and be missionaries, didn't you?"

"I'd be a pastor then, like Pastor Matthew?"

"If you wanted, or if you thought that God wanted you to help your people be better farmers, you could go to an agricultural school and learn better farming methods. When you came back, you'd be a farming instructor and when you had a chance, you'd tell farmers about Jesus."

"Hmm, I hadn't thought of that. We farmers need help, lots of help."

"Many missionaries work as doctors and nurses and tell people about Jesus when they can. I don't see why a farming instructor couldn't do the same thing."

How could I fail to love this sensitive hunk of real man?

Without realizing they'd done it, she found her right hand in Phillip's hands.

Habbie interrupted with a loud cough and Roz returned her straying hand to her lap. Phillip did the same.

Phillip frowned and said nothing for a long while. "No, I want to be a pastor. I want to read well so I can understand the Bible better. I want to learn how to care for my people. Yes, that's what I'll do if I have the chance."

"Then, my-soon-to-be-husband, that's what we'll plan to do. It will be easier for you to learn things if we start teaching you English since all your U.S.A. learning will be in English."

"Will you teach me?"

I never thought about being a pastor's wife until this minute. How am I going to manage all the people problems a pastor's wife has? I'll need a lot of training, just like Phillip.

Though the fire in the fire pit grew cold, a new warmth lit Roz's insides. She took that warm glow to her pallet. As she drifted off to sleep, she thought, this is love; I know it is.

Her sleep that night approached sleep in her own bed back home. She woke up feeling better than she'd felt since her kidnapping.

Thirty-five

The tasks Habbie demanded of Roz became light work. In the days that followed, she pressed Habbie for recipes and housekeeping methods.

These days Habbie only demanded that the girls work the fields with the men once or twice a week.

Habbie patted Roz's shoulder to wake her. "Today you take Chaney and help your husbands with their work all day. Only I do woman's work today. We made extra *fuul* last night for today's meals."

She put a covered clay bowl about a foot across and at least six inches deep inside a burlap sack. Another sack contained the last of her most recent batch of bread.

"I bake fresh bread today," she said.

"Why can't I stay here? I can't do that work." Chaney's lower lip trembled. "Besides, I still got blisters."

"Chaney, we're going to do field work today. We have to, so don't make a big scene. Wrap the hem of your skirt around your hands if you have to cover your blisters."

Chaney still had her lip sticking out in a big show of pouting when they marched away from the house.

When they reached the field, Roz set the covered bowl of *fuul* in the brightest spot of sunshine. Habbie said this would let the sun warm it to at least lukewarm.

There had been dew or a slight sprinkle of rain and the softer ground made the work a little easier. They managed to finish that field by noon and trudged toward a nearby acacia tree, the only one for at least a mile. They'd eat in its lacy shade.

Daniel had a big grin on his sweaty face. "I didn't think we could do so much."

Phillip grinned as well. "We'll be able to plant our remaining field and have plenty this year."

They sat and, as the senior of the two females, Roz laid out their meal, just the sun-warmed *fuul*, bread and water. She used the burlap sacks in place of Habbie's nice rug, and tried to make the meal as pleasant as possible under the circumstances.

Roz found a warm contentment in all this. Never since her earliest years had she considered becoming a housewife and yet it appeared that being the pastor's wife would be her career.

A grasshopper lit on her shoulder. Her skin crawled and she had to force down a scream.

I'm not six any more. The Sudan has grasshoppers; I'm going to live here so I have to learn to live with them.

Roz used this grasshopper's big hind legs as a handle, and dragged it loose. She still felt the attack of the creatures in her mind. But she refused to let it defeat her. She looked around for a good execution station. A nearby rock would serve well and she hit the grasshopper with a smaller rock, twice.

Then she turned back to the impromptu table. She could do this. The hairs on her arms didn't stand up much more than half way. Yes, indeed, she could do this.

"Bread?" she asked Phillip. And then she grinned.

Chaney reached across their rough "table" and grabbed a piece of bread.

"It's not customary for women to eat with the men," Adam said.

Chaney snorted her disagreement and glared at him. "You're mean," she whispered.

Pastor's wives are peacemakers and if Chaney's reaction to Adam's statement gave any indication, she'd be getting plenty of practice at being a mediator before the sun set.

"Have some more *fuul*, Chaney." Roz said.

Adam's angry face looked as if he could knock planes out of the sky with just a glance. But he said nothing—this time.

After the meal, Roz carried the two burlap sacks and the empty bowl to the next field. It seemed easier to do it herself than asking the grumbling Chaney to carry anything.

Phillip told her, "We're not usually able to work all of our fields, but when we can, we keep plenty laid back. We can get through even the bad years."

Roz nodded. "You're a very wise family. I feel so protected knowing I'm going to be part of it."

If only she could tell her dad...

They reached the field. The three men just stood there in silence. Even she could tell something wasn't right. This field had no vegetation on it at all—not that any of this country had much.

A scratch on her right foot, then her left ankle made her look down. Grasshoppers covered her feet!

Her skin crawled; she wanted to close her eyes and run away screaming at the top of her lungs.

She knew; she knew about this.

Grasshoppers are called locusts here. Not the thumb-sized cicadas that are called locusts back home.

These grasshoppers were real locusts and this was a locust plague. Locusts meant to take her family's land. A sudden rage filled her and the sound a lioness might make came from her throat.

No insect would eat her land out from under her. She stomped her feet. But that killed too few, only left them squirming and crippled.

She scraped grasshopper after grasshopper into the burlap sack. They covered the ground and she grabbed them by the handfuls, ignored their scratching and the damp brown stains of their spit while throwing them in the sack.

Grasshoppers flew around her, scratched her arms, her legs, and still she threw them in. When the sack became so full they tried to escape, she whipped the sack down on a large flat rock, then she stomped it.

The sack still moved. A fist-sized rock lay nearby. With a growl, Roz picked it up and hit the sack again and again. Her arms burned with tiredness and the sack continued to move. She kept pounding.

She stopped when she realized that the bag had a number of holes where she'd beaten all the life out of the burlap.

She grabbed more grasshoppers, intending to fill the sack again.

But Phillip held her arms. Even that didn't stop her. She threw handfuls of grasshoppers into the sack. Then Phillip shook her.

"Roz?"

She came to herself. "I-I...I hate bugs."

Phillip laughed. "I see that you do."

She put her grasshopper-spit tainted hands to her face then instantly removed them. "I must look a mess." She picked up the ragged bag of dead grasshoppers.

"There's nothing we can do about this," Phillip said.

"I'm sorry. This won't be a good year, will it?"

"Ugg. Grasshoppers are icky," Chaney said.

"They're just bugs," Adam said.

A grasshopper landed on Chaney's shoulder. "Ohhh, get him off, get him off!"

But Adam laughed at her.

Chaney settled the issue. She bawled at the top of her lungs and loped toward the house.

"Please get your sister under control," Daniel said.

"Yes sir." Roz ran after the squirt and soon caught up with her.

"What are you thinking? There's snakes, scorpions and spiders waiting for a juicy bite of people flesh. You can't run like you did back home; you have to watch out for those things."

"You don't know."

"I know quite a bit," Roz said. "I've learned about this land."

"Sure, somebody always teaches you." Chaney's chin quivered. "But I've killed lot more snakes than you and nobody taught me."

"Look, all I want to do is be Phillip's wife and spend my days making a home for him and for our children. We'll have lots of guests and I'll be the hostess. That's what I'm going to do because that's what I want to do."

"I want to go home."

"Be home here. You've got a man who would love you if you gave him a half chance."

"I'll never be home," Chaney wailed.

"Be real. This is what is."

"He's mean and so are you." Her head held high, Chaney marched toward the house.

Roz didn't walk with her. Hands on her hips, she shook her head and Phillip walked up.

"At least Chaney's learning this language," Roz said. "She's got to know it to make her complaints understood."

Phillip nodded. "We might as well go home. Nothing more we can do right now.

"What about the locusts?" Roz held the ragged sack of dead locusts away from her skirt.

"Dad thinks they're moving toward the north and east."

"Then they'll miss most of your land. I'm so glad."

When they reached the house, Habbie used a large number of words to express her displeasure with the sack of dead locusts.

But Daniel laughed. "Dear wife, you should have seen her. I didn't know she cared so much. She is truly our daughter and loves this land even as I do."

"If she loves it so much, why did she tear up my sack?"

Still laughing, Daniel said, "It will be all right. When we go to Um Ruwabah, you can buy another sack. Even we can afford one."

Habbie turned away, grabbed the broom and swept the floor Roz had swept yesterday afternoon. The entire time Habbie swept, she muttered. Most of her words couldn't be understood, but she said Roz often.

Thirty-six

In the evening a few days later, Roz and Phillip were going over the multiplication tables. Then the younger couple started again.

Daniel strode from the house. He stopped about ten feet from the two battling youngsters. He crossed his arms and cleared his throat.

Both combatants glowered at each other but they stopped exchanging unpleasantries.

At Daniel's request Adam stayed with him and he ordered Chaney to talk to Habbie.

Then Daniel told Adam, "You will not be married when we go to Um Ruwabah."

Adam stared at his dad with his mouth moving but making no sound. Finally he said, "Why?"

"You are young, perhaps too young for the responsibility."

"I do my part. I take responsibility," Adam said with a scowl.

"You are not wise. A necessary part of adulthood is peace. If I let you get married now, you and your bride would regret it the rest of your lives."

Adam's jaw muscles knotted. "I've never been anything but peaceful, you know that."

"Until your bride came into your life. Since that day, you have quarreled every day. I haven't heard you say more than one or two words to each other that were not an argument."

"Why are you complaining to me? It's her fault." Adam's face developed a deeper color. "You should be having Mother control her."

"I will not talk of this again. Your marriage will take place when you and your bride have learned to be at peace. That will be at least a year from now. Besides, you're only fourteen."

"I'll be fifteen in two months."

"Even fifteen is young for marriage. Perhaps I pushed you too far and too fast."

Daniel walked to the east, away from the house. But Adam stood with his shoulders bowed and his head down. Finally Adam kicked a small stone and walked to the west.

Phillip said, "I've been afraid of this. My brother and his bride don't talk to each other. They only want to be the victor."

"I've talked to Chaney about it, but she insists it's not her fault. She says she won't be a slave to any man, not even her husband. That could be my fault, I guess."

Phillip sputtered, laughed and then said, "How?"

"When she saw how hard escaping from our owner would be, she had second thoughts. Then I explained what slavery is. Maybe I explained it too well."

"I don't think you could explain slavery too well." Phillip put his arm around her waist.

She leaned her head on his shoulder. "I don't either, unless the person is a child."

From behind her, Roz heard Habbie's cough. Instantly she sat up straight and folded her hands in her lap. Phillip did the same.

"What a pair!" Habbie said with a smile. She dumped a load of wood next to the fire pit. "Be patient. We'll be going to Um Ruwabah soon. You can touch each other all you want after that."

"Yes, Mama," Phillip said.

Roz jumped up. "Habbie—Mama, Would you like me to get some more wood or a bucket of fresh water?"

Habbie laughed. "I only want happiness for both of you. Daughter, learn who my son is. Phillip, learn who your bride is." Habbie went into the house and the only sounds were a distant hyena comic opera.

"I suppose we should go over the seven times tables. If we can, I'd like you to be able to say the twelve times tables before we're married," Roz said.

"Then we'd better hurry. I still don't understand how this will help me."

"But you trust me, don't you?"

"Of course I trust you."

"Okay, seven times one is seven," she said and nodded to him.

"Seven times two is fourteen." He continued through, "seven times twelve is eighty-four."

That night Phillip completed his eight times tables and began learning the nine times tables. Roz wondered if she would have learned so fast if she had never had any schooling.

The next morning, the men left to go to the most distant field, the one the locusts had eaten. They hoped to have it ready for seed in two days.

Habbie told Chaney to get water at the spring both for the bucket they drank from and as many buckets as she could manage for the garden. She told Roz to grind the grain into meal for the bread Habbie made every other day or so.

About noon, Habbie left the girls working and took lunch to the men.

Roz had finished most of the grinding on the rotary millstones. She congratulated herself on gaining a useful skill for life in this primitive region. She would make a good wife for Phillip, she knew she would.

Roz looked up from her work. Chaney ran down the hill as if a lion chased her. But she made no sound. Chaney often became upset, but usually upset meant screaming and crying.

This could only be bad.

Thirty-seven

Roz sprinted toward her. Chaney couldn't seem to remember to watch for snakes and such.

Habbie, I wish you were here.

Chaney, with the water bucket empty and swinging, ran at top speed toward Roz. Finally she reached Roz.

"I saw them!" Chaney wheezed and sucked in more air. "Other side of the hill, men with guns."

Her eyes were large with fright and her hand on Roz's arm trembled. "Lots of men—guns!"

"Wait here." Roz ran to the top of the hill, crawled the last yard or so and looked on the other side of the hill. She counted thirty-two men.

She backed down the hill a bit, then stood, ran to Chaney and grabbed the younger girl's hand. "Leave the bucket; we have to warn the family."

Chaney dropped the bucket and together the two girls sprinted toward the distant field.

They reached the field, but saw no one. The adzes lay at the ends of rows.

"Where are they?" It took a few seconds for Roz to remember. "There's got to be a tree, a cave, a rocky overhang, something around here."

"Where…why?"

"It's a better, cooler, place to eat and rest than in the sun. That's where they are."

"What do we do?" Chaney asked.

Roz said, "You go up that hill; I'll run to that rise over there. See if you can see them from the top and meet me back here."

"Roz, I'm afraid."

"Just be careful. Phillip told me what's happened to some of his Christian neighbors—and watch for snakes."

"What if those men already found our husbands and Daniel 'n Habbie?"

"Don't make any noise, and for Jesus' sake, don't tune up and bawl. Oh, remember to watch for snakes."

Roz ran for her destination. When she reached the top of the rise, Roz saw them. Below her, this hill sloped into the next valley. All four: Daniel, Habbie, Phillip and Adam, sat under a rocky ledge that gave shade much as an awning would.

Relieved, she climbed down the beige shale near the family's picnic area. The rattling of stone announced her coming long before she made it all the way down. Phillip climbed up to meet her.

He asked, "What's going on?"

"Men with guns. Camped near the spring. Chaney went to look for you over that way. I'll go get her."

"Wait, I'll tell my folks and go with you," Phillip said."

"Hurry," Roz said. "She could step on a snake or something."

They had only just walked up the hill when they heard a scream.

"They've got her! I'd know her scream anywhere." Roz ran four steps before Phillip caught her.

"You can't get her back by yourself. Ought to have Adam help us. She'll be his wife."

Phillip made sense and she went with him to get Adam.

"We have a good hiding place. The folks will start walking there now. We'll get Chaney and all four of us will join them in a little while."

Phillip and Adam took canteen gourds and Habbie insisted that they take all the remaining food with them.

Adam said, "Come on; come on." Then he ran.

Phillip ran fast to catch up with his brother, but Roz stayed at his side. Back home, she'd been on a first-class track team.

"I've learned some things. You might need me," Roz said.

Without another word, the three ran in the direction of Chaney's scream.

The next hill matched the one that had been the picnic place...all beige sandstone and easily dislodged rocks. Adam started to charge right up the slope, but Roz caught his arm.

Disgust colored Adam's face and he whipped his arm away from her.

At a time like this, she didn't bother getting upset, just whispered, "If we try to go up that heap of stone, we're sure to start a noisy rock slide."

"She's right," Phillip said. "If they're on the other side, we might get Chaney killed and ourselves as well."

"What should we do?" Adam asked Phillip.

"Look, over there." Roz pointed to a break in the rolling landscape.

Phillip nodded. "It's kinda like a pass. We can go through there; we won't have to climb the hill."

Roz ran in that direction without waiting to see if Phillip or Adam would follow.

Phillip caught her, motioned to her to hang back and then he and Adam ran ahead.

With Adam in the lead, they were almost through the chasm between the two little mountains. Suddenly Adam dropped to all fours and motioned to Phillip and Roz to stop.

When Adam motioned for them to come, both of them crawled until they reached his position. Then she saw what he'd seen: Chaney surrounded by guards. She sat on the dirt, her hands and feet bound with rope thick enough to hold an elephant.

As if waiting for them to see her, Chaney screamed. The nearest guard slapped her so hard she fell over. Then he held his hand as if he'd injured himself.

Roz wanted to run to her, hit the man who'd hurt her. But with her first move, Phillip grabbed her.

"I can't just leave her there," she whispered. "We've got to do something."

"One thing we don't do is bust in without a plan," Phillip whispered.

Chaney didn't scream, but she still whimpered.

Adam looked over the area, and then he said, "I'm going to climb to the top of the hill. Maybe we can see where they're headed and rig an ambush."

Phillip objected. "But it's shale."

"If a rock falls—" Roz added.

"They make a lot of noise," Adam said.

"I'll go with you," Phillip said. "Catch rocks if they start falling. Roz, you stay here."

Roz started to argue, but decided against it.

"Okay, I can do that. Be careful." She squeezed Phillip's hand and looked for a hiding place in the weeds.

About twenty feet away, a clump of brush and two boulders looked like an ideal hiding place.

"I still think you shouldn't climb that hill, but I'll wait over there," she whispered. "If you're not here in an hour or so, I'm going to assume you've been captured." She patted his hand. "Then I'll have to rescue all three of you."

The men ran and she trotted to her chosen spot and crawled in.

I should have pitched a fit. How long before those thugs catch Phillip and Adam? What about Daniel and Habbie?

What would she do if this family and Chaney were all captured?

At that thought, she felt dizzy, lightheaded and her stomach seized. For some seconds she couldn't even breathe. After that, she waited and worried.

Finally Roz heard more noise coming from the enemy's campsite and crawled out of her weed patch. On seeing nothing threatening, she ran in the bent over posture she'd seen on TV when the soldiers, or the cops wanted to avoid alerting the bad guys. Soon she slipped into a weedy patch closer to the enemy camp.

She thought they had to be breaking camp. A group gathered around one man and he shouted something she didn't understand, and that group followed him. Their idea of a military march appeared to be a loose cluster of men all headed in the same direction.

The same thing happened not long afterwards. This second group tramped within thirty feet of her.

She lay very still and only breathed when they'd hiked about fifty feet further away.

I hope Phillip and Adam hid themselves well. They should be back soon—I hope.

An hour, maybe two hours later, Phillip and Adam should have returned.

"Dear Lord Jesus, please don't desert us. We need your strength and wisdom…I guess all I'm saying is: help!

"And I don't know how to say it any better."

Thirty-eight

Roz waited.

No noise came from the marauders' campsite.

She stayed nearby, just as she'd said she would, until the shadows grew longer. The men weren't coming; they must have been captured.

She'd prayed the best prayer she knew how. Now, she had to do her part, just as her dad always said. "Pray as if everything depended on God, then work as if everything depended on you."

Roz left the brush where she'd been hiding and prowled the area near the campsite. As she'd thought, none of those evil men remained.

She gave herself an order: "Find Phillip."

Even though they were first class survivalists, neither her mom nor her dad had been big on tracking. Her dad knew a little and taught it to her. She knew to go slow, look for footprints, pebbles that had been turned over and broken or stepped-on plants. She knew nothing else about tracking.

"Find Phillip," she repeated. She went through a chasm-like pass that must have been three blocks long and saw no one. Footprints, lots of footprints, but no people.

In case Phillip should be looking for her, she decided to leave V-shaped markers of pebbles or sticks along the way, just as her dad taught her.

She hadn't eaten since early that morning and hunger hurt. The mid-afternoon sun burned and she could do nothing about her hunger, or the heat. She kept walking.

When she saw a group of bushes about twice her height, Roz decided she'd walk through them and cool off a little.

She'd only walked a few feet into those bushes when a spider the color of her skin and the size of her hand barred her way. A scream tried to work its way out of her throat. Then she looked around. Other spiders, the kin of this one, waited.

These had to be the flesh-eating camel spiders she'd read about last year, the ones that can eat an inch and a half hole out of a soldier while he sleeps.

The hair on her arms stood straight up and with great care, she backed up and then detoured around the spider colony and continued on her too-sunny trek.

By then Roz could have drained a whole canteen and begged for more.

"Find Phillip."

The shadows grew longer and her thirst nagged her. She tried to swallow; it hurt… she ignored her thirst and followed the trail of broken twigs, turned over pebbles and footprints. Things would not get better until she found Phillip. And she wanted water so bad.

In the middle of the afternoon, she sat on a patch of softer grass and rested. The green grass looked appetizing enough to eat and she chewed a few succulent stems. At least it had a little moisture and a sweetly pleasant taste.

After resting and getting her breath, she'd only run a few paces when something hit her on her back. Startled and not knowing what it could be, she threw herself flat in the dry grass.

Over the tops of the grasses, about a block away, Phillip stood bent over as if winded. He'd been following her! She stood and held her arms open wide to greet her wonderful, very male, hunk of soon-to-be-husband.

But then she remembered he'd left her. Left her alone, defenseless, and worried. Anger rose.

She put her arms at her side and waited.

After he got his breath, he jogged to her and said, "There are gazelles that don't run like you."

"I was afraid you'd been captured. Why did you leave me?"

"Why did you run off? I've been afraid I'd never find you, or…"

Roz intended to tell him off for the worry, for the hunger and for the thirst.

But he stopped her. "I think you want to shout at me as much as I want to yell at you."

"You got that right."

He put his arm around her waist. "Can we call a truce?"

Roz leaned her head on his muscular shoulder. "Let's." She didn't want to argue. "I would like some water, kind sir."

Philip gave her the gourd canteen and said, "The marauders aren't very far ahead."

Roz gulped the wonderful-tasting water, replaced the wooden stopper and handed the gourd back to Philip. Then they started running.

"Have you got a plan?" Roz asked.

"We can't hope to attack them and win. We thought we'd wait until dark and see if one of us could sneak into their camp. We'll untie Chaney and then run for our lives," he said.

"Okay, that sounds as close to a plan as we're going to get. Who's going to be the one who goes in? Roz asked.

Phillip shrugged and never stopped running.

"I've already escaped from a camp once."

"You have? When?"

"My first owner, Sheik Kelmet. And he had guards around the tent Chaney and I lived in."

"But you escaped?"

"All the guards went to sleep—made it easy. Not wake them, all we had to do."

Phillip looked at her as if she'd grown an extra head.

"Maybe I know how to do this thing called escaping," she said. "I'll volunteer, unless you or Adam has your heart set on it."

"You aren't like any woman I've ever heard of."

"I'm no hero, but a little experience is better than none. My dad taught me lots of things that weren't in my schoolbooks. He really is a hero; has the medals to prove it. "

"He taught you well."

"So where's Adam?" Roz reached for Phillip's hand and they kept running.

"Adam's still following them," Phillip said. "That's his trail markers we're following."

"I hope he doesn't get too close."

"Me too. He's about as angry as I've ever seen him. I'd like to get back to him as quickly as we can. I mean, he's as adult as a kid of almost fifteen can be. Still—"

Roz picked up her running pace. "I get your point."

The trail Adam left went through an area with almost no grass, just a covering of fist-sized rocks.

"Careful," Phillip said. "Don't make a bad step and break a leg."

She squeezed his hand, but said nothing.

The terrain changed a little as she and Phillip ran. The rocks grew larger so that more and more of them could be called boulders.

At dusk Adam loped toward them. When he reached them, after he caught his breath, he said, "They've stopped for the night." He turned and started back the way he'd come.

But Phillip grabbed his shoulder. "Let's settle right here and rest while you tell us how many of them there are." Adam shrugged his brother's hand away and ran. Phillip followed and ran by his side.

Roz sank to the ground, knowing that her husband-to-be would bring his angry young brother back. All she could do at the moment was rest—and she needed rest. She looked up. The stars already twinkled as if God were sending her strength and encouragement.

"Thank you, Lord Jesus.

Thirty-nine

Carl took care not to run Harley much, just a gentle trot. Even with the extra rests he gave the elderly animal, the trip would only take a little over three days. Not too bad about the time and as a bonus, Ol' Harley had a smooth gait, almost that 'rocking chair' motion they prized in some horse breeds.

He'd learned about such things from Felix Carson, the owner of a major U.S. racing stable. Carson had hired Carl as a jockey after seeing his work in Egypt.

Carl liked being a jockey, but his jockey career in the U.S. didn't last long. He had a growth spurt early in his seventeenth year. The next two years Carl found work as a stable hand on Carson's farm.

Carson convinced him that a person could change his life by learning. Without education, Carl faced a life of shoveling horse dung. He wanted to be educated bad and crammed himself as full of it as a man could in two years. Then he met Gregorio Carnelli. That was a mistake.

Now twenty-seven, Carl still wanted a better life and this time he thought he might be able to get it. He'd be at Mufa's village this evening, or before the sun got hot in the morning. Then he'd take the next step in becoming the gun king of Africa.

Carl yawned and stretched often. Harley needed very little handling and in the bush Carl never got enough sleep. He yawned again.

A fly settled on his forehead and he waved it away.

While riding, he'd spent most of those last three days mapping out and revising the plan for the Okie's torture. He got a lot of pleasure out of the planning. The deed itself would be glorious.

He couldn't think of another way to give her pain that wouldn't kill her quick. So he'd done that part of his plan. A wave of tranquility came over him. He could feel his blood pressure dropping. His head drooped and his shoulders relaxed.

That insistent fly darted around his head and he batted it away several times.

If it hadn't been for the loud buzzing of those flies, he could have dozed even deeper.

Fly buzz or not, he daydreamed in full living color about how she'd look when he got through with her. His eyes wouldn't stay open, but he didn't worry. Harley had a real good trail sense. Carl yawned and stayed just conscious enough to avoid falling out of the saddle.

But those flies were really bad. Even though he didn't smell it, he decided there must be something dead around there. He kicked Harley to speed him up and get them away from it faster.

Carl realized his mistake only after the first sting.

He took more than a dozen stings before he could kick Harley into high gear. Harley actually ran for at least thirty seconds, and Carl thought they would completely outrun the little monsters. But the bees must have stung Harley in a sensitive place. For an old beast, his horse did a beautiful jump and buck.

Carl had never had such a long encounter with thin air.

He landed on the sand-like ground and slid at an incredible rate, feet-first. His foot hit that boulder and he felt the snap in his thigh at the same moment he cart-wheeled through the air.

He came to a stop ten feet farther down the trail. The first flares of a pain that would be with him for a long time came then.

"Gal, I'll end you if it takes the rest of my life," Carl muttered.

Then he put his entire attention into crawling farther from the few remaining bees. Using his two good arms and one good leg, he crawled another hundred feet before he took his last sting.

That Okie blonde, she did this to him—it was her fault. He wouldn't have dozed except for her.

"I'm gonna make you pay," he groaned and took stock of his situation.

At least he hadn't landed on his satellite phone. He took it from his belt and called Mufa.

Mufa would cost a lot. And he'd have to pay. Can't walk on a leg that feels like dice where the bone is supposed to be.

He expected to hear a laugh, and he did. A chorus of hyenas took that moment to tune up for their evening performance. He shook his fist at the sky. "You're not gettin' me." The next breeze felt cold, freezer cold and his stomach quivered. "There ain't no God!"

~ * ~

Mufa did cost a lot. The so-called doctor cost more. The requirement that he stay put cost the most. But he didn't have a choice. The cast weighed so much he could barely drag his useless leg out to use the so-called facilities, such as they were.

He couldn't get over this monstrous evil that had been done to him. Meribet—his sweet innocent Meribet—he couldn't rescue his love and Azibik would lose faith in his ability as a gun-runner.

No choice, none. And that blasted Okie gal did this to him. He'd give her back what she'd given and pay her interest as well.

Forty

About fifteen minutes after Phillip left Roz, he came back with Adam.

At first Adam wouldn't talk. They sat without saying anything for many minutes.

Finally Phillip told Roz, "There's only a dozen left. There were many more, but most of them have already gone back the way they came."

"Think they went back to their village? They're not going toward your folks' hiding place, are they?" Roz asked.

Adam ignored her. "See those trees?" He pointed toward the west where a clump of bushes and trees made silhouettes against the darkening sky. "That's where they are."

"They looked like they had settled for the night," Phillip told Roz.

"They took down a tree and they're making more fire than a hundred people would need. Tree's green, so there's lots of smoke. You can see it now."

Adam pointed out the plume of smoke rising above the black tree silhouettes. "They didn't put up a brush fortress like Dad always makes us use."

In the near dark, Roz saw the fire's smudge. She smiled and said, "They don't know much camp-craft."

"We'll get Chaney back," Adam said.

Roz nodded. Of course they would.

"I'm volunteering to rescue Chaney," Roz said.

"Now, hold it, woman. She's going to be my wife. I should bring her home."

"I can understand your feelings."

"Good. I'll go in a little bit." Adam crossed his arms and looked at the marauders' camp. The muscles in his jaws twisted, bulged and twisted again.

"However, I have experience at escaping and you don't."

Adam frowned. "What do you mean, experience?"

"When Chaney and I belonged to Sheik Kelmet, we escaped, even though the sheik had all sorts of people around to guard us."

"I think she should go," Phillip said. "We already know she's not like most women."

"My father taught me to stay in control of myself and to handle life even when things get bad."

"Why'd he do that?" Adam asked.

"For one thing, I asked. For another, he looked at it as my right as his oldest child."

Adam snorted. "But you're female. Your dad some kind of fat old man who never does anything?"

Roz had seldom wanted to hit anyone that bad, but she kept her cool.

"My father was a career army man who was escorting fifty-five people when they were captured by F.A.R.C. rebels in a country called Columbia. They beat his left leg to a pulp and broke all the bones, then they put him in a makeshift cell to die. With a severely broken leg, he escaped, put together a splint so he could move, found the rebel's explosives and rescued fifty-two people. The rebels had already killed the other three. He had to have his leg amputated above the knee. The U.S.A. gave him the Medal of Honor. That's the ultimate medal for bravery. You wouldn't know, but about nine of ten people who receive that medal die in the exploit that results in the medal. Not only that, today he holds down a job that would be a challenge for someone without a handicap." She paused.

"And if you ever say another word about my dad that isn't flattering…well, you won't like it."

The men decided to let Roz be the one to go into the camp. Even Adam agreed that she differed from most women.

The three walked most of the distance to the enemy camp. A thin new moon rose and the hyena troupe chuckled through the first act of their current opera.

All the men in the marauder camp were lying down for the night.

"If we have a knife…" Roz whispered.

Phillip gave her his treasured pocketknife.

"Keep my sandals."

Roz crept among the boulders. When she reached the edge of the marauder camp, she waited and watched the two guards.

As it had happened when she escaped so long ago, the guards sat on conveniently placed boulders on opposite sides of the camp.

One guard sat at attention with his rifle militarily vertical. After a long time, his head bobbed, but then he yawned and stretched. He repeated the bobbing and yawning twice more. She knew he'd sleep soon.

When the second guard put his rifle crossways on his lap, Roz's heart thumped hard. That man would also be asleep soon.

Then the first guard's head nodded forward and stayed that way. His rifle dipped low and finally his fingers released it gently to the dirt.

Roz's breathing quickened. In less than an hour, she'd know if she were just a braggart—or if she really did have a knack for sneaking into and out of an enemy's camp.

Near the second guard, Chaney, tied hand and foot, slept on her side with her hands for a pillow.

Poor kid. Must be exhausted. Roz shook her head and smiled a tight-lipped grin. *Chaney, you're going to be a lot more tired before this is over.*

Before long, the second guard's head nodded forward and his shoulders rounded in relaxation. He didn't move again and a tenor snore joined the other night noises.

Roz stayed in the shadows as much as possible and edged forward. The ridiculously large fire snapped and crackled.

After she'd found that newspaper article about her dad's Medal of Honor, she'd questioned him. Actually, she'd badgered him. She did her best to make him talk about his capture, his months of torture as an F.A.R.C. prisoner in Columbia, his escape and how he engineered the escape of fifty-two people.

He never did tell her much more than, "Don't let the enemy control what you think." He'd also said, "Fright makes your mouth dry."

She'd finally given up, but she knew that fright and a dry mouth hadn't stopped him and it wouldn't stop her. She was her father's daughter.

When she reached Chaney's side, she put her hand over the girl's mouth.

Chaney opened her eyes and nodded. Roz opened the pocketknife and sliced the ropes that bound Chaney.

Then she untied the girl's sandals and made her carry them. She pointed toward the nearest boulder. They crept about twenty feet beyond that boulder.

"Use your bare feet to make sure you're not standing on a rock that will move and make noise," Roz whispered.

"How am I gonna do that?"

"Stay on the bedrock." Then they rushed into the darkness.

After circling the camp, they came to the place where their future husbands waited.

Phillip handed Roz her sandals and put his knife back in his pocket. The men waited while the two girls put their feet back into their shoes.

"Let's go," Phillip whispered and put his arm around Roz's waist. Adam took Chaney's hand and pulled her up. Both couples ran—ran much too fast in the darkness.

Hope it's close to dawn. Hope all the hyenas ate well tonight. Hope we don't break a bone on these rocks.

Through the night, the two couples kept running. The men had their pocketknives open and ready if any hyenas or other predators wanted to make trouble. The girls picked up handfuls of rocks and threw them often enough to make the critters uneasy. Usually Adam and Chaney ran ahead, because it seemed to make Adam less surly. Not being in front didn't bother

Phillip and Roz. They usually ran with an arm around each other's waist. Roz knew that Habbie would have a fit if she saw, but it made sense. Each could hold the other up if that one started to fall. Besides, they were both good Christians and committed to waiting for their marriage. Still it definitely was not unpleasant.

At sunrise, Chaney stopped, bent over with her hands on her knees.

"Can't go any farther," Adam said.

Phillip panted, "We better not rest long."

They all agreed and sat among the dry grass and rocks for a very few minutes.

After a sip of water for all of them, Phillip said, "We'd best go." He took Roz's hand and they ran. Adam and Chaney ran at their heels.

All day they alternated running and walking. They rested little.

Close to sundown, they reached the hills where Chaney had been kidnapped. Phillip volunteered to go to their family's spring and fill the canteens while the rest of them gathered brush, made another stockade and lit a tiny fire. None of the wildlife paid them any serious attention.

At daybreak, again they alternated running and walking. By their first rest, the sun's heat claws raked them.

With Adam in the lead, they came to a hill with a deep cleft. The cleft turned out to be a hidden ravine and a secret entrance.

Boulders and shale had fallen in a long ago landslide. It looked solid, but left a large hollow in the middle. Inside, in the hollow, it even contained a rock overhang. Daniel had dug at the back of the overhang and added a rock wall that reached within six inches of the overhang, making it a manmade cave. Nearby, the greener area announced one of the rare springs.

The sound of Habbie's happiness at the return of both sons threatened to bring down the fragile cliffs and bury the whole family.

Forty-one

Earlier, at the marauders' camp, Mamed felt satisfied that he'd done everything well. He had captured one of the blondes. He didn't like her shrill screams, but it seemed that even stupid white blondes can be taught not to scream. A few slaps brought her to an acceptable silence.

He'd send his best men out to search for the other one at first dawn.

He went to Jeydil, his best tracker. "I want you looking for the other blonde at first light."

Jeydil never talked much. He merely nodded his head and went back to unrolling his pack.

"Take three men with you, spread your net wide enough to catch her," Mamed said.

After the evening meal, the camp busied itself with the serious business of getting ready for sleep.

Mamed appointed Ismail and Faheed, two of his best men, to guard the camp, and particularly, their prisoner. It had been a long day and he, as second in command, had tested his alertness and his wisdom many times. If he wanted to be their village's next headman, and he did, he must not fail. With the camp guarded by not one, but two of the best warriors in their village, he could rest. Azibik would be pleased with him. He would be pleased with himself—probably even Allah couldn't find any fault with his marshalling of his village's forces.

It shouldn't be that hard to find a stupid white female blonde in a place where stupid white female blondes don't belong. He heard that red-bearded half-infidel say that this one had excessive cleverness, but he dismissed the thought of a clever female and slept well...

...Until his ears filled with two male screams. Until that moment, things had gone well for him. Later Mamed wondered exactly where or when things began to unravel.

"She's gone! Gone!" Ismail yelled.

"Disappeared!" Faheed groaned.

Ismail knelt on the sand and chanted prayers. Ismail, the jokester, chanted prayers in the nighttime.

Faheed dropped to his knees and bawled. Two meter tall Faheed sobbed loudly. Faheed didn't cry, not even at his son's funeral last year.

By then, the entire camp had awakened.

Mamed wouldn't interrupt a man's prayers, so he didn't bother Ismail. He shook Faheed, tried to make him stop blubbering. "What happened?"

"Ohhh! Soooo beautiful. Sooo many beauties. Houris come to earth. Soooo beautiful! ...Houris." He said nothing for a moment and his face wore a puzzled frown. "We captured a houri?" His voice carried amazement and then he howled as if in pain.

Mamed couldn't get anything else out of the man except, "Soooo beautiful."

Azibik would be angry.

Would Azibik still let him be second leader?

~ * ~

Sighet al Azibik returned to his village with the uproarious warriors who had followed him. He had divided his meager forces so he could attack both remaining nests of Christians, but Mamed ben Aked, his most trusted lieutenant, had not arrived.

Mamed would do even better. Azibik had assigned his chief lieutenant the smaller of the two "nests," even though it contained the blondes. When Mamed brought the white females, he would be bringing, in effect, more rifles. When this Carl person returned, each of his men would have his own rifle. He'd even be able to re-assign two of the oldest rifles to his female guards. Make his village even safer. Truly Allah is good!

He walked into his hall, the largest room in the entire village. This was good. The rugs for the meal had been spread and the four ounce tea glasses and the pitchers had been set out.

This is good! He told himself.

Hamras al Khaibb, *the* grandfather, his mother's father's father, hobbled into the room.

"Did you succeed, my son?" he asked in his thin reed of a voice.

"Of course, my father," Azibik said. This ancient man had been a great warrior in his time and Azibik revered him. "You taught me well. The Christians didn't fight very much. We only rode our horses around the infidels' house and screamed war chants. We left a small break in our lines so they could escape."

"I taught your father that trick. Allah be praised."

"The Christian cowards did as Christians always do: they ran into the night."

"It is good."

"I let my men chase the cowards only far enough to drive the terror of Allah deeper into their black infidel hearts."

The elder man smiled and nodded.

"Then came the best part. We took their goods."

"Now you will leave them alone until they replace the goods? Then you will go back and take their goods again as I taught your father and his father before him."

"All my men have been so instructed."

"You did well, my son."

"We spent several days camping around the infidel house."

"But you followed my ways…you did not destroy the house?"

"We only scratched sayings from the Quran on the walls. Of course we marked the house walls as animals do."

"They will not forget you soon."

"They know that Allah watches. We left them a smell that will keep us on their minds for a long time."

"This is good. They will lose heart. Your next raid will find them weaker." The elder man looked around. "Why are we waiting? Where is the food?"

"We wait for the rest of our men. They will be here soon. The meal will be all the heartier for the capture of the two infidel blondes," Azibik said.

"We will have fresh female beauty to gaze at." Grandfather laughed until it became a cough.

"I've toyed with buying them from this half-infidel who will sell us guns."

Grandfather frowned. "Or, you could give the infidel his life as exchange for these females."

"His life depends on the quality of his guns."

Azibik's tea glass had just been filled for the third time when Mamed came. But the man's shoulders were as down as his face. Azibik knew before a word passed between them that the incident had not gone well.

He wondered how extreme should be his expression of disapproval. Since Mamed had done well by him in the past, he decided his displeasure should be measured and reasonably slight.

"At last, you are here," Azibik said.

"Yes."

"Your mission did not end well. Tell me."

"We captured one. And she displayed more beauty than we had been told. Truly like one of Allah's favored ones. We looked for the other fair one. But we did not find her."

The grandfather leaned forward and frowned.

But Azibik stayed calm. "Capturing one is good, but we had an order for two."

"Yes, my father, it is as you say."

"Well," Azibik frowned and sipped at his tea.

"We set up camp for the first night and put the fair one at the center of the camp. Then I assigned two to guard her, not one as we usually do. The guards assure me no sleep overcame them. She lay at their feet, well secured with heavy ropes, and then strange things happened and before the eyes of her guards, she vanished!"

Azibik had difficulty not spraying the entire company with tea. "She—what!"

"August one, I am not skilled with the Sacred Writings as you are. But I think we ought not repeat the attempt to capture these fair ones. I think these are houris come to earth."

Though shaken by this thought, Azibik knew he had to stop any such story. He had to do it immediately! He put his glass of tea down and stood, slowly, deliberately. "Come with me."

Mamed followed him into the courtyard that provided welcome privacy.

"The ever-virgin-pleasurers-of-the-blessed do not come to earth," Azibik said. "You will never say such things again."

"But sir, we were there. I, myself, felt the chilling power of the blonde one. Her cries froze my skin and her screams twisted my bones. Her shrieks must have been calls to her friends among the houri."

"I repeat, do not ever talk about a houri walking this earth. Never, do you understand me?"

"But—"

"This tale could cause more damage than you imagine. What about the ones who believe the tales of their mothers?"

"I saw—"

"If you wish to live in this village, you will not speak of this again. To correct your mistake, you will talk with the men you assigned as guards and, under your guidance, they will admit they slept or they walked away to relieve themselves, or other such actions.

"Sometimes men don't remember correctly and a little force, a slap or two, is necessary to help their minds along the most righteous path. Just remember, houris do not walk the earth. Do I make myself completely clear?"

"Y-yes sir."

"We'll rest a few days, then we hunt down those fake "houris." And you personally will capture them."

"Y-yes s-sir."

"Now come, have a pleasant meal. Rest yourself." Azibik patted the man's shoulder in the friendliest way he knew how. He must get the man on his side; make it easy for him to change his story.

Forty-two

The hill with the ravine and the long ago landslide sheltered Daniel and his family. It was far enough from their mud brick house to be overlooked in case someone should hunt for them. They had eaten well. And now the family sat inside the rock walls of their shelter. They'd made a fire at the entrance.

Roz sat at Phillip's side.

When everyone grew quiet, Daniel said, "We've been away for several days. Surely our enemies are gone now."

Phillip added, "We really need to get back and put the crop in. If we wait much longer, the land will be too dry. We'll waste any seed we sow."

Adam said, "If our wives help us with the field work, it won't take so long. Perhaps another three days here might be good. Just in case."

Daniel settled on staying two more days and both his sons agreed.

Forty-three

On the surface, the village that Sighit al Azibik directed and managed seemed quiet. Azibik knew better. Ever since the day they returned from the raid, he noticed that his men whispered to each other. Secrecy could not be a good sign. He decided he'd best have another talk with Mamed.

"Did you discuss our concerns with your guards?"

"My father, I talked to them most severely. And they keep saying they *saw* her disappear. As you instructed, I slapped them hard for that lie and they still refuse to say otherwise."

"Bring them to me."

"I will bring Ismail, but I'm afraid my eagerness to make Faheed change his mind did not go well. He is still unconscious."

"I didn't tell you to maim your men. What did you do?"

"I slapped him as you instructed; he fell against the wall and has not opened his eyes or spoken since." Mamed shrugged. "An unfortunate accident."

"Bring Ismail to me." Azibik turned away to avoid an incident he might regret. Mamed always did better than this.

Mamed and Ismail came. Mamed left the man with their leader. Azibik knew that if he didn't do something, the right something, this houri business would be a true disaster. It could even call his leadership into question.

"Tell me what you saw." Azibik frowned and put his nose within inches of Ismail's face. "I want the truth and I will have the truth."

The hairs of Ismail's beard trembled.

"The truth, man. I'm not an infidel. You must not lie to me as you would to one of those faithless reprobates. We faithful do not lie to one another. Allah watches us most closely," Azibik warned.

More trembling from Ismail, then, "I saw them. First I saw only the one we captured. Then another and then many. So beautiful," Ismail said. "Th-they surrounded her; touched the knots I—we, had so carefully tied and the ropes came apart as if their fingers were knives, very sh-sharp knives."

Azibik growled and turned away.

"Then a brilliant light, and they were gone. She also disappeared. They were so beautiful. Too beautiful to be of the earth."

Azibik ran at the man, grabbed his shoulders and shook him. "There are no houri on earth and there never have been."

"Do we need a martyr? I'll gladly give my wife and two sons to my brother, Gafaar. You know, the one who has only the one daughter. Won't take more than an hour. And then I'll be free to get myself killed and be with my houri forever."

"Houri don't come to earth," Azibik growled. "You're deluded."

"Just think, I'll be a martyr and Allah will give me at least one houri like the one we captured—maybe three, no four houri. Soooo beautiful!" He lifted his hands in rapturous worship. (Allah be praised!) Then without even spreading a prayer rug, and at the wrong time, he knelt on the floor, facing Mecca, and chanted his prayers.

Azibik had all he could take. He left the room.

Mamed waited just outside the door.

"Get your men together," Azibik growled. "We're going to fix this now…today."

When all the men assembled, Azibik made sure Ismail was among them. He had to teach that crazy wretch in the most apt terms that there are no houri on the earth.

"We have been getting bad information," Azibik shouted. "It is necessary to prove to all of you that there are no houri on this earth. This is for your good as Muslims.

"The woman who is the fake houri is one of those who live in the Christian house that Mamed raided. We will have no more harvests of goods from the Christians who live there. I wish it were otherwise, but it is necessary.

"If I let this continue, Allah would accuse us of defaming his Paradise and the beauteous houris who live in it."

He looked each of his men in the eye for a small part of a second." We will ride to that house; prepare your mounts."

Thirty minutes later, Azibik's men, Ismail among them, stood before his door. Each man had his horse's reins in hand.

"Mount up!" he shouted.

He led his army out of the village. Wordlessly, Azibik guided them toward that small house that had been occupied by Daniel's family. Perhaps Allah set this as the time to make them go. (Allah be praised!)

As usual, ten minutes of hard riding brought them to the last hill before they reached the infidels' house. "Leave your horses. We will attack on foot," Azibik said.

They crept up the hill and then as one man, they flowed over the crest. They shot their guns and screamed "Allah Akbar!" No one in that house would survive this attack. Azibik would make a point of not letting any blondes survive.

They surrounded the house. Azibik took his precious Kalashnikov inside and wasted a whole clip. He sprayed everything.

"When he knew for certain no humans were there, he said, "Tear it down. All of it. You, Ismail, start here and make the corner of the house disappear—to the ground—understand? Abdul, Sadiq—you start on this side. Tahir, you help Ismail.

"Amir, you and Hassan break those cooking pots.

"Omar, tear up that garden.

"The rest of you join in, break something. I want all of it torn apart and in pieces before we leave." He faked a laugh, "Tell me when you see a houri."

Everyone did as they'd been told.

Hassan and Amir tried to break the iron pots by jumping on them, by throwing rocks at them and by slamming them on the rocks around the fire pit.

Finally, Hassan said, "The only way we're going to break these heavy iron pots is by gun fire."

"Are you sure?" Amir asked.

"Why do you think I and my family spent four years saving, saving. Like a miser I saved."

"I thought you had gone completely, uh…"

"Nuts, you might as well say it; I know what they thought of me."

"That isn't your reputation today. You are a wise man and we all know it."

Hassan, with the grace of a wise man, smiled and nodded his head.

"Now we are all saving more so that we can also buy such magnificent weapons. Only you and Azibik have assault rifles. You are wise, and I am happy to call you my friend."

"Well, friend, here we go, fulfilling our appointed end."

Hassan, the wise man, put the rifle's barrel within an inch of the larger pot and pulled the trigger.

At the corner of the house, Ismail used a piece of firewood as a crowbar. In less than a hundredth of a second, the ricochet from the assault rifle's first bullet took Ismail out.

Mamed's young son, on his first raid, caught the ninth bullet with his right bicep.

The eleventh bullet's ricochet blew out Sadiq's chest.

The reloaded Kalashnikov hit Hassan with five shots as Hassan fired his fifteenth round. Amir, standing close by, also went down before Azibik could pull his finger off the trigger.

In the distance, a single hyena laughed.

Forty-four

Daniel's family expected to come back to a disaster at the little mud-brick house. And they did.

When they went inside the house, they could see the sky.

"The south wall needs rebuilding," Daniel said.

"The roof needs to be torn off and replaced with new," Phillip said.

Habbie came in and reported. "They pulled up the okra and part of the beans. But the peanuts haven't been touched and there's still enough time for a bean crop. If we have seed, we can try okra as well."

"Did they get your peppers?" Daniel asked.

"No." Habbie went back outside. And soon she laughed.

Habbie came back inside and brought her large cooking pot with her. "Look, they expected to wreck our pots using a rifle."

"Girls, this lets you know just how badly our enemies need a new way of thinking." She brought the pot closer to Roz.

"I don't see a thing," Roz said.

"Look right there…that shiny spot is where the bullet dug into the iron. It's a wonder someone didn't die here because the bullet wouldn't have been spent."

"Looks like cast iron doesn't wreck that easily," Roz said.

"The mark won't interfere with cooking," Habbie said.

But Chaney knelt in the dirt at the east corner of the house and wailed. Near the east corner, a large brown stain started about chest high and smeared its way to the ground. The dirt became darker than it should have been. There were more flies than normal there on the dirt and on the wall.

"It did—It did hit someone. They'll blame us for that too," Chaney wailed. "Just like they blamed my dad, my real dad. They beat him and beat him and he didn't do nothin'." Adam ran to her side and knelt with a perplexed look as if he wanted to hold her, comfort her, but couldn't.

Roz came and pulled the grief-stricken child to her. "It's all right, hon. We'll be okay. God will see that we are." She patted Chaney's shoulder, held her close and rocked back and forth with the child in her arms.

"Foolishness," Daniel said. "Who would be that stupid?"

He went through the empty doorway. "We have to rebuild the damage before the rains come. If they come."

"Adam and I will start making the mud bricks," Phillip said. "Shouldn't take more than about two, maybe three weeks to make them."

Habbie's chin quivered. "But you can't now; you have to finish planting the crops. We'll have to wait."

"We can live in a brush shelter for a while," Phillip said. "There are worse things."

Daniel pushed the debris away from a four foot-by-four foot area near where the west wall of the house had been. Then he used a piece of firewood as a scraper. Soon a plank door showed itself. When the plank had been cleared of the dirt, he pulled on the rusty iron ring.

"A place for saving," he told the two blondes, then he addressed his sons. "When you have your own farms, you must have such a place. There is safety in saving."

Then he took out two large burlap sacks and a smaller one.

"We have enough grain for the rest of the crop here." He patted the bags. "And enough to eat for a while if we aren't gluttons."

With tears in her eyes, Habbie laughed. "We? We have never been gluttons."

Daniel continued, "The grain and beans at the storehouse will last until we harvest the new crop and a year beyond, if we ration ourselves."

Daniel put his arm around Habbie. "At least we put the storehouse so far away they won't find it."

Habbie looked up at Daniel with tears still trickling down her cheeks.

"Praise the Lord God. Praise the Son," Daniel said and Habbie echoed his words.

"Praise the Holy Spirit," Phillip and Adam said.

"Amen," Roz said, and Chaney nodded.

Forty-five

In Azibik's village, the funerals for Ismail, Sadiq, Hassan and Amir went well. Their widows and children wept most piteously. Azibik used his reputation as a lay scholar of the Quran, almost that of a cleric, to state again that houri do not come to earth. He also wished the deaths had not been necessary to stop this rumor, but what Allah decrees is what Allah decrees.

Faheed breathed his last at sunset of the next day after the funerals. They immediately started the funeral process again.

At Faheed's funeral, Azibik repeated, "The Christians are to blame for all these deaths." Azibik said, "The Christians are the reason. Allah has done this to warn us against the Christian God."

He told them more directly this time that it was not his fault, nor Mamed's, nor anyone in the village. Azibik knew it for a lie, but a lie about Christians made it all right with Allah.

For a week after the burials, Azibik's village remained quiet. His men had anger, he could tell. He spoke at the evening meals; he blamed the Christians for the deaths. He knew he'd have to make both nests of Christians disappear. He hated that his village would have no more harvests of the Christians' goods. But what Allah wills…

Forty-six

At Daniel's house, the week went by without incident. The crops needed to be in the ground fast. The girls worked the fields every morning. Adam and Phillip kept working in the field until sundown. But the girls and Daniel spent their afternoons making mud bricks and doing the work of a mason by adding bricks to the structure. Occasionally for an hour or two, the girls helped Habbie and thereby learned housekeeping, Sudanese-style.

The tenth evening after the attack, Roz and Phillip walked away from the family, still in plain view as required by Habbie and Daniel, but private enough.

They sat on the flat-topped boulders Habbie had wanted for sitting while stirring the cooking pots.

Phillip added a single small log to the fire and the glowing embers soon became a bright blaze. It warmed the air just enough to let them stay outside comfortably.

"I like your dad very much," Roz said.

"He's the smartest man I know," said Phillip.

"Your dad is a lot like my dad." Roz said. "He's sweet and gentle, yet he knows how things ought to go and if he can, he makes sure they go his way most of the time."

She noticed Phillip frowning and added, "But you've got something on your mind, don't you?"

Phillip seemed to be having a private wrestling match with himself, but said nothing.

"We're almost married. If something is bothering you, my heart, tell me," Roz said. "I can at least sympathize."

Phillip looked into the fire and chewed his lower lip for many minutes. Then finally he said, "As soon as we're married, I want you to go back to your home and take me with you. I could do a lot for my people and I want to."

"I'd like that. You'll do well there. You've learned most of beginner's math and you're learning English."

"Could I do any less than learn your language? You've learned our language so well you sound like one of us. I'll be marrying the smartest woman ever to leave a footprint in this nation."

"Speaking of our marriage, our wedding is only a few days away."

Phillip nodded.

"I still don't know anything about the ceremony, or what's expected of me. There hasn't been time to talk about it," Roz said.

"You sound worried," Phillip said.

"I don't know the rules; I don't have any clothes except this black thing. I don't want to make a fool of myself or…of you and your family."

"You'll be told exactly what to—"

A bit of dirt spurted upward and an instant afterward, distant thunder rolled. Phillip knocked Roz off the rock, pushed her down and kept his arm across her shoulder.

"Stay down!" he ordered.

Another puff of dust spouted up about two feet in front of them.

"Those are bullets!" Roz whispered.

"Crawl into the house. Stay low," Phillip hissed and pushed her ahead.

While keeping her head down, imitating actions in movies about wars and army life, she crawled along the ground as fast as she could."

Another bullet whizzed over them and dirt thumped and sprayed upwards only a foot from the door. Just before they reached the still unfinished house, Phillip grabbed the water bucket outside the door. In a crouch, he ran for the fire and threw the water on it. Then he ran back to the house.

"The fire is out. We won't be so easy to see," Phillip said.

"We have to leave," Daniel said.

As if underscoring his words, another shot rang out.

Habbie cried, and gathered the things she wanted to take. She put all of them in the empty water bucket that Phillip had dropped by the door.

"I'm ready," Habbie said.

Daniel blew out the single oil lamp. "Let's go."

Another shot came from the hill overlooking their house. In the darkness, everyone crept outside and stayed next to the house. At the corner of the house, they ran away from the direction of the shots. But Roz couldn't find Phillip and another shot ripped the air. She caught up with Daniel.

"I don't see Phillip. We've lost him," Roz said.

Daniel merely patted her shoulder. "He'll come…you'll see."

She looked back. "What if he's hurt? Those shots didn't miss us by much."

"You'll see," Daniel repeated.

She walked on, hanging back just a little, but keeping the nearly invisible family in sight. Another volley of rifle shots rang out.

Chaney whimpered softly and Adam said comforting words. Roz knew she could depend on Chaney to keep whining. Soon Adam would get tired of soothing his bride, but she could hear that girl a block away, so she hung back a bit more to help Phillip if he needed it. She didn't understand why Daniel seemed so unconcerned.

Though she knew better, it seemed that at least an hour passed before she heard someone's footsteps behind her.

What if it's one of our attackers?

"Phillip?" she whispered.

"Shh."

She waited for him and when he reached her, she threw her arms around him. A metallic clunk followed. Then gently, as if she might break, he held her by the shoulders.

"I was so scared," she said.

"I didn't want to leave Mama's big pot like I did last time." He picked it up. "We'd better hurry. Dad's going to worry." Then he picked up the pot, took her hand and they ran.

He thinks that what he's done is normal. He doesn't know he's brave.

When they slowed enough that she could talk, she said, "I've always wondered if my husband would be brave like my dad."

He just laughed.

Only a brave man would laugh.

And yet she worried. Phillip wanted to come to America as her husband. Salt and pepper couples didn't have the trouble they used to have, but still...

Also, could she be sure she didn't have a little residual bigotry in her own soul? What about the school he'd go to?

She held his left bicep with her right hand while caressing that same arm with her left hand. "Phillip?"

"What?" He smiled, she could tell, even in the dark.

"I love you. Truly I do."

Phillip dropped his mama's pot again. "I love you." He tenderly gathered her to him.

They'd never touched like this before. A shiver tore her from the inside out.

"I never thought I'd feel about any woman as I feel about you," he said.

Roz put her arms around her beloved's neck, drew him down and kissed him. He kissed her back, hard.

Greedy for his caress, she returned his kiss, the same kind he'd given her. A new kind of dizziness whipped through her.

This isn't right. Definitely not right.

She drew back. "We mustn't."

He shook his head as if to clear it. Then without a word, he picked up the pot and, taking her hand, he ran.

When they caught up with the rest of the family, Chaney wasn't crying anymore.

Habbie hugged her son and with another thunk, the pot fell to the ground while Phillip hugged her.

"Thank you," Habbie said. "I would have hated to lose this; it belonged to my mother."

After Phillip picked it up, the family continued their walking and running.

"Phillip, do we know where we're going?" Roz asked.

With a quiet laugh, Phillip said, "We've had a place prepared for two years now. We call it our storehouse. Dad thought we might need it someday. As usual, he was right."

The hyena opera sounded closer than usual and the three men in unison took out their pocket knives. As one man, they opened the knives, but they never stopped walking.

"We're making a circle. Stay on the inside," Adam told Chaney.

"I can walk where I want."

Adam took her shoulder and not so gently pushed her to the more protected middle of the group. "Don't be an idiot," he said.

Roz took over the herding of Chaney. "He's giving you good advice. I recommend that you follow it."

"You're not the boss of me!"

"If I have to, I'm going to give you a sharp chop to the kidneys followed by an uppercut to your chin. When I do that combination, my opponent often becomes unconscious and they usually have a lot of sickness and bruising for at least a couple of days. Now do what you've been told or face consequences."

"We should be closer together. They attack the one who isn't close to the rest," Daniel said.

"We should stay together because we belong together," Habbie said. "That's important."

"Less likely to bother us if we keep moving like we're going somewhere and have something to do," Phillip told Roz.

"That's good to know," Roz said.

Chaney had no comment.

"Of course, if the hyenas are really hungry," Phillip said. "Then we'd have a problem."

The hyenas, with the faith God gave their kind, followed the family until the eastern sky began to glow.

~ * ~

At midmorning, the family reached its destination. It seemed just another of the sandstone-shale covered hills. But this one held a cave—not that it had the obvious look of a cave. On the hill about twenty feet up stood a boulder taller than an elephant and twice as wide.

Daniel went first. To get there, he climbed the rocky area next to the boulder until he reached the top of the boulder. Then he appeared to dive in. Soon he yelled from inside, "It's just as we left it."

With that, Habbie climbed up, followed by Chaney with Adam making sure she didn't fall. Phillip motioned for Roz to go up next.

She climbed, with Phillip behind her. When she reached the opening, she saw why the people before her seemed to dive in.

The hole opened near the top of that big boulder. They had to bend over and crawl into a cavity surrounded by rocks the size of large dogs. Inside, by the light of a torch, Habbie fussed over the few things they'd brought.

"But the plow, we left the plow." Tears streamed down Habbie's cheeks. "What are we going to do now?"

"The Lord will make a way." Daniel patted his wife's back. "It didn't do us any good without the donkey anyway. We'll stay away for a few days. By then the raiders will have moved on. Then we'll go back."

"I'm not sure I want to go back," Habbie muttered.

"Why?" Daniel asked.

"I can live with their attacks once or twice a year. Not twice, three times a month!" Habbie said.

"We have a good home. The land is fertile. Why should we let those people push us out?" Daniel said. "We tried moving once, and what did it get us?"

Habbie's face twisted and her chin quivered. "He died because of it." She looked as if she'd like to launch into a hysterical crying rampage. Instead, she went to the bucket that held the few things she brought.

Roz shivered. She knew Daniel had made a bad mistake this time. She'd seen some of the evil of this earth. But what could she do? She could speak Arabic well enough for normal things…but she couldn't argue persuasively with Daniel.

She decided to talk to Phillip. He could talk to his dad.

"I used to think that no real evil could touch me," she said.

"Yes, God is good," Phillip said.

"I thought that if I prayed, went to church often, and stayed close to God by doing the things the Bible says we should. If I did all that and if I didn't make friends with bad people, I thought everything would be just fine. I think your dad thinks as I used to think."

Phillip patted her shoulder. "Dad's a wise man. He's doing the right thing, I'm sure of it."

"But what if he isn't doing the right thing?" Roz asked. "I did all the right things, but they still kidnapped me."

"We'll survive. We always have. The Lord takes care of us." He crossed his arms and yawned.

"Sometimes He takes care of His children by taking them to heaven ahead of schedule. He almost took Chaney. One of the evil men who made us slaves nearly beat her to death."

"But she's still alive, and she doesn't look damaged."

"You'll never see her back. Since her beating she hasn't seen it. All she knows is that it's still tender. She doesn't know she'll live with scars the rest of her life."

Roz realized convincing him of their danger wouldn't be easy and the others would be even more difficult. She drew a deep breath and tried again. "I remember from my Sunday school class that a great many Christians were killed just for being Christians in the first hundred years after Jesus' resurrection."

"Yes, Pastor Matthew told us; it was a very bad time," Phillip said.

"But did you know that in this past one hundred years, many, many more Christians died just because they were Christians than in those first hundred years?"

Phillip stood frowning, but said nothing.

"Evil still exists. Evil still kills. That's why Jesus said, 'if they persecute you in one place, then flee to another.' One of my Bible teachers told me about it. It's in the book of Matthew."

"But what would we do somewhere else?" Phillip's words seemed almost a whine.

"Do you think this is the only farmland in the world? I've seen some good land that makes your farm seem a wasteland. Please, can we discuss this with your father?"

"I'll talk with him; tell him your concerns."

"Oh, one more thing. Couldn't we move south? You told me the land is lots more fertile down there. At least it gets decent rainfall. And South Sudan is Christian."

"There's Christians in South Sudan, but there's also 'Christian' politicians and 'Christian' soldiers. I think both are more instruments of the devil than the Muslims."

"I don't understand," Roz said.

"We're sure that 'Christian' soldiers murdered Timothy, my older brother. Mama saw them. We're almost sure that a 'Christian' politician ordered it. That's why we moved back up here. Up here, our enemy only makes life difficult. They don't kill us. Well, not often."

"You'd rather take your chances with an enemy who calls himself your enemy," Roz said. "I understand a little better why Daniel wants to stay."

"Men are supposed to protect their women. I can protect you just as my father protects my mother. Don't worry so much." He kissed her forehead.

Now those words and that kiss made her mad.

Her dad had kissed her forehead and he dismissed her concerns. She hated it from her father; she hated it from Phillip. But she couldn't do anything right then and she knew it.

"Yes, my heart," she said with all the sweetness she could manage. She kissed her index finger and touched his lips.

But 'yes' doesn't mean I'll stop trying to have us to move to someplace safe; or at least safer—if only I knew where that wonderful 'safer' place is.

Forty-seven

At Mufa's village, Carl felt he'd spent enough of his valuable time getting healed. He traded Ol' Harley and one of the few small diamonds he'd kept in his pocket all this time for another horse. Mufa made most of his living trading. Carl then had a much younger gelding, "Brownie."

The brown animal, bigger than most, had a white blaze and short white socks. "Brownie" was massive—one powerful horse. In fact, he looked more like a Clydesdale than an Arabian. Another diamond bought Carl's initial stock of guns and ammunition.

Brownie had no trouble drawing the cart loaded with rifles and ammo and, in addition, Carl and his heavy cast.

He'd be able to take Mufa's cartload of guns and ammo to Azibik without a hitch. Another diamond bought Mufa's cart and the harness for Brownie to wear. That left three more eensie diamonds.

In the future, he'd use a horse and cart to bring all the guns these Muslim people could buy. Not just in the Sudan, but all over Africa. Horses don't use gas and oil. Out here, you can't just run to the gas station when you run low.

But first he had a debt to collect from one Okie blonde. She wouldn't get away. Not this time. Surely Azibik had her by then.

Forty-eight

In the storehouse-cave, Roz thought about places that might be safer. She finally gave up—for then. Before Roz did any more 'thinking,' she decided she'd better help Habbie. Besides, talking with Habbie would give her a chance to discuss moving out of this area.

She went to Habbie

"What would you like me to do? We'll need to eat soon. Should we see if we can find sticks, or straw or…" Roz disliked using cow-patties as cooking fuel so much she could hardly say the word, "or, or dung?"

When Habbie turned, she looked as if she were as far from this cave as New York City is from the Pacific Ocean.

"We supplied this cave with wood, plenty of wood. And there is even a hole in the top of this cave to let the smoke out. But slowly, so that it doesn't look like a fire is burning. We're safe; no one knows we're here."

"Oh, then you've known for a long time you were living in danger?"

"Yes, we decided to stay. We will be fine."

Habbie's chin trembled. Even in the dim light of the single torch, Roz saw tears ready to fall. Why couldn't her husband see them?

Gently Roz asked, "Where shall we make the fire?"

Habbie took the torch and then said, "Come with me and bring the bucket. Put the things in it next to the wall."

Roz followed Habbie away from the slight daylight that came through the little hole where they'd climbed into the cave.

By the light of the only torch, they walked away from the rest of the family. The floor of the cave sloped downward. The torch revealed pictographs, much like the Indian paintings Roz knew about from camping in New Mexico. This family wasn't the first to use this cave.

Finally Habbie stopped.

At floor level, the torch reflected the wetness of the dirt, but there was no real pool. A crack between two layers of rock about four feet from the floor trickled in a thin stream to the floor. A flat rock sat at floor level.

"The bucket goes here; it's a better tasting spring than the one near our house. But it's so slow." She took the bucket from Roz and put it on the flat rock that sat at floor level. The bucket fit as if the rock had been made for it.

"Now we get wood." With those words, Habbie walked away, torch held high. They walked several more minutes. Surely, by the way the ground sloped, they had to be below ground level by then. The cooler air verified her theory.

They came to a tangle of branches that reached to the cave's roof and closed the tunnel to any further exploration.

"This is the wood supply?" Roz could hardly believe the family would have carried this much timber into the cavern on purpose. "You accumulated all this firewood in advance?"

"Yes."

When Habbie had loaded Roz's arms with branches, they began the long uphill walk back to the front of the cave. "I've wondered," Roz said. "Why does Daniel want to live in this area?"

"His father owned the land we farm before he did and he was born in the house we lived in. My man is a sentimental person. We tried moving away once." She shook her head. "Not a good time."

"But if you're in danger here, wouldn't it be better to go away and come back to this land another day?"

Habbie's chin quivered and she said nothing else until they reached the spring. Habbie jerked the pail up and some of the water sloshed out.

She glared at Roz. "You don't know what you're talking about."

"But you could get hurt, or, or killed."

"Daniel is a good man. He will protect us. Do not speak of this again."

By the ragged edge in Habbie's voice, Roz knew she'd pushed the woman as far as she could be pushed. "If that's your decision, I won't talk to you about it anymore."

"That is what I want," Habbie said.

Neither said anything further until they reached the front of the cave. Roz deposited the firewood against a wall. Habbie set the bucket on a waist-high rock that seemed to have been placed there for that purpose.

In a kind of alcove not far from the cave entrance stood a ring of rocks. Roz hadn't noticed that nook before. She inspected the area a little closer. Sure enough, there were ashes in the circle of rock.

"Get me some of the small sticks and three big ones," Habbie told Roz.

Obediently, Roz brought the wood. The rest of the family had moved back in the cave so they were only dim shadows against the dark. She wondered why they moved. After puzzling about it for a few minutes, she understood. Those not preparing a meal would be more comfortable a reasonable distance from the heat of the fire.

When Habbie had the fire going, Roz helped her make the simplest type of *fuul*, basically just lentils and grain and a handful of dried herbs for seasoning.

Habbie had brought only a few small sacks of grain, lentils and beans. "Is this all the grain we have to see us through?" Roz had heard about famines in Africa and wondered if her experiences would include extreme hunger.

"You'll see," Habbie said.

Habbie seldom made small talk, so the meal preparation continued in silence.

When the grain had softened and the lentils were mush, Habbie and Roz carried the heavy pot deeper into the cave where the rest of the family waited.

The flickering torch furnished enough light to see where the food lay, but no more than that. They had no flat bread with which to scoop up the *fuul* so they ate with their fingers directly from the pot. They had no comfortable rug and no large flat bowl for the *fuul* either. They didn't even have salt.

Roz saw a tear course down Habbie's cheek. No one else noticed, so she said nothing. At least, for now, they had food.

At the end of the meal, Daniel said, "We will stay here a few days. Then we will take you ladies home."

Just before she opened her mouth to object, Roz looked at Phillip. He shook his head. If Daniel decided to go back, she'd have to go. No choice on that.

Four days later, Daniel said, "The raiders will have left by now. We must see what they left us and plant our crops."

"Let's go," Phillip said.

"It's sunrise. We should be working soon," Adam said.

The family marched back toward their house.

Chaney said, "I want to look at the house from that hill. It looks like a picture from there."

Adam laughed and the two of them ran in front of the group.

The couple reached the top of the hill and Chaney screeched and fell to the ground.

Phillip, Roz, Daniel and Habbie ran to the younger couple.

"How could they!" Habbie joined Chaney in tears.

"I expected some damage, but this? No, that's not real!" Roz wanted to rebel against something, but what?

"Those new bricks we made didn't stand up to those marauders any better than the ones that were put there by grandfather," Phillip said.

Habbie walked through the place where the door had been and collapsed. Daniel sat her on one of the boulders by the ashes of their days-old cooking fire.

"We can make more mud-brick," Adam said. "Until we put the walls up, a brush shelter will be all right."

Habbie didn't stop crying.

"We should take any keepsakes the raiders might have left us and say goodbye to our old home," Daniel said.

When Habbie got some control, she picked up a large clay jar from the rubble. It had only one small chip at the rim. She dusted it off and ordered Roz and Chaney to take the pot to the spring.

"We need a last taste of the water from the home place. Then we'll go," Habbie said with a sniff.

Roz took the jar; she could at least do that much for Habbie.

When Roz and Chaney neared the spring, Chaney said, "I want to see the farm from the top of the hill for a last time. It's still pretty, even if the house is gone."

"Be sure to watch for snakes."

With an indulgent smile, Roz held the jar and watched the younger girl run ahead. Let the child have a few moments of childhood, she thought.

Chaney sprinted until she reached the top of the hill. Suddenly she dropped to all fours and began crawling backwards down the hill. The instant Roz saw Chaney's strange behavior, Roz ran toward her.

Roz said, "What's wrong?"

"They're still there," she whispered. Tears were already streaking down her cheeks.

Roz crept to the crest of the hill.

Sure enough, just below at least three dozen men cleaned rifles, took care of horses and worked on equipment. Two men tried, unsuccessfully, to start a fire. A small antelope awaited butchering and cooking supplies lay close by.

Roz crawled back to Chaney. "Let's go," she whispered.

Forty-nine

When they reached the rubble where the family's house had been, both girls were so out of breath they couldn't talk.

"Go!" Roz panted.

"Raiders," Chaney said.

"Lots of raiders. Other side of the hill," Roz said.

Habbie grabbed everything she'd found. Adam took Chaney's hand and pulled her with him. Phillip ran in tandem with Roz. Daniel hurried Habbie along just behind them.

"We don't have darkness to hide in," Phillip said.

He put his left arm around her waist and lifted her so that her feet barely touched the ground.

Gratefully she put her arm on his shoulder and let him half-carry her for a step or two. Then she said, "I'm okay. I run just fine."

"Hurry," he said.

Roz looked over her shoulder. There were no man-shapes coming over the hill just yet. Would the family get away this time? She prayed for strength for the entire family. They couldn't be caught for slaves.

I've been a slave. Never again. If it kills me, I'll never be a slave again.

Adam, just ahead of Phillip, pushed Chaney into a little gully and dived over himself. And moments later Roz also found herself diving into the little dip in the ground and tumbling to the rocky bottom. Phillip followed her.

Daniel and Habbie came over, each tucked into a ball, so they were out of sight quickly.

Roz lay in the tiny depression panting, hoping they'd been in time. "Did we get away?"

"I think so," Phillip said.

Daniel climbed to the top of the gully and slowly raised his head just far enough that his eyes were above the ground.

"Praise Esus' name; they aren't coming," Daniel said. "We'll have to stay here until dark; then we'll go back to our storehouse." He scooted down the small slope far enough to put his arm around Habbie.

Habbie buried her face in Daniel's chest. Her shoulders shook but she made no sound.

Who wouldn't cry when marauders came through whenever they wanted? And no one stops them.

Phillip put his hand on Roz's shoulder. She rolled over enough to look into his brown eyes.

He couldn't have been more handsome. And this man was her intended husband.

A shiver ran through her and settled in her most private places. She couldn't tell if the feeling had any part of love in it. Definitely, it felt like lust. She wanted this man to husband her and she didn't want to wait much longer.

Why am I having these lusty thoughts? Not a good time to flake out. Not a good time at all.

After a few moments, she decided that maybe this feeling, these thoughts, were a result of all the fear, the danger, she'd gone through. Had she gotten fed up with being every evil person's toy to be pushed, mashed and shoved around? Maybe she was just angry.

She thought about it.

All of us ought to get mad.

I ought to be furious. They could murder me before sunset. Only right to get what little pleasure I can out of this situation.

She made sure she couldn't be seen over the rise. Then she took Phillip's hands in her own. "I love you, my heart."

"You, who were born to luxury. You, who were kidnapped and came to a land where life is hard. You get chased by thieves and looters."

Roz nodded.

"You tell me that you love me. You know I can't ever take you out of this misery by my own actions. And you love me?"

"I love you, Phillip." The heat inside her flared and her lips demanded kissing, serious kissing.

He kissed her hands and would have kissed her lips, but Daniel cleared his throat. With a smile, Phillip patted her hand.

"I'm going to talk to my father," Phillip said. "Next week we would have gone to Um Ruwabah where our church is. But if there are many raiders, it could be months."

"Months? But our marriage—" How could she tell her straight-laced groom-to-be that she might figure out a way to rape him if she didn't find ways to stay away from him?

"We may not be able to go there for a long time. I think we should get married now—If you want to?"

"Yes, that's what I want, but how?"

"My father will hear our vows and we will be married in the old way. When we can reach our church, we'll repeat our vows for Pastor Matthew."

He crouched low and crept to Daniel's side. She lay back and looked at the cloudless sky, almost content. She still wished she could let her dad know about her impending marriage. He'd want to know, no, he'd want to be here to give her away. And she wished she could tell her worrywart brother that she was fine, just fine.

She pictured the wonderful scene when she would enter the American Embassy with Phillip at her side. Probably they would have to pass some of those strong poles that keep car bombs and such things at bay.

Then they would enter the gate, and march up to the front door. It would have glass framed by a heavy, well-crafted door of dark wood, or maybe it would be inch thick glass without wood around it in the modern style. But modern or not, the gold lettering on the glass would inform the world that the tiny piece of land belonged to the U.S.A.

She could see herself holding the door open and urging her shy husband to enter that small slice of her homeland.

Phillip returned and whispered, "We'll stay here until it gets dark, then we'll go back to the storehouse. My family will hear our vows there. We'll rest." He smiled, unfolded his tall body and lay on his back. "Uh, at least…" His grin grew wider.

But Daniel frowned and cleared his throat.

Phillip immediately became businesslike. "We'll rest one day and at first light the next day we'll start for Um Ruwabah. No one can predict how long it will take to get there."

"Any idea? I mean how long did you travel last time?" Roz asked.

"It could be just a few days, like last time, or it could be months, months of hiding and danger. Sometimes our Muslim neighbors seriously try to make us leave our land, like they've done this month," Phillip said.

Being so close to Phillip seemed like being next to a wonderful tornado that would enclose her entirely if she let it. "But we'll be married tonight," she whispered.

"Tonight, we are one." He touched her hair with one finger and then used that same finger to stroke her from neck to finger tips.

Roz tried to keep her breathing more or less normal. "You're forcing me to say that I'm having difficulty being so close to you."

She rolled over onto her stomach and put her elbows into the scratchy grass and sand. Her chin found a place in her hands. That deep burning inside roared into a fire that reached to her cheeks.

"Well, I'm having trouble and it's your fault, you handsome hunk."

Phillip's face developed a mock look of surprise. "Heavens, what will mother say?"

Roz giggled. She laughed with the man she would marry. How wonderful to know her good man had a sense of humor. She intended to be the best wife anybody could be.

At the last glimmer of sundown, the family began their march to their cave-sanctuary.

Phillip held her hand for most of the journey.

The moonlight gave enough illumination to make out a group of hyenas. They tried coming close to the family, but the men opened their pocket knives. That click seemed to tell the beasts to back off.

"Ohh, what's that?" Chaney pointed at a couple of cat-like creatures with big ears. They'd joined the parade only moments before.

"Doesn't matter. They want to eat any leftovers after the hyenas get through with us," Roz said.

"Ugh!" Chaney ran and Adam caught her.

"Don't run! Predators chase things that run," Adam growled. "You want to do something, throw rocks."

Chaney still couldn't throw small rocks very well. After trying a few times, she picked up a much larger rock and hefted it as she might have done to kill a snake. After the third large rock failed to do any good, she walked at Adam's side and once in a while she threw small rocks.

The entire family threw rocks. The hyenas chortled and giggled while they trailed the family for many miles. The cats looked wise and stayed just outside the range of the family's rock throwing.

Finally, a hollow sound much like thumping a melon preceded a startled yip. Almost at the same time another yip showed that the family had the hyenas within range. After that the hyenas drifted away. But other creatures still followed them.

The hyena troupe laughed from a greater distance and Daniel said, "Faster, we should walk faster." And they did.

The moon neared the end of its ride across the sky and the dark grew even more intense. The large-eared cats slinked off perhaps an hour later. By then the east bestowed the faintest hint of gray to the sky.

"It won't be too much longer," Phillip said.

Two hours later, just as the sun began its heated campaign to make things tough, they reached the cave.

"Looks the same as when we left," Roz said.

"Probably. Wait here." Phillip joined his dad in climbing to the small opening.

Daniel climbed in and minutes later Phillip waved them to come up; climb in.

The family entered the cave and found it just as they'd left it. Not long after they'd gotten settled, Daniel stood near the entrance and asked the family to come together.

"We have gathered to hear the wedding vows of Phillip and Roz. Roz, do you vow to be wife to Phillip in all respects? To love and honor him with your life?"

"I do."

"Phillip, do you vow to be husband to Roz in all respects. To love and protect her with your life?"

"I do."

"Under the old ways of this family, I declare that you, Phillip, and you, Roz, are one. Phillip, kiss your bride."

"We'll have breakfast soon, and then we have to start our preparations to leave this place."

The day seemed impossibly long. The family bustled about getting ready to make this momentous move. Roz had no private time with her new husband. Finally the evening came. The family ate, and then Daniel said, we should sleep now. Let us pray for Phillip and Roz's new family. And also, that life will go well for all of us."

After supper, Habbie said, "This way." She carried the only torch.

Phillip circled Roz's waist with his arm and they followed his mother. "It's not what I wanted for our wedding night," he said. "I wanted—"

But Roz interrupted, "to be in my husband's arms is what I wanted. I love you, Phillip," she whispered in his ear. "I want you, my heart."

He replied with an indrawn breath and a tighter squeeze on her waist.

Habbie led them to a place near the spring but far enough away to be dry. A sheet-sized cloth lay on the floor of the cave.

Roz couldn't remember Habbie being away from the family. Yet her mother-in-law had come here to prepare their bridal bed. She had respected

Habbie since that first day, but now her love for this lady overflowed in a tight throat and tears.

"This is your place for tonight," Habbie said.

Roz hugged Habbie, "Thank you, Mama. I love you almost as much as I love your son."

Still holding the torch in her right hand, Habbie hugged Roz with her left arm, kissed her and then kissed her son. Habbie took one more look at the two, and with a smile, she disappeared, and took the torch with her.

In total darkness, total bliss and more fervor than she'd imagined, Roz and Phillip spent themselves on each other and slept.

Roz woke feeling full of achy muscles that had never ached before. She shook Phillip.

"Wake up, my heart."

He thrashed about and she crawled backwards, out of the way of his flailing. She'd noticed he woke up in fight mode every morning. Six people can't sleep in one room without learning each other's ways.

When she stopped hearing the sounds of his exertions, she said, "We should join the family before your mama has to come get us," she said.

Fifty

When the newlyweds reached the family's place at the front of the cave, the fire's last embers still glowed and everyone slept.

"Not as late as I thought," Phillip whispered.

"In the morning we'll need our sleep," Roz whispered. "I've dreamed of sleeping in my husband's arms for a long time." She didn't kiss him; if she did; she knew they wouldn't want to sleep.

She took the sheet from Phillip and spread it out for them. They both lay down and slept holding each other as if each were the other's life preserver.

Later Roz woke. She didn't immediately know what had awakened her; she only felt that something had tangled itself at the base of her neck. The hairs still stood straight up.

She already knew that lying absolutely still had to be the right thing to do when waking in a dangerous situation. She listened and moved only her eyes.

Then she heard a silky rustle, almost like a taffeta dress, but softer.

Snake!

Shivers tried to work themselves out of her shoulders. She wanted to leap up screaming. She did nothing.

Where?

If she could see it... She'd seen enough African snakes to recognize most of the really deadly ones. She heard another slight rustle. By listening, she placed it near Habbie and Chaney.

If she didn't do this right, that snake would bite one of them.

Phillip, sleeping at her side, seemed comatose. No help, not even from her husband. He'd thrash around and that snake—. Habbie and Chaney had to depend on her.

She'd have to wait until the snake moved again.

Ages passed before she heard that silky sound again. It seemed to be on the other side of Chaney. Then Chaney coughed.

A sound like water in a hot frying pan erupted from the snake. She'd seen a snake that made that sizzling sound. Phillip told her those tiny brown snakes with that pattern on them were more deadly than the fat tan ones with brown stripes and spots.

Surely this wasn't the same; surely it didn't have that pattern, like a brown argyle sock.

Stop dreaming. It's about three feet long and its scale pattern looks like a little brown argyle sock. I don't have to see it.

With every ounce of muscular control she possessed, she completed a slow motion roll from her back to her stomach.

Please, Lord, don't let Chaney or Habbie move again until I can help them.

Ever so gradually, Roz rose up on her elbows until she could see over Phillip.

Chaney lay curled in her usual fetal position with her back turned to Habbie. As she usually did, Habbie lay cuddled in the strong arms of her husband. Maybe two feet separated Chaney and Habbie.

That snake stretched its small length like so much rope in that two foot width between Chaney and Habbie.

Chaney made no further movement or sound and the snake stopped hissing.

It's probably enjoying their warmth. They're so exhausted they don't know that living death has joined them.

What should she do? Throwing a big rock at its head would probably get either Chaney or Habbie bitten.

But I know what will work.

Fifty-one

With desperation fueling her efforts, Roz crawled backwards, away from the sleeping family. She did it in such slow motion that a sloth would have admired her.

Finally she bumped against the cave wall. She'd crawled away a good seven or eight feet. Surely that little snake couldn't strike at her from that far away.

She stood and took off her black dress. Embarrassed to appear nearly nude before her husband's family, Roz stood still for a moment. For another moment, she tried to calm her shaking body.

Get it done! Every second is another second when something could go wrong.

With that, she held her dress in front of her. Ever so slowly she walked toward Chaney and Habbie.

A slight hiss sounded. Then quick, before the snake could strike either of them, she shrieked and threw her dress over the snake.

Chaney and Habbie sat up.

"Move!" Roz yelled. "Snake!"

Her black dress wriggled as if alive. Daniel's walking stick lay nearby. She grabbed his stick and hit the dress. Again and again, she hit it —until Philip took her hand. "It's got to be dead now, my heroic wife."

He removed her garment from the ground. The twitching, broken remains of the snake lay before them.

Roz shuddered. "I couldn't think of anything else to do."

Then she remembered she wore no clothes. Her dress, caked with snake's blood and dirt, lay in her husband's hand.

"I have to wash my dress."

Warmth covered her from her toes to her hair. She snatched the dress from Phillip's hands and ran down the dark tunnel.

Habbie called after her, "Wait, you'll get lost. I'll go with you."

When she bumped into the cave wall as the tunnel turned at a bend, Roz stood still with total darkness surrounding her. Habbie made sense; but then, Habbie usually made sense.

Roz still felt the head to foot warmth that had to be a blush. But she told herself that being nearly naked wasn't too much of a breach of good manners since her dress did save lives.

It seemed to take an age before Roz saw a light moving, getting brighter.

Habbie came saying, "You saved my life. My own mother died from a snake's bite."

"I'm afraid all I feel right now is embarrassment."

"There are many tunnels and we know that two of them have been used as cemeteries. We would not disturb the dead. Never, never by yourself, go down any of the tunnels except the one that leads to the spring. If you go there, you know how to follow the walls."

They reached the spring and not having a bucket; Roz wet her dress in the trickle and then wrung it out many times.

Finally Roz said, "I guess it's as clean as I can get it right now." She flapped the dress around in an attempt to dry it.

"It will be cold, but if you put it on, it will dry faster," Habbie said.

"You're right," Roz said. Then with Habbie's help she worked her way into the cold thing. "You're right about its being cold too."

"It will dry," Habbie said and held the torch high.

"Not as fast as when we do it in the noon heat, but you're right. It will dry." Already Roz felt the chill.

In silence, the two began the long walk back to the rest of the family. Roz couldn't think of anything to say that hadn't already been said.

When they reached the front of the cave, Daniel told Habbie, "It's time we should go."

"We'll eat boiled grain. It won't take long to cook; I'll make extra for our next meals. It will see us through. We'll fill the canteens and be ready."

After the hasty meal, Habbie took the bucket and said, "Roz, Chaney, come with me." Then she turned with her torch held high and again walked down the tunnel.

Roz followed her for a few steps, but had to go back and get Chaney.

"Come on," Roz said.

"You don't have to be so bossy!" Chaney said, with her lower lip in a pout.

Without another word, Roz led her after Habbie.

Habbie went into a cave branch Roz didn't remember. There, Habbie came to a pile of gourds shaped like crook-neck squash. Each of the gourds connected at the neck to another gourd by a thick leather cord.

"We fill these with water," Habbie said.

Each of the three women took a double handful of cords with the attached gourds and went to the spring. Habbie put the bucket under the trickle. When the bucket filled, they put the water in the gourds.

They stoppered the gourds with the wooden plugs that were in them. "Careful, don't press too hard. Gourds crack," Habbie repeated many times.

When they'd filled all the gourds, and lugged them to the cave entrance, again Habbie said, "Follow me." With the torch in hand, she led Roz and Chaney into the same branch of the tunnel as before.

"We've used this for several years as a granary," Habbie said. "It hasn't been bothered by any of the mice and other pests we usually see, just a few snakes. We think we don't see mice because snakes eat them. Pat and hit each sack hard. That will make the snakes go away."

"We need to take all of it with us, don't we?" Roz said.

"If we're to live until we've planted ourselves in some other land, yes, we do. If we're to have seed to plant, yes, we do."

Just then a slender gray snake worked his way into the light.

Chaney screamed, looked for a rock but found none. Instead she picked up a small sack and threw that. The snake slithered away.

"That's our main source of flavor. The herbs do better if not jostled too much." But even in the near dark, the girls saw Habbie's grin.

The wheat, lentils and beans filled heavy sacks, extremely heavy sacks. Roz couldn't help grunting when she lifted hers. She didn't say anything, just shambled to the front of the cave and put the sack down. She wondered how far she'd be able to carry that load.

Chaney would never be tall or very strong. She arrived at the front of the cave staggering under the load. She fell on top of the bundle, unable to move any further.

If the squirt had to carry that sack, they should just forget leaving. She couldn't carry it a mile, not in a year.

For that matter, how were they going to get these sacks out? Just hefting them to the opening would be a tremendous job. After that, they had to get them through a hole that Daniel barely squeezed through.

Surely they had a plan.

They did have a plan. First Daniel and his sons moved a few boulders inside the cave. This created stairs. Then they removed three rocks that made the opening so small. They did it as if this were a standard procedure they had done many times before. Then they hefted the sacks through the hole. After that, they replaced the three rocks at the entrance.

Thoroughly sweaty, the three men returned to the inside of the cave. Habbie stayed at the opening guarding the grain. Roz and Chaney brought the gourd-canteens of water out and put them with the stack of grain sacks. How would they carry all of this? Roz wondered.

She found out when Adam emerged from the cave. Immediately the end of a pole stuck up. He pulled it through the hole and laid it down. The end of other poles followed. After he pulled those poles up, Phillip appeared with an armful of smaller poles and rope. Then Daniel came out, also carrying short poles.

Daniel said, "Let's not delay any longer."

"But, we should see if the raiders left the plow," Phillip said. "I'll run to our old home and see."

"It's too dangerous. They'll either kill you outright or you'll lead them to us and then we'll all die. We can't use the plow without an animal anyway."

Phillip didn't say anything for a minute. He stood frowning and staring at the ground.

His father clapped him on the shoulder. "When it's time, we'll get a new metal plow, or we'll use a fire-hardened branch. My mother's father used one of those all his life and he grew more than enough to feed his family."

Phillip still frowned. He shook his head. "We need that plow. We used a branch once, remember? Not nearly as good as the metal plow. Takes longer, too."

"Daniel took his son's shoulders and then drew him close in a hug and a pat on the back.

"I'll be extremely careful," Phillip said.

Fifty-two

"We're going to start without you. Be more than wary," Daniel said.

Habbie also hugged her son and wiped tears as she turned away.

Phillip turned to Roz. "Be careful. Help Mama and don't argue."

"Me? Argue?" Roz giggled. "Hurry back…and you be careful. I don't want to be your widow until you're at least seventy-five."

Phillip hugged her and kissed her so hard and so long that she felt dizzy and then Daniel coughed. Without another word, Phillip turned and ran toward the farm.

"Let's hurry," Daniel said. "We should be miles from here before night comes."

Daniel and Adam used ropes to tie the shorter poles onto the long ones. A carrying frame emerged from their work. Then they piled the grain and most of the gourds on the frame.

After lashing the sacks and gourds down so they wouldn't fall off, Daniel seemed satisfied.

"Now we go," said Daniel.

Daniel and Adam lifted the ends of the carrying frame to their shoulders. Both bunched cloth under the pole where it pressed on their shoulder. Then they walked away with the women falling in beside them. No one talked.

Habbie walked at Daniel's side. She cried without a sound and Daniel held the pole on his shoulder with one hand and wiped her tears with the other. He kept walking, but he drew her close and comforted her.

Suddenly feeling an overflowing gratitude, Roz couldn't move.

How wonderful my husband must be. He's been taught to be a man by Daniel.

If they could get to an area where Christians were accepted, then she would have everything she wanted. Except she wished she could let her dad know that she still lived, of course.

Phillip caught up with the family about an hour before sunset. He carried only a piece of metal that in places shone like a mirror. It was just the plowshare. He didn't bring any of the wooden parts.

Roz hugged Phillip and smothered him with kisses. Daniel motioned for the pair to remove themselves to the far side of the only tree in the area. And they did. The other family members rested.

"I've been so worried."

"Were you?" Phillip had a huge grin. "I only saw one man, and I flattened myself on the dirt. He just kept walking, never saw me. We're safe." He folded himself around her and Roz allowed the warmth of his body to comfort her and let her relax in a never before felt safety.

"When I reach heaven, it won't feel more wonderful," she murmured.

"I love you as I never thought I could love."

Moments of bliss never last long enough and soon Daniel called them. They tied the plowshare onto the carry-frame, then Phillip took one end of the frame and Adam took the other.

She walked beside Phillip without a word for a long while; then asked, "Where will we go?"

"We're still trying to reach Um Ruwabah, where the church is. We'll have Pastor Matthew hear our vows when we get there," Phillip said.

"Where are we planning to go afterward?" Roz asked.

"I've heard of a few places in the north where there are more Christians than any other group," Phillip said. "The problem is that none of those places have good farmland and our family will nearly double the population. I'm worried about that."

"Why isn't it good farmland?"

"They get little rain and the land is filled with rocks. We needed the plow so we can cultivate more land. Even if each piece doesn't grow much, if we cultivate more pieces, maybe we won't starve."

Is there anything else people do there? Do we have to farm?"

Phillip just frowned and kept walking.

Near sundown they came to a thicket of trees and brush.

"Here's our usual place. See, part of our last shelter is still here. It's a good place," Daniel said.

Everyone gathered brush and firewood. They used parts of their last shelter to prepare this one. A small fire warmed more of the boiled grain Habbie had made the day before. In this batch, she added some lentils and seasoned it with the herbs she'd brought.

When they woke the next day, Roz thought maybe she had a solution to the problem of the dry land.

As she walked at Phillip's side, she explained her idea. "Before my family moved to Oklahoma, we lived near Amarillo in the western part of Texas. It's pretty dry and lots of people raise cattle. Maybe we could get some cows and be meat-farmers when we reach our new place."

"I wouldn't know how."

"We'd have to have some help until we learn what to do. I mean, back home coyotes are the only predator. They're too small; they can't take down many cows. Makes ranchers awful mad when they kill even one calf, though."

Phillip said nothing.

"Do they do any ranching at all where we're going? If they do, then they'd know what to do about hyenas and snakes. If not, we'd have to find a solution to the problem ourselves."

Phillip didn't talk. He shifted the carry frame to a new spot on his shoulder, kicked a stone and kept walking.

Roz really wanted to talk with her husband. But Phillip just kept walking.

Roz looked up at Phillip. "Are you ignoring me?" She gave him her most flirtatious smile.

"I don't like what you're talking about."

Puzzled, Roz could only say, "Why?"

"It's not seemly. The woman doesn't decide where we go or what we do. That's the man's business."

"But we're a team. That's what marriage is. Making two different people into one unit, a team. Besides, I only meant to discuss the subject of where and how we'll live. Talk, that's all I meant."

"You'll have more than enough to keep you busy, even make you brave, once the children come."

"I'll still want to talk to you. I mean, really talk."

Phillip just kicked another stone.

Roz stood with an open mouth and looked at him. She wondered if this were the same man she'd given her heart to? She knew that some men have an apparent change of attitude after they marry and get a woman to themselves. It's as if a woman doesn't matter after they've been conquered. Other men take women for granted. Whichever category he fell in, he wouldn't get away with it.

Roz said nothing. She couldn't do or say anything that would help right then. She kicked a stone.

What else could she expect? Women had been fighting this attitude from their men since Eve gave Adam the forbidden fruit. Maybe women deserved the attitude. Who knew?

She did know he wouldn't get away with it. After all, any woman worth beans had an attitude too. And she valued herself as worth several beans.

Fifty-three

Mufa told Carl that he was getting in some better guns and advised him to wait a few days. Carl decided that would make sense, Azibik would be more satisfied and satisfied customers are good for any business, even gun-running. He'd wait a few days, a few more days of healing for his leg.

He called Meribet and assured her of his love. She told him of her fear and he promised to rescue her as soon as he could. His phone had no more charge left after that call.

After another evening of messing with his little generator, Carl called George.

"Made my last deadbeat call," George said. "Found me some good workers. They held him down so I could work him over royal."

"That's good."

"Only had to break his big toe. Then the wife ran into the room. Gave me all those gold dowry coins she'd been wearing."

"Leave her man alone. That's all you had to do," Carl said with a laugh.

George laughed. "You got that right."

"If you got nothing else, I have a job for you…if you're interested."

"I'm not one for saying no, less'n I hear your proposal and don't like it."

"You'll like this. You remember that blonde gal?"

"She got us beat and 'punished' by the sheik…that blonde?" George asked

"That one, yeah."

"I don't remember her. 'Cept I'd skin her alive if I caught her."

"How'd you like to track her down, you and your men?" Carl said.

"Who's paying?

"I am, that's who."

"What a deal."

"You don't get to skin her, though. You got that. I'm the one what does the skinning."

"Awww..."

"Tell you what, you can have first dibs at her. Use her all you want for a few days," Carl said.

"That's how you're skinning her?"

"After you, all the men I can find will get a piece of her. That's so she won't object too much when I cut her up a little and stake her on an ant hill."

George laughed. "Do me a favor; I wanna be there when you stake her out."

"You're sure? Don't want vomit at my celebration."

"I wanna watch her, wanna see them ants take out her eyeballs."

"Then we got a deal?" Carl asked.

"That gal's on my list. I wanna pay her back big time," George said.

"You'll track her down and keep her for me? Remember, you don't get to see her ended until I'm there."

"This deal be my pleasure. Mind my asking why you ain't usin' her?" George asked.

"Blondes make me puke. Only good for one thing."

"What's that?"

"Dying real slow." Carl's mouth watered at the thought. "While you're tracking her down, I got another deal I got to take care of, got to."

"How long's your other deal gonna take?"

"Nigh onto a month. If you find my blonde before I get back, keep her alive, but I don't care about anything else you want to do to her. I just want to see her die...die sooo slow."

~ * ~

At Mufa's town, three more days passed before a rusty pickup came. It had a motor that sounded as if it would totally disintegrate if it had to go another mile. They'd loaded it with wooden boxes in columns about six feet tall. These were securely strapped into the pickup's bed. The guns had finally come in.

Fifty-four

Daniel's family walked in silence through the barren landscape. The animal trail that some jokester had named a road only helped a little. Finally, Daniel called a rest break.

Phillip said nothing to Roz or anyone else. The land around them grew flatter, sandier, and less rocky.

"Is the land where we're going as sandy and dry as this?" Roz asked.

Phillip nodded. "Too dry to farm." He looked at the ground a moment. Then he walked to the only large boulder in this area and with his arms crossed, he leaned against the overgrown rock with his back to her.

She'd managed to make Phillip really angry. Maybe she had been a little pushy, but she'd only wanted to talk with him.

Husbands and wives were supposed to love each other. Uncertain about what to do, she looked at Phillip's stiff back. She'd rather be caressing him, but he didn't want her. That hurt.

She remembered the few incidents in her own parents' lives when they'd disagreed and yelled at each other. It had frightened her. She'd hoped to do better.

What she ought to do was see if she could get this straightened out now. Bad temper and sullen attitudes wouldn't be normal in her marriage. Not if she could help it.

She walked around until she faced Phillip. "Can't we talk about whatever is bothering you? If it's my fault, then I apologize."

Phillip looked up, a startled look on his face. "Your fault? What are you talking about?"

"You told me I'd interfered and messed with men's prerogatives. Then you stopped talking and turned away from me."

Phillip almost smiled then. "I didn't mean it, not much anyway." His hands made fists and the muscles in his forearms knotted. "I'm discouraged, that's all."

"You aren't happy about moving. Is that it?"

"I'd hoped to talk to Pastor Matthew about taking me on as an assistant in training."

Daniel interrupted with, "We should go."

Phillip folded the toga-like fabric he usually wore and held it on his shoulders while he lifted the carry-poles and set them back on top of his shoulders. "Now I can't be a pastor's assistant."

"Why?" Roz asked.

"My father could have supported us out of the old farm until I had a church of my own and a congregation who could pay part of our expenses. After I got a church, I'd always planned on farming a little to make ends meet."

"They do that some in the U.S.A. too. Bivocational, I think they call it.

"But my father's new land won't feed him and mother, and there's Adam and Chaney. It sure won't feed four very well."

Roz walked faster just to keep up with Phillip.

"Even when the crops are good it won't feed them well. When there's a bad year, they'll go hungry. There won't be any extra for supporting us. We have to work our own farm full time and save some back to help the folks in their old age," Phillip said.

Roz couldn't think of anything to say that would help. She nodded and walked by Phillip's side as silent as her man. Much later they stopped for rest again.

Phillip walked away and Roz walked with him. Neither spoke.

Then she saw that his hands made fists again.

She took his right balled-up fist and caressed it open.

"I definitely think you should come to my country. You can get the training you need. I'm sure our farm experts would help you. And then we'll come back and help your people."

Phillip didn't say anything. Daniel gestured for the group to move and Phillip walked back into position and picked up his end of the carry frame. He still said nothing.

"We can talk while we're walking," Roz said.

"We'll be so far away," he said.

"I know, my heart. But your parents are both healthy. They are, aren't they?"

He smiled and nodded.

"Then now is the best time." Roz said the words with such authority that Phillip laughed.

"All right. We go as soon as the folks are settled on their new farm. We'll have to help build their new house, find a source of water, get the crops planted…"

"Of course, my heart. We have to make sure they're okay. God wouldn't want us to in any way abandon your parents…or your little brother.

That evening, they built another fort of thorny brush and slept inside it near the fire. As they usually did, Roz and Phillip made an intertwining ball. Roz couldn't remember more happiness at any time of her life.

No animal made a serious attempt to break in. Roz woke briefly when the local hyena pack passed so close she could smell them. They seemed to be chasing something and ignored the humans.

The following day had been cut from the same cloth as its predecessor. The land grew more like pictures of the edge of the great Saharan sand desert.

"I'm glad we're not going to be farming this." Roz let the dirt she held drift through her fingers.

Phillip didn't say anything. He put his head down and walked along saying nothing.

"Are you ignoring me?" Roz asked.

"I just, I don't want…"

"You're upset about leaving? Is that it?"

"Partly." He frowned, and said nothing for a few seconds. "I don't want to talk all the time. I don't feel like it. Is that okay with you?"

Roz hushed; instead, she tried to be a connoisseur of this desert place. She kicked a rock. If he didn't want to talk, then she wouldn't talk. Instead, she held his hand and they just walked. Once in a while they smiled at each other.

It's his way. I have to live with that. Actually, I don't talk a lot when I'm upset. We're two peas and now we're a pod.

After they took a break, they began walking again. She held his hand and just walked—no talking—with the man she loved.

About noon the next day, they began traveling downhill and the land grew less sand-like. It felt like dirt, extremely dry dirt.

When sunset's oranges and pinks covered the dusty landscape, they crested a small hill.

Roz walked by her husband's side. Occasionally they held each other's hands. It seemed the two were being stitched together, bonded each to the other. Roz thought of her parents' marriage. She had admired their soft steel love that outlasted any trouble, but until now she had always thought it would be impossible for her. With Phillip, just exactly the right man for her, she could be soft steel with him.

In the distance a peaceful-appearing small town spread before them. It looked like a Christmas card that said, *O Little Town of Bethlehem.* All it needed were three wise men in the foreground.

This family had three men. Who could say whether they were wise or not? She knew her husband valued the same things she did.

And yet, Phillip had no hint of sissy about him, male to the core; that was her man. She squeezed his hand...

Rifle fire...

Explosions, destroyed stillness…gunfire.

Phillip and Adam threw the carry rig and its contents to the ground. All of the family tried to hide behind it. But they couldn't all fit.

Phillip grabbed Roz's shoulder. "Have to crawl to those trees over there." He pointed to a clump of scruffy brush and small trees.

Fifty-five

A bullet zinged over their heads. "Trees, I see 'em." She did her best military crawl. He urged her to move ahead of him.

Behind her, Chaney sobbed.

Daniel, Habbie, Adam and Chaney crawled toward a large boulder.

Phillip ignored the boulder and headed straight for the ten or so scrubby trees he'd pointed out. Bullets screamed over their heads and made little puffs in the dirt.

Roz looked back. About a dozen men, not an army, but more than enough to murder her family. She redoubled her efforts to reach the trees.

The bullets stopped. And then she heard a shout, a raspy voice. She knew that voice—Carl. Why? Why did he keep chasing her? Did he think the things she'd done were that bad? She didn't know. She did know that God was on her side, not his.

She kept crawling toward the trees. More bullets. But not as before…they all seemed to come from one gun.

About ten feet from their goal, Phillip groaned, and then lay still.

Roz crawled back to him. "You're hit!"

"I'm all right." He tried to crawl, but his right arm wouldn't move.

Blood poured from the wound in his shoulder. Roz looped her right arm under his left armpit.

"I know this is going to hurt bad," she said. "But we have to move and I don't know anything else to do."

She dragged him toward the trees. Philip pushed with his legs.

They reached the first tree and then they ran, stooped over to show less of themselves. At the furthest tree, they stopped a moment and flopped on the ground.

"It will be too dark to see much of anything in about a half hour."

"I hope so," Phillip said. "Might escape in the dark."

Roz added silently. "If we aren't eaten by something."

The bullets still fired, but not in their direction.

"Let me see," Roz said.

She pulled his shirt aside. The bullet had gone through his shoulder from back to front.

"Take your shirt off; it's all we have for a bandage."

With a groan, he peeled the shirt off. To the occasional gunfire, she tore his sleeveless shirt into suitable strips for old-fashioned tie-on bandages

"I took a first aid course in high school. Looks like that course is going to be much more valuable than I ever thought any course could be.

"My teacher, Mrs. Bateman, thought her dog-eared 1940's book on bandage-making was a treasure." Roz reserved one front panel, but tore the rest into strips. The front panel became pads to cover the two wounds, front and back. The strips held the pads in place and reinforced the damaged muscle and bone.

"A couple of the boys fussed at making those old-fashioned things. No tape, no antiseptic, just cloth to tie over the wound." Roz knew she talked too much, but couldn't stop herself. "I can still hear Mrs. Bateman. 'Think, young man, you could be fishing somewhere in Alaska and your friend manages to fall and open a twelve inch gash in his thigh. You're miles from any other human, there's no phone service and all you have to work with is a shirt and your brains.' She had a high-pitched voice, like a kid, but she was so, so serious. You had to listen to her."

He didn't say anything, just nodded.

"I was after an easy A. But I never forgot Mrs. Bateman's words about 'a shirt and your brains.'" She finished tying the pads in place.

"Now, I get to use what I learned to preserve my husband's life. Not a bad dividend on an easy A."

After she'd made the bandage, she unraveled Habbie's careful stitches in the hem of her dress and tore that unseen part of her skirt free. The sacrifice of this unseen fabric would help Phillip. She tied it together and hung it around his neck to make a strap-sling with the bottom of the sling at about the level of his elbow. The excess fabric of the strip cascaded down his back. She thought about tearing it loose, but didn't.

Carefully, with Philip trying not to cry out, she put his useless right arm into the sling.

Philip said, "We have to go into town. Dad told us to meet there if we got separated."

"Can you tell which way is town?" Roz asked.

In the distance a single thump of gunfire sounded. "We go that way, away from the raiders." Phillip whispered, but made no move.

"We'd better go," she said and helped him stand.

Phillip sounded weak and in pain. She put his good arm on her shoulder and they walked on.

They came to more scrubby trees—trees that of themselves seemed hostile.

This dismal little forest might hide all sorts of vicious creatures ready to tear the life out of them. She stumbled over a fallen limb and pulled Phillip down with her. He tried to contain his groan but failed.

"I'm so sorry!" Roz picked herself up. Phillip didn't recover so fast. She tried to help him up but he brushed her hands away.

"It's all right." He struggled to stand upright and managed only with the help of the sapling against which he'd fallen. He held his injured right arm with his left hand.

"Wait a minute." She untied the sling and used only enough of the strip to make the sling the right length. The rest she tore off. It wasn't quite long enough so she bent down and tore a strip about four inches wide and a foot long from the bottom of her dress. She tied this strip to the rest and then tied it horizontally around his chest and right arm at elbow level. "It will help keep your arm still. Should have known to do this already."

Phillip said nothing, but even in the near dark, Roz could see the agony on his face.

"If the bullet damaged the bones in your shoulder, I don't know anything else to do."

Phillip nodded.

"I don't even know for sure that your arm should be absolutely still; all I know for sure is that your injury is way beyond my first aid skills."

Phillip didn't even nod. He just walked on and she could tell that each step set off more pain.

Roz didn't know how long before they'd reach the town. Since they'd been able to see the town without too much of the graying that distance causes, surely it couldn't be more than ten or fifteen miles. At a normal hiking rate of about twenty miles a day, if they stopped now, made a shelter, waited out the night and started walking at first light, they'd be near the town or maybe in it by noon tomorrow.

But they wouldn't be hiking at a normal rate, not with Phillip's injury. She worried about the rest of the family as well.

No more gunshots. But did that mean the raiders had given up? Maybe they'd killed the rest of the family and were now looking for the two of them. She didn't know.

The town meant safety; that much she knew.

Phillip didn't stop walking.

"My heart, let's stop walking. I know how to build one of those brush forts; we'll be safe inside it. You should rest."

Phillip shook his head, no. and kept walking.

No choice. Roz stayed at his side and helped him when he stumbled.

Fifty-six

Phillip staggered occasionally. As they walked, he staggered more often and she took his good arm, put it back on her shoulder.

Soon he leaned on her so that she bore much of his weight. They didn't talk; it would take energy to speak.

After they'd walked for what seemed hours, an exhausted Roz pulled Phillip to the top of a small rise. "We have to stop," she said.

"Can't," Phillip said through clinched teeth.

"Must." Roz led him down the other side of the slight hill, then gently pushed and lowered him to the ground. She collapsed beside him. "Your wife has run out of steam."

A sliver of a moon rose in the east; it didn't give much light but Phillip got to his feet. "We have to get away from here. Moonlight will let them see us."

Still sitting where she'd collapsed on the ground, Roz said, "Maybe the moonlight will let us find the rest of your family. We're hidden by several hills and at least four thickets. Let's sit a little while; I need rest and you need rest real bad."

Phillip didn't answer. He staggered off with the stones crunching under his feet. Roz caught up with him just in time to keep him from falling. They walked on at the slow pace Phillip could maintain. Then Phillip sank to the ground.

"Leave me. I can't make it."

"We'll rest a little; then we'll go if you think so." Using almost no pressure, Roz put her hand on his bandage. Soaked. His big danger was loss of blood.

Soon Phillip stood and Roz stood with him. He put his good left arm on her shoulder. "Never thought I'd have to lean on anyone, certainly not my wife."

"I'm strong. Let me carry as much of your weight as I can." She put her right arm around his waist and held him tight against her. The moon would set soon, and then they'd be in total darkness until the sunrise.

In Africa the sun is your biggest enemy and Roz dreaded the coming of the day. Yet in this black night, hyenas laughed at some cruel joke and the other night hunters created another sonata of disharmony. She shivered.

When Phillip collapsed again, they sat where he fell.

"Thank you for not leaving even though any woman in her right mind would leave a man like me."

"You saying I'm crazy?" She giggled, hoping to lighten the mood, even though fear ate at her. She kissed him. "Maybe I'm insane but I'm staying. We'll make it to town. Surely there's someone there who knows enough about medicine to help you."

She felt the bandages. If he didn't stop bleeding soon, he'd bleed completely dry.

"The moon won't last more than another thirty, maybe forty minutes. If we don't break our necks or get eaten, we're in good shape," she said.

Phillip muttered a weak grunt.

They came to another small group of trees and scrubby underbrush, much of it thorny. "Here, hon." Roz stopped. "Sit right here." She placed him next to one of the larger trees. "I'm going to make one of those brush shelters. You have to rest; it wouldn't hurt me either."

He agreed and in the near blackness she felt around for the thorny brush she needed. When they reached the town, her hands and arms would need some help, but she could make the two of them safe for a little while, at least safe from hyenas.

The snakes and human marauders? Maybe nothing could make them safe from those. Roz piled the brush in a ring three feet away from the tree where Phillip lay.

"I should be protecting you," Phillip whispered.

Roz pretended not to hear. She didn't like the weakness in his voice. She put all her energy into building their defense. She'd make him as safe and comfortable as possible—all she could do.

She had one last bit of brush to put in their tiny fort when the moon completely disappeared.

Her head swam and she called the feeling by its true name: Fear. She'd dealt with fear before.

It seemed years ago she'd spent days in the underground room the slavers used as a staging point. She knew it had been no blacker there than here. If she survived that sightless time, she could survive this one.

After she put the final piece of brush in place, she knelt at her husband's side. "Phillip?" When he groaned, "Yes," she said, "That's done. We'll be safe, at least from the animals."

She thought he said, "Good," but maybe he just groaned.

If only she had some water, she could have increased the amount of liquid in his body. It wouldn't have been blood, but any liquid would help.

In a little while she said, "I love you, my husband, my heart."

He made no response.

She knew he'd lost consciousness. This good man would die unless she got help for him. Without a sound, she wept as if there were no end to tears.

A noise outside the little brush fortress stopped her crying. A yodeling laugh made the hair on her neck stand at attention. Another laugh sounded on the opposite side of the brush fortress. She could smell them now.

Then she heard a sound much like her dog back home digging in the dirt.

Fifty-seven

"NO!"

Roz yelled the words and the digging stopped. But the hyenas would come back. She climbed the spreading tree around which she'd arranged her defense.

"Please, Lord, I need a big branch," she prayed, then added, "and I need it quick."

She yelled and kept on yelling, but the hyenas laughed and there were more of them then. What if they dug under her brush wall before she could get her club?

Hurry!

She found a branch that seemed right. As far out as she could feel, it had no leaves so she thought it would break off easily.

But it didn't break.

The hyenas laughed and snuffled just outside her fortress.

"You scruffy cowards. Get out of here!" She took a deep breath and screamed. The laughter stopped.

"Don't quit!"

She found some smaller branches that would break off and threw them with all the force she could manage. Once she heard a surprised yelp.

"We'll be just fine, my heart," she shouted. "This isn't hard; I can handle it."

Hurry!

She climbed a little higher and, while holding onto the branch above her, she put most of her weight on the branch she'd wanted. That snapping sound meant her target branch had broken. She climbed down the tree far enough to grab it and wrestle it loose.

Hurry! Phillip needs me.

She didn't remember climbing down.

Hurry! Make Phillip safe.

She heard a hyena digging and pounded the dirt where he dug.

After hitting the ground with her club dozens of times, she heard a dog-like howl of pain. She grinned; one hyena wouldn't dig for a while.

"See, hon. We'll be all right, just like I said."

She listened for the sound of hyenas scratching and kept on pounding the dirt.

"It'll be okay, dearest."

Keep them out—Wish we had a fire.

"Don't worry, my heart, we'll be okay."

More digging.

She pounded and kept pounding. *Would it ever stop?*

Finally, as the first light of dawn fought its way into the sky, the last of the beasts ambled away.

Totally spent, she collapsed where she stood on the opposite side of the tree from Phillip.

"Hon, they've gone. We're safe for now. But I've got to get you some water." Using the tree to help her, she climbed to her feet.

Beyond this small stand of acacia trees, the dim gray light showed bare dirt, thorny brush, an occasional clump of dead-looking grass and more brush. No water, not even a cactus.

"Dearest, you were right. This is wasteland only a person born here could love."

Phillip said nothing. He'd said nothing, only groaned a time or two after they'd reached this tree.

"Phillip?"

She edged around the tree to face him. He didn't move and flies clustered on his face. She knelt to brush the flies away.

"Phillip?"

Roz put her hand on his chest and felt no movement and he felt cooler than he should.

"Phillip?"

She put her fingers on his wrist…

Cold, he was cold.

So cold.

Trembling, she checked the pulse in his neck, as she'd seen on TV.

She refused to believe he had no pulse.

"No!" She shook him and got no response.

Bitter, bitter tears. She loved him. She couldn't live without him; she just couldn't.

Flies clustered on his handsome face. She brushed them away.

What should I do? Dear Lord, what do I do?

Silence—The only answer, silence. Yet, she felt—something. She couldn't even call it a feeling, yet she knew, she knew—what? Only that God cared. Only that He also grieved. She cried about that too.

Why, Lord Jesus? Why?

Next to her beloved's body, she leaned against the tree and sobbed…until she remembered that here in this hot land, his body wouldn't last the day before decay became obvious.

She cried and brushed away flies until the early morning sun shone on her face. No more delays. She had to take care of his body, give it the respect it should have.

How? She had no tools, couldn't dig a six-foot deep hole without so much as a shovel.

If a person came by on the trail they might have tools…but no, there were never many people on that animal track. Even if there were, even if they didn't look threatening, she couldn't ask for help. She'd have to let them be close enough to show her non-native-ness and in this country that would get her killed.

Why not? I'd be home with Jesus and Phillip is already there. Mother is already there... All my grandparents are there...Aunt Peggy and Uncle Charles...My cousin, Kinsey...and Aunt Mavis' stillborn baby, Haley...
Phillip is there...

Before she knew she'd done it, she walked half of the fifty or so feet to the trail. Then she collapsed and dissolved into tears again. It took almost an hour to remove that bad idea from her psyche.

She went back to Phillip's body and she still had no way to dig his grave. She cried about her lack of tools and her helplessness. Then she had a vivid memory from the many "Old West" movies she'd watched. The hapless victim had always been buried under rocks because the hero also had no shovel.

She could do that much. Still crying, she left her husband's body and a short distance away, she dug a shallow trench with her hands.

When she thought that the trench would fit Phillip's long form, she went back and as gently as she could, she dragged him to his grave.

No matter how often she shooed them away, flies covered his face and his wound. She had to relieve him of the flies quickly.

"My heart, this is the best I can do. I'm so sorry." Beginning at his feet, to delay the finality as long as she could, she covered him with a layer of earth. At last she'd covered him as if with a blanket. Only his beautiful face remained uncovered.

She wiped away the flies, gazed at him once more to imprint his face in her memory.

"I'm so sorry, my heart. I wanted more, much more, time to love you." She kissed his cold lips one last time.

Weeping, weeping, weeping, Roz showered down double handfuls of dirt on her beloved's face. She fought herself over an illogical, no, crazy, urge to wipe the dirt away—it seemed so wrong and she knew it was right.

Finally he seemed to be a mound of earth. She pulled more dirt, as much as she could, over his grave. Her husband would at least have a layer of soft earth between his body and the rocks.

Then she searched for weighty boulders that were small enough to carry. Couldn't let the hyenas get him. While she carried the rocks, she noticed her hands bled from scraping up all that soil, especially where that croc's tooth got her. It bled almost like Phillip's wound.

"I won't leave my husband unprotected."

There weren't many rocks in this area. She carried those nearby. Then she had to travel so far to find more that she wondered if she could find her way back.

She judged the noontime because the shadows were short, and she still had only a single layer of rocks covering her beloved's grave.

Hurry!

She licked her cracked lips and tried to find enough saliva to swallow. Unless she got water soon she would be in serious condition herself. By her light headedness, maybe she already was.

Can't stop. Phillip's grave…

Hurry!

She'd seen no succulents. But she hadn't been looking for them. She told herself to look for water holding plants while she looked for rocks.

The burning heat left her barely able to put one thought next to another one and her feet weighed more than the rocks she'd carried. But she couldn't stop She had to find more rocks.

Hurry!

Whatever else, his grave had to be protected before sunset. Mustn't let the hyenas get him.

She found a plant with fleshy leaves as long as her little finger and about as thick. It spread across the dirt for a good five feet.

Trembling with both fear and anticipation, she broke off a leaf, brushed away as much dirt as she could and bit off the first bite, about half the leaf. Bitterness filled her mouth. She wanted to spit it out. Instead, she chewed just enough to allow it to go down and swallowed.

It sat well enough on her stomach so she wouldn't be tossing it up. Thirst threatened to overwhelm her, but Roz waited another minute or so; the plant could be poison.

When she found that she still felt well, she put the rest of that leaf in her mouth. She'd had no nausea or any different dizziness than what she already fought, so she swallowed it down, fiber and all. The rest of the plant went with her and she swallowed some of the leaves periodically all afternoon.

By sundown Roz found enough rocks to cover Phillip's grave so it looked like the ones she'd seen in the movies. She tore another strip from her skirt and broke two sticks off a nearby bush. She put the sticks at right angles to each other and tied them to make a rough cross. Phillip ought to have at least that much of a marker.

The hyenas laughed their insane braying and from somewhere near she heard another sound, the roar of something large. There weren't supposed to be lions here but it sounded lion-like. She inserted the end of the cross between the rocks at his head and ran back to the brush shelter she'd already built.

After she replaced the open section of her defense, she chewed the last of the succulent plant that had sustained her that day. In the morning she'd say a final memorial service over her husband's grave and walk the trail at the bottom of the hill into the town, to safety and to water. Surely she could reach it. Surely she wouldn't die of thirst before then.

Fifty-eight

What would she do after she reached the town? How would she survive? The people in that town mustn't know her blonde—white—non-native status.

Phillip would have protected me, even if we could never find his family again. He would have made it all work out.

Fear grew in the dark. It pressed on her like the rocks on Phillip's grave.

Roz collapsed against the tree. All her hopes, gone. Tears flooded until she couldn't see and her sobs grew louder and louder still.

"Why? Dear God, why?"

Roz wanted to lie down and cry until she had no more sense than a cricket—or a grasshopper.

I'm not a grasshopper. I'm a hero's daughter and a hero's widow.

Multiple twig snaps and panting made a trail that started to the north and continued to the south.

Roz stood and felt the ground for the branch she'd used as a club to protect Phillip. Just finding it seemed a victory. Holding it stiffened her backbone.

No crying. Guard yourself.

The hyenas came and Roz told them. "You didn't get him and you won't get me. You're wasting your time." They didn't listen; of course.

She clubbed their feet until they gave up sometime in the deep darkness between evening and morning. With relief, she backed up until the tree stopped her. Grief and tiredness overwhelmed her and she fell rather than sat against that comforting trunk.

"Dear God, thank You for making the hyenas go away."

Even the thought of her all-powerful God watching over her didn't stop her from feeling empty. She cried and thought she might still be crying when the sun came up.

"Why, Lord? He was a good man. He was your man. Why?"

Tears again overwhelmed her and she couldn't even sit up. Roz lay on the dirt next to the tree, the dirt that Phillip had lain on the previous night. Completely overcome, she dragged her fingers through the soil, perhaps through Phillip's blood.

Then she heard something in the dry scrub to her left.

A large animal, too large to be a hyena, came through the brushy plant-life, stopped and approached her shelter. She could dimly see its outlines through thin places in her defense. She screamed at the beast and wished she'd had matches with which to start a fire. The creature stopped. Then Roz realized she'd been more than foolish. If he broke through her shelter, and he could, she wouldn't get the privilege of lying in a grave.

With the club in her hand, she scrambled up into the lower branches and prepared to climb much higher.

"I'm a hero's daughter and a hero's widow." After a moment she said, "I'll get home if it kills me."

Then Roz screamed, "I'M GOING HOME. IF IT KILLS ME, I WILL GO HOME!" And she climbed a little higher.

She listened for more noise. No sound came to her and in the quiet dark she kept watch. Here in the tree, she knew nothing could reach her.

But Roz couldn't keep herself alert; her concentration faded.

She shook herself awake. "I'm going home."

Not so much as a hyena chuckle disturbed the land. Despite her self-order, Roz found herself fading into sleep.

"Don't be a fool. Stay awake!"

But soon, she faded again.

"Stay awake!" She flexed each arm and each leg, did as much of a jump as she could on her tree branch, looked at the sky for the first light and listened to the night. Nothing disturbed this silent little forest and again she faded into unconsciousness.

Her left hand lost its grip and for a sickening moment, she swung over empty air only held by her right arm and the accidental tangle of her feet.

Thoroughly awake, she scrambled higher than even lions could climb. As she climbed, she broke off branches to cover herself against the cold. She removed her dress and tied herself down just in case she did the unlikely and really slept.

The first light brought her back to full awareness. The little trail at the bottom of the hill already shone with sunlight. She'd better travel as much as she could before the sun became unbearably hot.

She pulled the brush shelter apart and went to Phillip's grave. For a while she said nothing, just knelt there with the numbness of disbelief comforting her.

She couldn't leave him. She just couldn't.

~ * ~

Eventually she knew she'd have to go.

The sun grew warmer.

"I must leave now, my heart. Please know you will live in my heart until the end of my days." Roz meant to say her last words to her husband with dignity, but she collapsed on the sand and the beige dirt grew dark with fallen tears.

When she recovered enough, she said, "My mother's already in heaven. Look her up; she'll show you around. And I'll see you again when my time comes." She knew nothing else to say and stood.

"Lord Jesus, he's my husband. Please grant him thy peace. Please watch the place of his passing. I loved—"

A hand touched her shoulder and she spun around. Daniel, Habbie, Adam and Chaney stood there.

She cried, "Why couldn't you have been here? Why? Why!" She beat on Daniel's chest.

"Daughter, what is this?" He held her hands to keep her from beating him and from breaking the water gourds he carried around his neck.

Tears running down her face, she whispered, "My husband is dead."

Habbie screamed, "No, no, no!" She moaned and collapsed in a writhing mass in the dust. Adam dropped to her side, echoing her cries.

Roz wanted to join Habbie, wanted to have the relief of public grief and people to comfort her in this unbearable heartache. But she couldn't give in; she must be brave at least long enough to tell his father what happened.

"They shot him when they attacked. We ran as long as we could. I did my best, but it wasn't enough." She leaned against her father-in-law. "I'm sorry, so sorry."

But Daniel said nothing. Just nudged her out of his way to kneel and put his arms around both his wife and his remaining son.

Roz and Chaney stood outside the family circle. Chaney, as usual, cried. And as usual, Roz patted her shoulder and tried to comfort her.

But the family closed them out.

It hurt; Roz couldn't breathe. Sure, they were Phillip's parents and sure, Adam had become their only son. But they'd allowed her to be Phillip's wife.

And now she became the outsider again.

Not this time; I won't be alone. Chaney won't be alone either."

She took Chaney's right hand in her left and knelt between Adam and his mother. She pulled the crying girl down with her. After removing Adam's hand from his mother's shoulder, she put his hand on Chaney's shoulder.

"Your wife-to-be needs you," she wailed to him.

Then she put her arm around Habbie and let herself weep on her mother-in-law's shoulder without restraint.

Through her tears she saw Daniel with a startled expression on his face. He stretched across his wife's back to pat her arm. Her father-in-law looked old, much older than she'd thought.

Daniel's got enough on his shoulders with Habbie's grief. I shouldn't burden him with mine.

But she couldn't stop crying.

Too soon, Daniel helped both Habbie and Roz to their feet. "We have to say goodbye to our Phillip."

Habbie went into another paroxysm of crying. But Roz sighed a shuddering intake of breath and wiped away her tears.

Straighten up, no more bawling.

That order to herself stopped her outward grief, but only for a moment. Unable to help herself, she threw herself on the rocks of her husband's grave and again emptied herself of tears.

Daniel made Habbie stay with Adam and Chaney. And with a worried look on his face, he pulled Roz upright.

"We should not leave the cross; Muslims will defile his grave if they find it."

He pulled up the crude little cross and laid it flat. Together he and Roz covered it with the beige soil. Afterwards Roz put her head on the ground and darkened the soil that covered the cross with more tears.

Too soon Daniel forced her to stand and said, "We have to leave this place and reach Um Ruwabah before sundown." He pushed her to Adam and Chaney. Chaney, bless her, cried in sympathy and patted her on the back. "At a time like this, we need the strength of our Christian brothers and sisters," Daniel said.

Then Daniel tried to lead the weeping Habbie away. But Habbie would not be moved. Finally he lifted Habbie from the dirt and tried to drag her away from the grave.

But Habbie refused to leave and became a dead weight that would not be moved "We must go," Daniel said. But Habbie stayed.

"Adam, help me with your mother."

The words Habbie said made no sense. Slowly the two men dragged her from the nearness of Phillip's grave. At first Roz did nothing. Her stunned mind wouldn't let her think about anything other than the increasing distance from Phillip's grave. Chaney's crying wasn't helping.

But finally she saw Daniel's burden. The poor man seemed ready to give up. She had to help.

"Your wife-to-be needs you," she told Adam.

Daniel's right arm held Habbie's waist. Still crying, Roz supported her weeping mother-in-law with Habbie's right arm drawn tight against her neck. She held it there with both hands. "We must go, Mama. We need our Christian family. We have to have the love of our brothers and sisters in Christ."

Habbie nodded and managed to walk with less assistance. But she didn't stop crying. Chaney wailed like a professional mourner and, with Adam holding his wife-to-be upright, the family trudged along.

When they'd gone for what seemed many miles and when Habbie needed more support than Daniel and Roz together could manage, Daniel called a halt.

Without shade from the fierce sun, they sat by the side of the animal trail called a road. Habbie only kept on crying.

Roz made no sound, but she knew she had been permanently broken and would never be whole again.

Best get used to it. I can do it. I have to. I'm of hero stock...

She didn't feel like a hero and burst into fresh tears.

Phillip, why?

Roz couldn't swallow and her throat hurt with thirst.

"Please, might I have some water?" She croaked the words and Daniel said nothing, only took the two gourds that were tied together around his neck and handed them to her.

Nothing had ever tasted so good. It tasted warm, from the heat of the day and the heat of Daniel's body. But it was water! So good.

"Thank you." She gave both gourds back to him. One of them contained nothing.

When he looked at her with questions plain on his face, she said, "I haven't had anything to drink in two days. I ate some fleshy leaved plants, but that's all I've had for two days."

He nodded. "You've taken too much water too fast. You're going to feel sick—nauseous—for a while, but it will pass." He patted Habbie's shoulder. "We need to go." He lifted his wife and the family trudged onwards.

Fifty-nine

Four days ago, Carl had the doc cut his cast off and fit him with a splint that buckled on with genuine brass buckles. Doc didn't like it, but under Carl's threats, he did it.

Since he didn't look so helpless, Carl had gotten a few men together and tried to chase down that Okie blonde. He found the house where she had lived. But someone had fought a war there and only a bit of its shell remained.

That didn't stop him. One of the men he'd hired was a good tracker and kept Carl's team on her trail. Carl hadn't known these men and hadn't figured on their superstitious belief that they must be inside a village or at least in some kind of shelter before dark. They'd deserted him near sundown even though they'd found her and in an hour he would have been roasting her over an open fire.

The hard way, Carl learned to make sure a man would fight if he said he'd fight.

This time he'd do better and get a more trustworthy crew. The trackers Mufa recommended lived in an out of the way place called Um Ruwabah. Mufa's place lay about forty miles from that village.

At Carl's request, Mufa sent a note telling the men they could get work if in two days they met near the well in the square at two-thirty. Brownie could easily cover that distance in less than a day.

Then his satellite phone rang; he hoped this call from Meribet found her in a better mood.

Her first words seemed pleasant enough. Then he asked her about how she liked being a restaurant owner.

"All-all right. But...D-dad."

What do you mean, your dad?

"I'm not supposed to tell anyone, not even you."

Carl's insides twisted. He had to rescue his lady and do it soon.

"Listen real close. Don't want you making mistakes. We've got a big problem here. I want you to leave your dad's place right now and then call me."

"I don't—"

"Just do it. Don't tell your dad or if he asks where you're going, lie to him, say you have a beauty shop appointment or something. Sweetness, it's important that you do this. I'll wait for your call."

Meribet's call came ten minutes later.

"What's all this secrecy about?"

"Sweetness, I have to tell you some things and you aren't going to like it, any of it.

"First, I've made a bunch of money as a hit man for your dad. You can hang up now. What I've done...I won't blame you." He took a deep breath and squeezed his eyes shut.

"Do you think I'm a teenager? Think I don't know what my dad is? Think I don't know what you've been?"

"You do?"

"I've known since you told me you wanted to be something else than what you were. You'd been taking college correspondence courses. And then you started working your way up on Daddy's ship."

"You knew? And you still talk to me?"

"I was so proud of you, that you'd stop, that you'd change your life for me."

"Sweetness, I'm glad we're on the same page there. But the important thing is that he's grooming you to take my place."

He could hear Meribet sobbing. "He shot a man. Made me stand next to him so blood sprayed all over me. He said I'd just been initiated into him and his gang."

"Your dad is what they call a real piece of work… He's even worse than my mom."

"What can we do?" Meribet sounded like a little child.

"I want you to go back to your dad's house and plan to live with him a very little bit longer, say two, no might be three weeks. Can you do that?"

"I-I n n…Yes, I can."

"I'll try to get there sooner. By the way, if you really want anything that's in your rooms at your dad's place, rent an apartment somewhere and take it out a piece at a time. I know you've got lots of good jewelry. You'll want that. And clothes, you'll need some clothes. Put the things you want in the apartment you rent. But don't let your dad's men follow you."

"I can do that."

"I'll be coming to get you, but it's going to take a little time…a couple of days, could be twice that to reach a town with an airport that flies well maintained planes. Don't want to crash in mid-Sahara. Then, I gotta get to a town with flights that cross the Atlantic. Probably two days to fly home. After that, you'll never have to see your dad again."

Meribet inhaled loudly.

"You do want to never see him?" Carl asked.

"I know what he is and if I stay, I'll have to be just like him."

"I'll be there in about two or three weeks. All you need to do is be real sweet to your dad, even if you'd like to rip his heart out."

"I can do it; I'm a good actress. You'll see."

He looked at his watch. No way he would reach Um Ruwabah by two-thirty. That blonde piece of hell—

Sixty

The family reached Um Ruwabah about the middle of the afternoon. Few people walked the street and no one looked very friendly to Roz. She checked Chaney's scarf and made sure no blond hair showed.

"Am I okay, no hair showing?" she asked Chaney.

"Chaney looked at her critically and then poked some hair back under Roz's scarf.

"Let's go," Daniel said.

Daniel stopped at the town center. On the other side of the well, a group of men milled around, obviously waiting for someone.

"Just in case, we should fill our canteens," Daniel whispered. "Do it quickly. These people are not friends."

"Roz, Habbie and Chaney filled all six of their remaining gourd canteens. "We won't drink any now," Habbie said. Then the family hurried away. On the far side of town, at the last house, Daniel knocked at the door.

A small covered hole opened and moments later, the door opened and a dark male person only a little taller than Chaney said, "Come in, quickly—quickly." He drew them inside.

They walked in and the heat grabbed Roz's skin, wrung it so dry that no moisture remained.

How can anyone live in this heat?

The man slammed the door. "You're early; your time is next week."

"Pastor Matthew, we have no home."

"Come in, refresh yourselves." With a grunt, he picked up a six foot plank almost twice as thick as a two by four. "We'll talk about it later, after you've rested."

"We've lost Phillip."

"Timothy, and now Phillip. Two sons lost; I'm so sorry," He shoved the plank back into the heavy metal hooks across the door jamb, thereby locking the door. "I know how it feels."

"I know. You lost Samuel. Was it last year?" asked Daniel

"Two years; they shot him almost two years ago."

"We trust that God knows what He's doing." A muscle twitched in Daniel's jaw. "We must trust."

Roz noticed that the windows, placed high in the walls of the mud-brick house, had all been closed with fresh mud bricks except for a fist-sized opening that had a bit of cloth over it.

Daniel introduced Pastor Matthew Aliburi to Roz and Chaney. Then Pastor Matthew led them to a corner of the house that looked like Habbie's kitchen corner. A large pail sat on a shelf. They all drank as much of the warm water as they wanted. The gourds they brought remained in the kitchen area.

Pastor Matthew gave each of them a piece of flat pancake-like bread. "Come to the roof; it's cooler there." He motioned to a rough ladder attached to the wall not far from the kitchen nook.

Twenty-two people sat on the flat roof. They huddled under the shade of a cloth awning that stretched across the middle of the roof.

With Daniel's family, that meant there were twenty-seven people on this roof. Roz tried to walk lightly.

Pastor Matthew cleared his throat. "Friends, some of us want to move from this area and now our Daniel and Habbie are homeless. Their son, Phillip, is with the Lord."

A murmur went through the group and the pastor waited until the group grew quiet again.

"With the coming of Daniel's family, we are definitely out of compliance with the law that no more than seven men can gather at once. We must be quick."

Without another word, a man and his two sons left the shade of the awning and walked down the stairs so far that only their heads could be seen from the roof. Without a word they stood in the blazing sun.

Then Pastor Matthew said, "It's time to decide. Will we stay here and perhaps bring some of our Muslim neighbors to the Lord? Or will we move south, to the new state of South Sudan—a place that might be safer?"

A murmur went through the crowd and Daniel said, "We will need to start over somewhere. Though we found the south no safer than the north, wherever the rest of you want to be, we will go with you."

More murmurs, occasionally someone said stay, and then the entire group looked to Pastor Matthew. He cleared his throat. "We must talk to next week's group, but so far we agree; we stay here. And we try to be friends with as many of our Muslim neighbors as we can. Perhaps we can bring some of them to our Savior. Is that what we want?"

One by one, each of the men said, "Yes, we should stay."

"Now we must address the needs of Daniel's family. They have only what they wear. How can we help them?"

"I have more than enough land. You can use part of it," a tall Egyptian-looking man said. "I'm so sorry for your loss." His son of about six nodded his head and frowned.

"I, too, am sorry for your loss." A chubby man in a thwab that looked clean, but old and threadbare, said. "I know it is a small thing, but the Lord has given me ability as a trader and I have two plows. I give you one of them."

"We will provide you with clothes," said several of the women. Three young girls looked solemn and so very grown up as they nodded in agreement.

"My wife says we will give you one of her cooking pots," said a broad-shouldered black man whose olive-skinned wife sat cuddled next to him. She held her man's upper arm with both hands and blushed as he said the words. His daughter of about ten also blushed.

"We had an excellent crop last season. We will give you seed and enough for food until you make your crop," said the man who stood on the stairs. His sons of about twelve and eight nodded. "We are also sorry for your loss, my friend."

"My donkey's last colt is old enough to be plow-broke. You may have him if you want to break him," a man with gray hair said.

"Stay with us until you find a place and get your crops in," Pastor Matthew said.

Roz had never really seen Christian love in action as she had seen it this day. All of these people were desperately poor, yet they shared the little they had.

When she got back home, she'd tell others about the horrible poverty here. She'd also change her major. She didn't know what her major would be. The enrollment counselor would help her figure out the formal wording and the classes she'd need when she again enrolled at OU.

Then for the first time she realized that with widowhood came freedom to go home and stay home or not as she chose. Would Chaney want to go with her? Would she be taking Adam to America as well?

Sixty-one

For now, she would be the best widowed daughter-in-law she could be. Silent tears fell.

When Pastor Matthew finished his last prayer, most of the people left.

The Egyptian-looking man introduced himself to Daniel as Ashir ben Alisalim. "I am a new Christian," he said. "My neighbors will not harm us. They have always known me as, uh, different and they have not bothered me. His son shuffled closer and took his father's hand.

Pastor Matthew said, "You should be prepared for them to be offended."

"My becoming a Christian proves what they've always known." Ashir laughed, a hearty booming sound that improved Roz's mood just to hear it.

"They will treat you as they treat us. Your reputation for being this country's most quarrelsome man won't protect you for long," the pastor said.

"I know," Ashir said. His grin showed white teeth with incisors like tombstones. "But it's not as pleasant to argue as it used to be." He patted his son's shoulder and the boy looked up with a grin very like his dad's.

"Bless you. That change in your outlook is one way you know you have truly become a Christian," Pastor Matthew said.

"I will come back to town soon," Ashir said. Then he turned to Daniel, "If my wife doesn't object too much, you can build a shelter next to my house."

He turned to the pastor and with eyes shiny with tears said, "Please pray for my wife. She will not listen to me when I tell her about the Christ."

Pastor Matthew said, "The Bible says that when we have an unbelieving spouse we must be especially kind to them and pray for them."

"Perhaps I argue, not just talk, with her," Ashir said. "It will be as you have said." He stood straighter and looked as if a weight had been lifted.

With those words, Ashir and his son walked down the narrow outside stairway and Ashir whistled while the two marched along the road to the east. A woman, Pastor Matthew, a boy of about six and Daniel's family stayed on the roof.

"The Lord God willing, he will succeed in bringing her to Christ," Pastor said to Daniel. "Now, we will make a place for you. We have been sleeping here on the roof. Less danger and less heat. The house is not safe when it's winter and it's too hot in the summer."

"I saw that you have stopped their throwing rocks and garbage through the windows since we were here last," Daniel said.

"They call us evil names, toss rocks and we must pay more for anything we have to buy, but in this village they don't kill us," Pastor Matthew said.

"I think that, as a group, we have the skills to make most anything we need," Daniel said. "We don't need to buy much."

"We have learned to buy a little even if we could make what we need. It helps the people in the markets and the tradesmen think more kindly toward us. If they think well of us, maybe others will."

Daniel nodded.

"The militia watch us for any violation. If we were to do anything illegal we would go to jail for a long time."

"I'm glad we weren't caught with so many men here." Daniel said.

Pastor nodded and said, "Your family can have the east wall and we will take the west. We sleep close to the barrier wall at the edge of the roof. Rocks don't hit us very often if we stay close to the wall."

Night came and Roz slept fitfully. At some point, a rock landed only a foot from her head and she heard another rock thud onto the roof, but not close to her.

In the dark Roz prayed again. This time she knew that God heard her and that she'd eventually get back to America and that Bobby and her dad were well. But she also had this urgent need to become more courageous. Did God cause that desire for courage?

Probably.

Courage only comes with practice; her dad had already told her about practicing courage, and it bothered her. She didn't want to practice going through danger; a feeling that could only be called rebellion filled her.

That's cowardice!

The thought of courage brought thoughts of Phillip, and Roz lay there, beating at her sorrow and looking at the stars for many minutes.

Eventually she decided that if God wanted her to practice being courageous, she would practice being courageous every time she had the chance.

It will hurt...

Phillip died in pain...

Let it hurt, at least I'll have pain to share with my husband.

She slept.

The sun rose, but Roz continued to drowse until Habbie patted her shoulder.

"It's time," Habbie said.

Roz yawned and sat up. "What shall I do?"

"Help make the bread."

Obediently, Roz went to Sharifa, who kneaded bread dough in a shallow wooden box. As Sharifa directed, Roz made the bread patties and put them on a wicker tray.

The salt and other bread ingredients found their way into the cuts where Roz's hands had scraped out Phillip's grave. A little pain to share with Phillip, a good thing.

Thank You, Lord.

Roz also examined the red line from her little finger to her wrist. With everything else she'd had on her mind, she hadn't thought about it. The worrisome gash had stopped oozing pus and seemed to be healing. Even making Phillip's grave hadn't disturbed it that much—a true miracle!

Thank You, my wonderful, glorious, healing Lord!

Sharifa told Roz to bring an armload of wood and a large handful of kindling. Sharifa carried matches and the tray of uncooked bread down the stairs to a small round oven.

When they reached the bottom of the stairs, Sharifa said, "At least they have not destroyed my new oven." Nearby, six rocks outlined a fire pit with embers and ashes in it. Sharifa had Roz put the wood between the two cooking places.

Just as Roz had found on her camping trips, natural, non-petroleum-assisted, fires are hard to start. It seemed forever and three matches before the kindling blazed to life. Using a paddle, Sharifa fanned the blaze. Finally the logs caught and the blaze filled the little oven.

Roz held the wicker tray. But she spent most of her time looking for anyone who might be lurking.

When Sharifa put the last toasty bread patty on the tray, she grabbed the tray from Roz's hands and raced back up the stairs with Roz right behind her.

Upstairs, Sharifa's cooking pot had already been emptied into a bowl much like the one Habbie used at the old home place. In a few minutes, Daniel's family ate with Pastor Matthew's family.

For the rest of the day, the four women did household chores. They made *fuul* in a large batch so that the women didn't put themselves in danger quite so often. The men moved a loom under the awning that remained in the middle of the rooftop and each woman took a turn at weaving.

Daniel and Adam went with some men who came up the outside stairway. Only Pastor Matthew stayed at the house.

Even if Phillip had lived, Roz probably wouldn't find out where the men went or what they did. They didn't think women needed to know much. She shook her head as Aunt Hazel would have done. Men!

Daniel and Adam came back. Less than an hour later, Chaney and Adam had yet another fight.

Then Chaney sat next to the east wall and sniffed. Adam turned his back and refused to talk to her even though Daniel spoke to him about it.

Roz had no answer for this problem. "Lord, what am I to do?"

The Lord watched, but gave no directions.

Sixty-two

Days passed. The following Sunday another group of people came to the house and Pastor Matthew gave another sermon.

To obey the law about the number of men who could gather in one place, Daniel and Adam left the roof top. They took Pastor Matthew's axe with them. In the evening, they came back with a couple of good sized logs. They came up to the rooftop for the wedge. Then they split the logs into useable firewood and brought the firewood up to the roof where it would be kept safe.

The following Monday afternoon, Chaney stood with her hands in fists yelling at her husband-to-be. Adam couldn't understand the curse words she used, but Roz's mouth flew open.

The muscles in Adam's neck bulged. With his hand open, Adam raised his right arm and advanced on Chaney.

Chaney screamed, "You better not slap me! I'll kick you where it hurts."

Habbie rushed between them. Her voice rising above Chaney's screech, she shouted, "That will do."

Habbie grabbed Chaney's upper arm and pushed her to the loom. She made Chaney sit on the loom's seat.

"Start weaving, young woman, and don't stop until I tell you!"

Daniel took Adam down the outside stairs and they didn't come back for at least an hour.

With every fight, Chaney seemed less reasonable. Roz worried.

Mostly Roz wanted to go home, wanted to take Chaney home, but how? The wells gave this town a good water supply. She'd asked; the wells supplied the only water, no live creeks.

The nearest thing to a creek were small, very dry gullies or wadis. The wadis almost never had water, Sharifa said.

How would she find the Nile?

Knowing she had to leave sooner or later, preferably sooner, she decided to talk to Daniel and Habbie. They probably wouldn't mind if she left, but what about Chaney? Would they let her go?

They wouldn't want to lose Adam's wife, would they? Yet she'd sworn that Chaney would go home with her.

After supper she approached Daniel. "I've been thinking about our lives here. I'm creating a problem for you, aren't I?"

"Problem? I don't know what you mean," Daniel said.

Habbie looked up, questions plain on her face.

"Your custom is to buy your son's bride, but now that Phillip is dead, what does that make me?" Blinking didn't keep her tears from falling.

"I'm only another mouth to feed and I can't bring him back." She swiped the tears away.

"You are the wife of our son. You had no dowry and no family here in my country," Daniel said.

Habbie nodded.

"We're Christians; we won't desert you," he said. "We'd never exile you from our family."

Habbie nodded again. "You will always be part of us," she said, "You're all of Phillip we have left."

This isn't going to be easy.

"What I'm trying to say is that I need to go home, uh, back to the U.S.A. I'll take the memories of my husband and of his parents who have adopted me."

"You can't," Daniel said.

"You mustn't," Habbie whispered. "We want you here. Christians are too rare. We must stay together."

"Phillip wanted to be a pastor," Roz said.

"I know. He told me," Daniel said.

"We were going to my home and return after he learned from teachers in my country. I've decided that I'll get some more learning and then I'll come back here, if that's what God wills."

"But who will listen to a woman?" Daniel said. "You can't be a preacher; you couldn't farm. You would only be putting yourself in danger for no reason."

"I don't know what I could do. All I know is that I need to go to my home." She tried to think of an understandable way to say what she needed to say.

"Besides, I've worried about my father and brother every day since my capture. I need to be with them. At least let them know I still live."

Daniel nodded. "Yes. You should do that."

Roz added, "Also, I need training so that when I come back, I can be something other than another mouth to feed."

Daniel looked at his feet and said nothing.

"Even though it's needed, I don't want you to go," Habbie said. Her eyes shone with tears.

Daniel sighed, closed his eyes a moment and then said, "What do you want of us?"

"Your love, a water gourd, no two water gourds, and someone to show me the way to the Nile, uh, the big river.

"You can't walk to America. The men around here would, um…" Daniel paused.

"I know; I'm a female foreigner among people who have no respect for women and who despise foreigners."

Daniel nodded. "It would be very bad."

"If I find the river, I will be all right. You have to admit that my speech has improved. You'd hardly know I wasn't born speaking this language."

Both Daniel and Habbie nodded.

"I'll wear the burka so they won't know I'm a white." She put her hand next to Habbie's. "My skin is almost as tanned as yours. Maybe I could just wear a scarf and always look down so they won't see my blue eyes."

"It will break my heart to lose you," Habbie wailed and grabbed her.

Roz hugged her mother-in-law, holding her tight as if they could never be parted. There remained only one thing. She had to convince them to let Chaney go as well.

As if that thought were a cue, Chaney shouted at Adam. "I will not!"

"Yes, you will," Adam said.

"When we marry, I won't wait to eat until you have eaten all you want. Not never!" Chaney yelled.

"I'll have an old-fashioned wife; or none at all," Adam yelled back.

"Then what would you say if I said I want out?"

"You can't. I don't believe in divorce. After we say the words before the pastor, you're mine for the rest of your life. Get used to it, woman."

Chaney squalled and her many tears glittered enough to be seen across the rooftop. She turned away from Adam with her hands knotted into fists. Roz knew it wouldn't be long before Chaney would be screeching loud enough to be heard on the other side of town.

She said, "Daniel, Habbie, is it possible that Chaney isn't the right bride for Adam? In her way she's as stubborn as he is. They'll both be miserable for the rest of their lives."

"She may not be an ideal wife, but she's still Adam's bride," Daniel said and Habbie looked expectantly at her husband. Daniel had a resigned look on his face.

Roz knew that if she asked, he wouldn't refuse to let Chaney leave.

"Do you want me to take her with me? She would do well in her home where she has what she needs," Roz said. "She hasn't done anyone much good since she's been here."

"Do you *want* to take her with you?" Daniel asked. "You don't need an extra burden."

"I can do it. We've made our way across a lot of your worst land already. I think she would do almost anything to reach her home."

"I'll talk with Adam," Daniel said.

Roz couldn't hear all of what they said. She tried not to watch them too much but couldn't seem to avoid frequent glances in their direction.

Chaney contented herself with sitting on the floor and leaning her head against the retaining wall. She never stopped whimpering.

Pastor Matthew, Daniel and Adam left the roof.

They came back about a half-hour later. First they talked to Habbie, and then they walked to where Roz sat.

Pastor Matthew, Adam, Habbie and Daniel sat down next to Roz. "It is done," Daniel said. "We will provide you with burkas and as much food and water as you can carry."

"But we wish you would stay," Habbie said. "Adam wishes it too." Adam, with his lips a tight line, nodded his head.

"Probably the sooner we leave the better," Roz said.

"Yes, this is the best time. In six months it will be high summer," Pastor Matthew said. "You do not want to be in the desert then."

"I'll talk to Chaney. Thank you so much. You've been wonderful parents to me."

Sixty-three

Carl's phone rang. Had to be Meribet.

"I'll meet you in Madrid," she said.

"Madrid? What are you talking about?"

"Yes. Madrid," Meribet said. "That's where I live now."

"But you can't—"

"Oh yes I can. After Dad gave me a little Beretta pistol and made me go to the gun range every day, I had to get out."

"Sweetness, you were safe with your dad."

"When he'd been preparing me to be a monster just like him? I don't think so. Oh, I have a new name. I'm now Bette Graham."

"But…how…"

"Mama chose it for me. I think it has a nice ring to it, don't you? I wanted something a little zingy and Bette, where you pronounce it 'bet' works just fine and she said she gave me a blessing in making my last name the same as Billy Graham's."

Carl's mouth hung open; he wanted to object to something, but which something?

"I've got all my papers including my passport. Cam Carlton is a really good forger and a very nice guy."

"But he'll go straight to your dad. He pays most of 'em."

"Don't be such a worrier. We went to the best man in New York City. Someone my west-coast dad doesn't know exists. My PI checked him out before we went."

"PI? Oh, yeah, private investigator. But we? We, who?" Carl asked.

"Mama and me. She wants me safe and she doesn't want me worrying all the time."

"But…sweetness, this is a big world and you don't know all the dangers out there. And I—I uh…"

She cut him off. "Here's what I want you to do. If or when you can get to Madrid, I want you to find a seat on one of the benches in the big park with the lake. I'll take a walk around the lake sometime between two and four o'clock, not every day, but at least once a week."

"My poor sweetness, I'm so sorry you have to be in a strange country where you don't speak the language."

Laughter poured from the phone. "Of course I speak Spanish. I started speaking Spanish before I spoke English. My babysitters were almost always Spanish because they worked for less. Daddy always had a genius for cheap. The accent here is a little different, but I get along. My new friends think my accent is cute. And I have a nice job."

"A job?"

"Sure, don't want to depend on Daddy any more. I sell real estate. Juana says I'm a genius."

"Juana?"

"Juana's my boss. So far, my first month I've already made more than enough to pay my rent, food and everything else I need. That's just my first month. I'll do better next month when I have a little 'pipeline' going."

"But…but, why? How?"

"When you get here you'll have to come see the view from my apartment." She paused a minute and then added with a definite point to her words. "*After* you get your own."

His stomach dropped about a foot. He knew he'd lost her, but said, "I'll be there as soon as I can."

"I know you will. Bye now."

Sixty-four

At the dimmest light that preceded sunrise, two figures in black burkas slipped down the outside stairway from the roof of Pastor Matthew's house. Each carried a bundle and two sets of gourd canteens.

A young man in khaki shorts and a red plaid toga-like garment followed them down the stairs. Then he took the lead. The three hurried toward the northeast, away from town, and continued to walk until the baking sun directly overhead shrank the shadows to almost nothing.

"This is the wadi that leads to the big river," Adam told Chaney. "If you keep going, my almost wife, you'll find what you call the Nile and return to where you came from."

Chaney started to cry again.

"Thank you, Adam," said Roz. "We would have been lost without your help."

"Adam," Chaney sniffed. "I'm sorry I'm not the girl you wanted."

"Me too." Adam didn't smile.

"We'd best go. We have a long, long way to travel." Roz grabbed Chaney's hand and pulled her away from Adam.

Chaney, predictably, began wailing before they topped the next hill. Roz turned to take a last look at her husband's brother, her kin.

Then she gripped Chaney's wrist and strode away. They had to reach Cairo as soon as their legs could take them there.

"We don't have to run all the way," Chaney protested.

"Only thing that makes sense," Roz said. "Get to Cairo as fast as we can, find the embassy and call my dad."

"I don't care…we don't have to run."

"Daniel said we have a long walk before we reach the Nile."

"Okay. We walk fast."

"Probably be a day, maybe two before we have any water except what what's in our gourds."

Chaney said nothing, just sniffed a lot. At least she didn't cry.

Near nightfall, Roz gauged the nearest large tree as at least half a day's walk.

"Now we get to see if we can build an adequate brush shelter."

With a sigh, Chaney said, "Yeah. I thought you were going to say that." Without another word, she pulled up a couple of small shrubs." And yelped, and yelped again.

Roz knew this wouldn't be fun but she did what she had to do.

"Be sure to save the thickest stems and roots. That's all we have for our fire."

"You don't have to be so bossy."

When they finished with their fortress, they ate their meal, such as it was, and Roz said, "We get to sleep by the fire, for a change."

"I'm sleepy already." Chaney arranged her burka so that it kept most of the sand away from her body and lay down. "Good night, don't let the bed bugs bite."

With the fire to keep them away, the laughter of hyenas and the sounds of other animals didn't disturb Chaney. Roz slept lightly and added to their fire once, but no hyenas tried to dig under their defenses.

They rose with the dawn.

"I'm hungry," Chaney said.

"Be better if we move away from here before we eat. Something might have smelled us and want to have warm blonde for breakfast."

Chaney looked around. "There's nothing here. Let's eat first." She sat down on a small boulder.

Patience, Roz told herself. "Take a piece of bread out of your sack and eat it while you walk."

"Can't we have some of that bean muck they like so much?"

"It's not bean muck; it's called *fuul*."

Roz strode off, confident that Chaney would follow. The burka would make the heat worse and she wanted to get as far as she could before the temperature became really suffocating.

When she reached the top of the rise, Roz turned to see how much she'd have to slow down to allow Chaney to catch up.

Chaney wasn't catching up. Chaney sat on the same boulder she'd been sitting on, but she didn't eat. Chaney had frozen. A deer in the headlights had nothing on the squirt.

A scrawny male lion crouched about fifty feet from Chaney. His thin mane clumped together in mats, his ribs and the top of his hip bones stuck out.

Without thinking, Roz ran toward the lion. She screamed as loud as she could and picked up a rock.

She could never hit the lion from that far so she threw it high. Height would equal extra distance. The noise of the rock's fall might get its attention off of Chaney, at least Roz hoped it would.

It landed about twenty feet from the lion. He jumped slightly and turned to look. Roz, closer then, lobbed another rock at the beast and kept screaming. The second rock hit a boulder, bounced off and landed within a few feet of the cat. He flinched at that one too.

Roz picked up another rock and aimed it for the animal's head. It landed with an audible thud on his ribs. He roared, and roared again. Then he turned and as majestically as a starving cat with a limp could, he walked south, away from Chaney and Roz.

While wondering what had possessed her to attack a lion, Roz stopped.

"Chaney, come on!"

Roz knew her patience had evaporated, again. She wanted to shake the little nit or at least tell her what she thought of her.

Don't. It wouldn't...wouldn't help at all.

Chaney sauntered toward her, looking in all directions including behind her.

"Move it!" Roz stood with her hands on her hips.

At her urging, Chaney managed to walk a little faster. When the squirt had gotten within a couple of yards, Roz took off again. She walked fast without caring whether Chaney would keep up or not.

When the shadows announced that noon had come, Roz stopped. "Look, I'm sorry this is so rough for you. We have to get through it, that's all."

"You're mean," Chaney said.

"Maybe you think that lion wanted his ears scratched or his tummy rubbed."

"Don't be silly," Chaney said with a sniff.

Roz walked faster. "You could say you made a mistake when you stayed around our campsite instead of walking away."

Chaney didn't say anything.

Roz didn't need to look under Chaney's burka to know that the squirt's lip stuck out or at least, trembled. Chaney would be crying before long and that wouldn't help either of them. Roz changed the subject. "It's almost noon. We should stop and eat."

Chaney said nothing.

"There's a rock ledge that makes a nice shadow over there." Roz marched toward the promising shade. "We can have bread and *fuul*, rest for a little while."

"We won't rest long, will we? I want to go home." Under her breath Chaney muttered, "Away from you."

Roz pretended not to hear the last words. "Me too."

They reached the promised shade…Roz put her pack down and threw the front of the burka over her head, making it a kind of cape. Chaney did the same.

Roz dug the bread and the flattish gourd containing *fuul* from the bottom of her sack. "We need to eat mostly *fuul*; it doesn't take long for things like that to spoil."

Chaney didn't comment.

"I'd hate to waste the food our friends gave us. They couldn't really afford it, you know. Besides, I'm famished."

"You wouldn't let us eat earlier. Serves you right if you're starving." Chaney glared at her.

Roz slathered a piece of the flat bread with a generous amount of *fuul*, put it in her mouth and chewed, hard. Chaney wasn't likely to get any more pleasant.

"First thing I'm going to do when I get home is have a hamburger and a soda. I hate this stuff," Chaney said.

Roz set her mind on enduring Chaney's complaining and infantile antics until Chaney became the problem of the embassy.

After a day or two, the embassy would do whatever emergency procedures they had to do—anything to get this child out of their hair.

Roz ate and drank, and then lay back in the sand. A little rest let her feet stop feeling as if they had no callus or even skin to cover tender flesh would be good. Chaney stopped complaining and also lay back to rest.

In her dream-free sleep, Roz didn't hear the marching boots until they were too close for the girls to hide. They barely had time to put their burkas back in place to cover their blond hair and light skin.

Sixty-five

Roz shook the skirt of her burka into a more civilized pattern. Then she heard a deep rumbling laugh. Through the screen-like eyehole of her burka, Roz saw a tall man so thin he could have squeezed through the barrel of his rifle.

"Good day, sir," she said in her best Arabic and bowed as she had seen other civilians behave toward soldiers.

"Good day." The man lifted his cap, and mopped his forehead with his arm. Then he laughed. "What's two females doing out this way?"

"W-we were looking for firewood and got lost. We've found the wadi now and we'll be home soon. Thank you for coming to our rescue."

With that Roz grabbed Chaney's arm, both packs and all the gourd canteens. She walked away as fast as a Sudanese woman ever walks.

A thunderous snarl of many shots roared and Roz pushed Chaney to the ground and fell on top of her. The rumble of laughter sounded again followed by snickers from various soldiers and a few more laughs.

"Come here," the thin man said.

Slowly, Roz rose to her feet, helped Chaney up and walked back to the group, or squad, or whatever. When she reached the man, she bowed again.

"Yes sir?"

"I didn't tell you that you could go."

"Yes sir, I mean no, sir."

"You were not out looking for firewood." The man laughed. "What do you take me for?"

"One of the brave men who guards our nation. And I was afraid."

"Afraid. Of soldiers? Now, why would you be afraid of soldiers?" The man brayed yet another laugh.

Roz decided that maybe this time Chaney's tears would be the best way out. If she cried loudly and for long enough, maybe they could get out of this alive.

She sniffed. "You have guns." Then she wailed "We were afraid."

"You should be afraid of most military." He didn't laugh this time. "I, however, am not such a person. I follow Allah and observe the five pillars at all times. I make sure my men do the same."

Roz didn't say anything. Just sobbed even louder and bobbed her whole body in repeated bows. With her burka covering her from head to toe, she knew she'd have to make her movements large or the man wouldn't know how she was supposed to be feeling.

"Now, why are you women here in the middle of this desert place?"

Roz cried loudly and Chaney needed no encouragement to keep up her usual wailing. "My husband was killed by men with guns as we were going to our new home on the Nile. I buried him three days back."

"So you buried your husband, then you began walking?"

"Yes sir," Roz launched into a loud crying display with much bobbing of her torso.

"Stop that crying. I'm not one to take advantage of your problems."

Roz continued to cry but she said, "Yes, sir." Then she cried some more. Chaney, bless her, never stopped crying.

"What's the name of this village?" The leader spoke with as much kindness as Roz thought his brute's voice could carry.

This dangerous game wore on her, but Roz kept it up. "I don't know!" She howled and cried as if absolutely overcome. "My husband has relatives there and after the raiders destroyed our house, he said he'd wanted to live near them for a long time."

"The war," the leader said to a greasy-looking man wearing a military beret.

"We picked up the few things the raiders left us and now we're here." With that she yowled in a loud voice and kept on screeching.

"That will do, Mama."

But Roz didn't stop.

"I said quiet!"

Roz bowed herself to the ground as she'd seen Habbie do at Phillip's graveside. She huddled on the ground. All the while she whimpered and made herself shake.

"Come with us, Mama, we'll take you to your village. I'm sure I know which one." The man laughed. "You'd probably lose your way again and die in the desert, just like a woman."

He turned to the dozen or so men in his command. "These women are under our protection." A few of the men giggled, but most simply stood in some semblance of military 'at rest' posture.

Roz didn't have a good feeling about this, but what could she do? If she grabbed Chaney and ran, these…thugs, would shoot, no doubt about it.

They walked behind the men, as any woman in this country would do. As soon as she could, Roz leaned over and whispered to Chaney. "Your Arabic is better than it used to be, but if they heard you, they'd know you aren't from this country. So just pretend you're a mute and can't make any sound but crying noises."

"Why?"

"You like being alive, don't you? These men have assault rifles, the kind that shoots lots of bullets fast."

When she heard that, Chaney started whimpering again.

"Whatever you do, don't start a big crying scene unless I do. I don't know what they'd do."

What might these intensely Muslim, black, extremely macho men do to two white American Christian females?

Nightmare!

She kept that thought in mind through the rest of the afternoon. Near sundown they stopped. Each man took a small piece of blanket from his pack and knelt on it. Then they mumbled prayers. To avoid upsetting them,

Roz and Chaney sat with their heads bowed. After that, they made camp, each man eating rations from his own pack and Roz and Chaney ate from their packs also.

Roz sighed with relief when no one gathered thorny brush to make a corral. While the men scavenged the area for wood and then started several small fires, she made sure that she and Chaney would sleep at the edge of camp.

She looked busy as she removed small rocks that might gouge a person while sleeping. She knew the soldiers would never realize that she lined up the rocks to point the way to the wadi. No man who thought women were less than stupid would suspect a woman of anything that needed thought. In the middle of the night she could feel the rocks and know which way to go. Mustn't be wandering off into the desert.

By the time she had her direction pebbles pointed correctly, the leader had assigned two men to sentry duty. Soon everyone except the sentries bedded down and the camp grew quiet. She had Chaney lie down inches from her and let the youngster sleep.

Roz lay down but she didn't sleep. She'd positioned herself so that she could see both sentries. She lay there watching them, willing them to sleep.

These soldiers had no reason to chase them. If she could find that little ditch of a wadi and walk toward her right—and if she and Chaney really moved their feet this night—and if no lions or hyenas found them—and if they didn't step on a snake, or sit on a yellow scorpion, they'd be all right.

Please, Lord, let us be all right.

The three-quarter moon rose to its majestic place in the sky. Probably the moonlight gave them the best chance of success they could have. She'd been worried about finding the wadi by falling into it. That scenario could easily have happened on a darker night.

Now that they had moonlight, surely they wouldn't stumble. She lay still while hoping she gave a good imitation of deep sleep.

When the moon reached its high point, she thought the sentries were sleeping, but she couldn't be sure, not yet. In the distance hyenas laughed and one of the men on guard moved ever so little. She waited a while longer. No one stirred.

She rolled over and knelt by Chaney; she gripped the girl's shoulder and held her hand over Chaney's mouth. Chaney nodded and made no sound.

The two grabbed their packs and a set of canteen-gourds each. Then they crept in a wide circle around the camp toward the ravine. After that, Roz held Chaney's hand and ran. They needed to be in the wadi and miles away before the sentries discovered they were gone.

When they reached the edge of the gully, they slipped, scrambled and fell down the steep slope. At the bottom they picked themselves up and ran to the right, just as Roz had planned.

"Hurry," Roz whispered, "We don't have long."

"I am hurrying. You don't have to be so bossy."

Roz ran and as she ran she realized that she'd developed even more endurance than she'd had in college. Even the horrible things she'd been through had a reward.

When the moon neared the horizon, Chaney said, "Stop. I can't go on."

"We have to move. We can't be anywhere near those soldiers. Besides, I want to be a long way from those hyenas we heard."

A whimpering Chaney started running again.

About an hour later, just before moon-set, the light grew so dim they couldn't see the rocky path they needed to travel. Roz told Chaney, "We'll have to stop. Can't have us breaking a leg or something." She sat down on a rounded boulder.

While feeling her way to Roz, Chaney said, "I'm thirsty."

"Go easy on the water," Roz said. "We only have one of our canteen gourd sets each. We left the rest because they might bang together and make noise, remember?"

"Dumb."

"You'd rather take a chance on getting captured because we were afraid we might get thirsty? I don't think so."

"I still say it was dumb."

"We'll get by. Just have to walk fast and get to the Nile soonest."

"Dumb."

Chaney drank from the gourd and then she said, "We need to keep on going. I want to get home."

"Me too, but we can't get hurt. No way we'll get home if we hurt ourselves."

Chaney said nothing. Instead, she picked her way through the mass of boulders filling that part of the wadi.

"Chaney, don't do it!" Sometimes she wondered why she bothered to bring this child along. But then, she'd promised God and she wouldn't break a promise to Him—or anyone else.

With a sigh, Roz climbed the boulders and by hearing alone, she followed the pigheaded little fool.

Sixty-six

With his lighter, more mobile splint, Carl entered Azibik's village. Attached to his newly bought cart, with its load of guns and ammo, Brownie, the big brown horse pranced along. Sahli, the man Mufa had appointed after Kazir "ran off," rode Ol' Harley. But Carl saw no man. Not even a dog. This was nothing if not strange.

"Hold it, let's wait here," Carl said.

Sahli frowned. "Don't usually see villages so quiet."

"Give me Harley's reins. You slip off, go around back; see what you can see. I'll go up the street as if this silence is normal."

"Wait, what you…"

"No time, just do it." Carl slapped the trace reins on Brownie's back. Brownie ambled down the street.

Sahli didn't say anything, just flipped Harley's reins in the direction of the cart's seat. Then he vanished, just like that.

Carl took the reins. He wished he could disappear so quietly. In a few months he'd be able; he promised himself.

A bullet plowed into the seat. It missed him by less than a foot.

"Hold it right there," a boy's voice yelled.

Immediately, Carl knew that voice was wrong. Who gives guns to boys of six and puts 'em on guard? Where were the men?

Shrubs bordered the far end of the most distant house. The barrel of a rifle stuck through the thick maze of branchlets.

"Hello, son, I'm a friend. You don't need to be afraid. I'm just delivering some goods to your father."

The rifle pointed up and the boy wasted a bullet.

"Don't talk. Leave," the boy said.

"Didn't your daddy teach you not to waste your ammo?"

Carl click-clicked with his tongue to make Brownie amble a bit faster.

"Turn your animals and leave."

"Really, it ain't ever a good idee to be careless with your bullets."

"Turn those horses!"

He ignored the order and slapped Brownie a second time with the trace-reins. Brownie's amble became a canter.

"Never can tell if that bullet you wasted might a been the one that woulda saved your skin."

"Leave us."

A hot whoosh whipped above Carl's head.

This kid is serious.

"Boy, you don't want to raise my blood pressure. You wouldn't like it and neither would I."

Another slap of the trace-reins and Brownie's canter switched to higher gear.

A scream hit the air and a minute later, Sahli dragged a struggling body into the street.

Carl snapped the reins hard and Brownie reached the struggling pair in seconds.

Not a boy?

Carl stopped Brownie and leaned down to look at this child-warrior. She wore a green and blue plaid shirt and jeans. Her long black hair hung down her back in a single braid.

"Gal, what you doing out here with a gun?"

At that moment, Carl realized that every door held at least one female and all of them were armed with something. Bows and arrows, crossbows, another rifle. The roof held more of the same. A door opened and three heavy-weight women in burkas walked through. Each carried a butcher knife in one hand and a skillet in the other. A platoon of teenage girls armed with bows marched up behind the cart.

The young woman that Sahli held stopped struggling. "I told you to leave us."

"Let her go, Sahli."

"We ain't leaving," Carl said. "Sahli, climb up on Harley. We're going to sit right here until Azibik comes back."

The girl pulled her shirt down and hitched her jeans up.

"He won't be back until tomorrow noon. One or another of my mothers or sisters will get tired of guarding you. You'll be dead before you draw another breath."

"Awww, gal."

"Don't matter, my father's going to tell us to shoot you, almost always does."

Is leaving the better part of smart? He pondered that question for perhaps a whole quarter minute.

He answered himself: *Yep.*

"Okay, Miss. We won't disturb you anymore. We're going out of your village. We'll wait for Azibik in that field over there."

"Better be out of range of our rifles and crossbows."

Carl couldn't believe what he heard.

If that Okie hussy taught them…Naw, no time even for her to do this.

"If our bow-girls decide to, they'll see if they can do the deed closer than fifty yards, maybe slit both your throats while you sleep. They're real good at camo."

"But all we wanted…"

The smile on the girl's face held no warmth.

"We always have a contest; winner's the one who puts her weapon in you."

Carl growled and slapped the trace-reins hard across Brownie's back. The horse bucked slightly and broke into a trot. After they passed the last house, Carl guided the animal through the field.

A stand of acacia trees grew about three miles from Azibik's village. That ought to be far enough from these mad women. He and Sahli would camp there.

Sahli said nothing until they neared the trees.

"I told Mufa I'd help you. But I didn't agree to die at the hands of a village full of crazy females," Sahli said. "I'm going home."

"But..."

"Don't worry. I'll light a big blaze and put some wood in the cart so you can drop it on the fire without climbing out of the cart with that brace. Leave your animal in harness. You and that horse should be safe enough from the animals. Then I'll leave. You'll have to figure out how to be safe from those women."

A single hyena laughed long and very close.

Sixty-seven

The moon neared the horizon and Chaney raced down the wadi with Roz behind her. As they went, the rocks in the wadi became larger. The two ran among foot-sized stones and chair-sized boulders.

Finally, Roz caught up and grabbed the hem of Chaney's burka. When she tried to wrestle herself free, Roz clutched the younger girl's shoulders.

"Stop it! Wait 'til it gets light. If we keep running in the dark, we're gonna break—"

"I wanna go home!" With that, Chaney sat down and cried. Roz sank down by her side.

Roz wanted to cry too and maybe she did. Even so, they were on their way home. That was something, an important something.

Both girls dozed; perhaps they fell into true sleep. The stupor that overcame Roz lasted until the sun lit the eastern sky. She sat for a while and contemplated the future.

A long time ago, Lord Jesus, I told you I wanted adventure and courage. You did what I asked, but Lord, I'm not sure I like being adventurous. I still want to be brave. But I'm here, and I'm Yours, such as I am. I know that I'm here for a reason. I need all the help You'll give me. Please, Lord God, help us.

The sounds of the desert were no different...the sky remained gray with a pink edge to it, but Roz knew; she knew that her Lord was in charge and this was exactly where she was supposed to be.

She waited for the early sunrise to become more intense. Then she stood; she could do this. God would guide her through it. They would reach Cairo…eventually.

She shook the sleeping Chaney and said, "Let's go."

By the time the sunrise became pink and orange, they'd reached the other side of the large boulders that had hampered their progress during the night. They traveled more comfortably, only needing to walk around the occasional large boulder and step across the smaller rocks.

"All that matters is getting to Cairo," Roz said.

Chaney reached down and lifted her burka and tossed it back into its cape-like form. She kept walking.

Trying for gentleness, Roz said, "You won't like it if someone finds that you're a 'Yankee.'"

"So?"

Roz said, "They'd want to skin you while you're still alive; you know that."

"Why is everybody so mean?" Chaney put her burka back in place.

"We'll walk a little longer," Roz said. "It won't hurt me to be hungry. I think I'm still a few pounds heavier than when our former 'master' made us eat so much."

"Maybe Sheik Kelmet did us a favor," Chaney said and then sniffed.

"At least he made it possible to live on next to nothing for a while."

They walked on and before noon the ravine walls of the wadi opened out into a field of grassy green.

"Will you look at that?" Roz said. "If there are crops and the land is flat, you don't need a GPS to know the Nile has to be close."

"Now we walk along the river bank? Have all the water we want?"

"Follow the river, but far enough away so we don't get eaten. If there's water in this country, there's crocs."

Chaney turned her burka-covered face toward Roz, "Get eaten? I'm the one who's going to eat. What you talking about?"

"Crocodiles," Roz said in exasperation. "Where's your brain?"

"I forgot."

While gritting her teeth, Roz said with all the pleasantness she could muster, "Why don't we eat a piece of bread, refill our canteens and rest a while over there at the palm tree next to the river."

"Where that crocodile is?" Chaney laughed.

Roz laughed too. They kept walking. A caravan of a man and a boy with two camels and a donkey passed them.

"Have to remember women don't assert themselves." Roz guided Chaney to the side of the road and let the caravan pass.

Soon after that, they found a group of palm trees and scrub bushes.

"It's almost private...surely we won't be seen." Roz put her burka into the cape form and sat down.

"I'm so hungry," Chaney said. She fanned her burka back as well.

Both girls dug in their packs for the last of the bread. "Now if we can just keep ourselves out of trouble until we reach Cairo, we've got it made," Roz said and tore off a piece of the dried out bread.

"You really think we can walk so far?" Chaney asked.

"I'm going to make every effort I ever thought about." Roz ate another bite and took a sip of water.

"Me too." Chaney gave an emphatic nod and took another bite. "To be treated like a real person again. It'll be great!"

"Me too. As a kid, I didn't like school. I had to sit still and do things I didn't know how to do and I definitely had no interest in learning how." Roz leaned against the base of palm and looked up at the cloudless sky. She took the last bite of bread and chewed. "I guess I didn't care whether they treated me like a real person or not."

"I don't care about school. Just do what my mom says and try to keep my little brother out of my hair."

"Dad wanted me to be somebody special. After a while I wanted it too. Not that I cared about good grades all that much at first. Now I really like being somebody special. I'm trying to graduate with all A's. That will mean I'll have *summa cum laude* on my diploma. That means I'll be special."

"Yeah. I have to keep mom from getting mad and beating Bubby when she's lit," Chaney said. "Maybe I'll try harder to do good in school."

Roz got up. "The sooner we start walking; the sooner we reach Cairo," Roz said.

They put their burkas back in place and walked the rest of the day. The only interruption was an old pickup that carried three men in the back. It kicked up a lot of dust.

They coughed, but kept walking.

Sixty-eight

George did a double take as his pickup passed the two burka-clad women.

"What gives?" Pete asked. He was the best tracker in Sudan, so he had the prime position up front.

"Those two don't walk right." George chewed his jaw while he thought about it. "Could it be after all this time I've found 'em?"

"The gals we been chasing?"

"Yep. I swore that no one would get away with putting anything over on me. No one ever has except my twin and that blonde."

"That's only two."

"Can't take out James, not while Mom's alive, but this gal…" He chuckled. But he didn't slow down or stop.

"Why ain't we picking her up?

"She's got to be the slipperiest female ever known. If it's her, don't want to alert her. Gonna need expert help. Not gonna let her escape from me twice."

He didn't add that if it wasn't her, up the road a ways he'd see about what came so naturally to these attention-starved Muslim women. He just showed 'em a little common politeness and let nature do the rest. No sense disturbing the landscape whichever way it ran. He did need to call Carl, though. Shouldn't destroy useful connections.

He pulled his satellite phone off his belt and handed it to Pete. "Here. Punch the second number on my speed dial. Tell the guy that answers that we've probably found her."

Pete did as he'd been told. "We follow the trail on the west side of the river," he said into the phone.

"He say he meet us in Debara in three days, maybe less. And he yell we don't try to catch her." Pete handed the phone back to George.

George laughed. "And why did he say that?"

Pete's face broke into a grin. "He say she too slippery."

Sixty-nine

At their next rest, Roz rubbed her feet and said, "My feet still hurt. Do yours?"

Chaney also messaged her feet. "They don't stop hurting very much."

"Well, they've got to last until we reach Cairo."

"We're gonna need some food before we get there."

"I know," Roz said. But she had no answers, just questions, just needs.

Dear Jesus, please don't let it be too hard for us.

It seemed for just the merest tenth of the blink of an eye, she felt assurance.

The feeling of protection continued even though that same old pickup came down the road, going south this time. The three men in the back seemed more alert than necessary.

At the pickup's passing, Roz's backbone itched as if an alarm had been triggered. Yet she still felt this protected feeling as well. She didn't know what to make of either feeling. She didn't mention it to Chaney.

That evening they stopped walking just outside a village. They hid themselves in a field covered by a grass-like plant almost three feet tall. The heads of grain had started to form in that grass. Surely there were no hyenas this close to a place with lots of people. It would be a good place to sleep.

The loud music of a cricket philharmonic with crocodiles performing hissing roars as a bass section lulled them to sleep.

As the dawn turned from gray to pink, Roz woke to the bawling of oxen and the creaking of primitive wheels. A man with gray hair and a beard to match led the way and behind him came three men who had to be his sons. Each man drove a cart loaded with hay.

"Chaney, wake up! With any luck, here's our ride," she whispered.

Roz pulled her burka over her head and slapped as much dirt as possible out of the black cloth. Chaney did the same. Then she and Chaney fell in line with the wagon of the gray-bearded man. "Pardon me, good father," Roz began.

He had a wary look on his face; she'd better talk fast.

"My husband and our parents were killed and we're making our way to Cairo, where my father had other relatives."

"Cairo?" he said with a frown. "Where is this Cairo?"

"It is far away. Very far away." She breathed a silent 'thank you' to God for not needing to explain that Cairo lay in another country. "May we walk with you to have the safety of your presence? You will not need to concern yourself with us."

"If you want—" The ox on the right side veered off toward the field of grain. Its willing yokemate bawled and also pulled the wagon toward the grain. The man yelled.

Roz grabbed Chaney and rushed to the opposite side of the road.

The man hit the creature on the right shoulder with the three-foot club he carried. When that didn't stop the obstinate cow, he hit it on the nose. The ox got the idea and the pair of bovines returned to their placid pace down the path.

When the man ceased to breathe fast, Roz walked back to him,

"Thank you, good father, for allowing my sister and me this measure of safety. We will take our place at the rear as we should." She added, "My sister does not speak, she is very nearly mute, but I understand her when she makes an attempt."

With that she took Chaney's hand and the two girls stood at the side of the road until the last of the carts passed, then they fell in line behind the carts. "I told him you couldn't speak so that you could be understood. The best thing is for you not to say anything."

"I thought we'd get to ride."

"I hoped, but at least as long as we seem to be part of that man's family, we won't have to worry about being attacked. That's something."

"This is hard." Chaney sniffed, her shoulders bowed and she shuffled along.

Roz patted her shoulder. "We'll get through this. You'll see."

Chaney sniffed many times.

Finally, Roz said, "You know the twenty-third Psalm, don't you?"

Chaney sniffed and nodded. "Sorta."

"Well, you know the part, 'he leads me through the valley of the shadow of death.'"

Chaney nodded.

"That means we're not going to have everything easy."

"That's the truth," Chaney said and sniffed again.

"But even when it's hard, Jesus is up there ahead of us leading us out of the valley. We just have to get through it."

The only interruption to the placid day was that old pickup, going north again. It forced the ox carts to the edge of the road and passed them.

They hadn't walked much more than a mile when they saw it parked by the side of the road. Their little four cart caravan passed by. Roz had that itchy feeling, but saw nothing threatening. Three men struggled to put up a tent and the other two men had walked into the near desert a block or so. They seemed to be looking for something. Probably wood for their fire, Roz thought. There were a few trees in that direction.

Again that night the girls slept near the river, but separate from the elder man and his sons and not close enough to the river to be food for the many crocodiles.

They arose at daybreak and followed the man and his sons.

An hour later, that pickup dogged them again. It came so close to running the girls over that Roz grabbed Chaney and the pair of them walked in the slight ditch on the left side of the road.

Then the unmannerly person squeaked around the wagons by running on a part of the untraveled area on the right side of the road. When the driver reached the elder man at the front of the group, he stopped.

"Pardon, uh, I'm trying to find the, uh, town of Debara. Debara? Know where that is?" The man's Arabic was less understandable than Chaney's.

The father said nothing. Then the ox on the right side veered off toward the grain field again and the father applied himself to controlling his animal as he had done before.

The rude man in the pickup shouted, "Debara. Uh, where?"

The father just looked at the man.

But Roz knew that voice. She whispered, "Chaney, do your best impression of a Sudanese woman. And for heavens' sake don't say anything. That's George."

"Debara?" George demanded.

The father pointed out into the desert. There did seem to be a slight trail that lead out that way and George gunned his pickup out of the palm-shaded roadway into the sun and the desert.

They didn't see George or his pickup again. About noon, the man and his sons turned away from the river toward a small mud-brick house to the west of the road.

Roz put her arm around Chaney and the pair watched the men when they reached the house.

A young woman wearing a scarf greeted them and an older woman, also wearing a scarf, met the gray-haired man who led the troupe. Two small boys came out and danced around one of the younger men.

These men are home. Why have I been denied a home? I didn't ask to be kidnapped; I certainly didn't want Phillip to die.

She wanted to yell at someone.

Since no one volunteered to be yelled at, she hummed her dad's little ditty.

"Stay alive, stay alive."

Seventy

"We're on our own again," Chaney said with a sniff.

Knowing Chaney's penchant for tears, Roz said, "Not to worry. One day we'll be opening the front door of our houses. You'll see."

Then she mumbled to herself, "If it kills me, you'll see."

The day grew hotter. By sundown it seemed that the whole world had turned into a mirage. Even the palms wavered in the heat. Evening and coolness finally came. Their sleeping place that night lay at the edge of a field of wheat that had begun to turn yellow with ripeness.

Roz remembered from a story in the Bible that you could eat grain straight out of the field. If she remembered correctly, you just rubbed the grain in your hands to loosen the outer husk or chaff. Then you blew gently so that the chaff fell from your hand. After that, you put what was left in your mouth, chewed and swallowed.

She pulled off a head of grain, rubbed the grain between her hands and blew away the chaff. A small pile of grain remained. She put it in her mouth and chewed.

"This isn't too bad. It's food." She showed Chaney how to 'hand thrash' wheat.

After her third handful, Chaney said, "It's food. But it's not very good." Then she tucked her feet under her burka and lay back. "G'night, Roz. Don't let the bedbugs bite."

Roz looked up at the stars. They'd make it to Cairo. They'd already reached the Nile. Now they couldn't get lost. That was progress. They'd made real progress.

Thank you, Lord Jesus.

Seventy-one

Outside the village that contained only women, Carl got through the night with no real mishap. After receiving the message from George, he pondered leaving, but decided that wouldn't be the right move for the future "Gun King of Africa." He'd stay right there, get his business with Azibik done. *Then* he'd finish his business with that Okie blonde.

Yeah, he ought to play these times that way.

Once he heard some rustling and a few twigs snapping. He followed his ears and aimed his rifle at the last twig snap. A human-sounding grunt rewarded him. After that he fired twice, but got no sound as pay back.

About sunrise he tried to hit his fire with another piece of the firewood that Sahli left in the wagon for him, The fire was only about six feet from his left front wheel but somehow, he mis-aimed. Coals scattered everywhere.

Brownie danced, but settled down before dragging the cart through the fire. Sahli had done well in choosing this place. If there had been any grass here, he'd have been in a disastrous wildfire.

Shortly before noon, Sighit al Azibik and his men returned, just as his warrior-girl-child said he would. With any luck Azibik had his two hussies and he wouldn't need George and his trackers.

At the meal Azibik invited him to share, his host explained that he found nothing in the Quran that forbad a man from teaching his women to defend themselves.

Azibik said that it had been his most enlightening moment. (Allah be praised!) He realized that if his women could defend themselves, he didn't have to leave men behind to guard them.

"You've trained them well," Carl said.

"That is another reason for needing more guns. If they have a few more rifle women, they'll be safer."

"Since you weren't able to find my slaves, we need to work out a payment arrangement."

They worked out an arrangement. The guns and ammo he'd brought netted him a nice sum of cash. Enough for the rest of the payment on his island. He'd still have his savings in the bank in Alexandria. Somehow, he'd talk Meribet into living on his island. He needed to give time a chance to work it out. That's all.

Two of Azibik's men volunteered to help Carl find the Okie. "I have to tell you she's the craftiest female of her generation. We don't catch her soon, all your wives will learn her secrets and no man on earth will have a decent night or day again… ever."

Another man joined his crew after hearing those words. He arranged for his new crew members to meet the rest of his crew in Debara in two days.

He planned to use that time to find a decent hiding place for his payment from Azibik. He did; it was an eensie cave in a sandstone hill. No one would ever think of looking there. He took the time and the frustration to do GPS on his phone and wrote the numbers on the inside of his belt. He wouldn't be losing that belt or using another one. He'd always have his private bank's location with him.

The four trackers he'd hired might yet find her trail. Surely six or seven men plus his four skilled trackers, plus George and his crew, could catch one Okie female. Didn't matter how smart the flamed slut was. He'd find her and put an end to her.

Let her God bring her back from the dead.

Seventy-two

When the morning light woke Roz and Chaney, they ate a few handfuls of "hand-threshed" grain, made sure there were no crocs at the shore and filled their gourd-canteens with the muddy Nile water.

We're probably getting all sorts of parasites from this mud we're drinking. Can't be helped. We'll have to get rid of the parasites after we reach Cairo...if we can.

A small gray grasshopper landed on Roz's shoulder. She picked it off, intending to throw it down and stomp it. Then she realized that the hair on her arms didn't rise, not very much anyway. While holding the pest by its large hind legs, she turned it to face her and examined its enormous compound eyes and the mouth parts that were already dripping that brown spit.

It's just a bug, not a demon that will kill me, or leave me unable to cope with life.

She grinned, told the creature "Boo!" and let it go.

"If you're ready, we ought to move it," Roz said to Chaney. "We've got miles to go."

"And miles and miles after that," Chaney added and skipped for a few steps.

Roz didn't say anything, just walked, fast.

"You think maybe Carl's found someone else to beat up?" Chaney asked. "George is looking for somebody in Debara. Not here, not looking for us. And we haven't seen any of Sheik Kelmet's men in a long, long time."

Roz laughed. "We'd better hope so. I don't know about you, but I'm really tired of escaping."

"Me too!" the younger girl said. "All we got to do is walk into Cairo. That's how many more days?"

"I think we'll be there in about twenty-three days. But I've probably lost track," Roz said, "The important thing is that we'll make it. God will see that we do. I've got faith in Him."

"Me too!" Chaney took Roz's hand and the two walked on.

Seventy-three

Just outside Debara, Pete's uncle Fisal had a goat ranch of sorts. Carl met George and his trackers there.

Carl left his cart.

Early the next morning, Carl told Fisal, "I'm going to need my cart back, but I won't mind if you use it while it's here." Carl knew the man wouldn't bother it because he didn't have a horse. No goat or even a herd of goats could pull the weight Brownie handled so easily.

Carl told George and his gang. "I've decided. I want one last chance to chase her down by myself. Want you and the trackers to stay here. That's insurance in case she escapes again."

"Not going to forget to call, are you? Wanna see her get et alive by ants," George said.

"Do I forget things like that?" Carl's grin had a hint of an insane Cheshire cat. "Keep your phone handy." He limped over to Brownie.

Carl didn't bother fussing about the beat-up excuse for a saddle that George had picked up for him. He didn't complain about the useless eensie saddlebags either. At least they would hold the roll of duct tape he liked to carry as insurance. He climbed aboard Brownie, splint and all.

George handed him the coil of rope he'd demanded.

"It's good stuff," George said. "Nylon's the best there is."

In his mind, Carl could feel her struggling as he tied her with this nylon rope. With a feeling of relaxation that began at his breastbone and spread clear out to his fingers, he rode off heading north. George had seen her on the Nile trail.

Carl pushed Brownie to a gallop and kept him at it until they reached the Nile. The horse was tired and thirsty by then so he led Brownie to the Nile. He had to shoot a croc that came close while the horse drank and then he let him graze for a bit. Carl's broken leg had begun to ache and so he also needed a break. After that, he mounted up and about two hours later, both his legs had gotten tired, and the broken one ached real bad. He thought about stopping to rest. Then ahead, in the distance, maybe a bit more than half a mile, he saw two burka wearers! Had to be the Okie and that maid of hers. They stood on the river bank looking at something down below.

Carl made a mental list of everything he'd need, or want, to do a satisfying torture. Then with a curse, he peeled off into the desert. He didn't usually miss details, or fail to plan. He'd need to put a sliding loop in that rope…

In the desert, Carl made the loop. Then from the other end of the rope, he cut eight shorter lengths. A tall bush provided eight stakes. He crammed the stakes and short ropes in his too small saddlebags and coiled the long rope over the saddle horn. His next action would be pretending those girls were calves at a rodeo. He'd seen exactly two rodeos while he lived in the states, but he thought he knew how to rope a calf. Can't be that hard to throw a rope over a stupid calf—or two stupid women.

Just as he intended, Carl's rope circled both girls. It only took eight tries.

Seventy-four

Chaney stood and screamed, but all Roz's energy went into getting out of this trap. She'd need more freedom of movement. She wriggled out of her burka and twisted it around her left arm.

Wearing only her undergarment, she grabbed Chaney's arm and ran from their attacker. The rope hit them several times, but she managed to dodge out of it or throw it off each time. Finally the rope slipped over the pair and this time he backed the horse, just like a rodeo calf roper. She couldn't get loose in time.

Dear Jesus, what are we to do now?

It wasn't an audible voice, but she heard it clearly just the same.

Tell him again, how to be saved.

"Won't do any good. But I'll do it if it kills me," she muttered. "And it could—kill me. But You know that."

Carl tied the other end of the rope that held them to the saddle horn. Then he slapped Brownie on the shoulder. The horse moved and the rope squeezed tighter while Carl half-dismounted, half-fell. He limped to Roz.

"You got away from me for the last time." He struck Roz with his open hand.

She would have fallen, but Chaney's attachment to the rope kept her upright. The stinging pain to her face brought involuntary tears.

"I forgive you for that slap and all the other stuff you've done to us." She couldn't keep the quiver out of her voice. "I have some good news you need to hear."

He hit her again, in the stomach this time.

Dizzy and sick, she managed to whisper, "I forgive you."

With a growl, he grabbed her left wrist and though she struggled, he tied one of the short ropes to it. Her right wrist got the same treatment. Roz noticed his hand's tremor and wondered at it.

"Lay down, both of you."

When they didn't lie down, he hit Roz in the stomach again. When she sank to her knees, Chaney also fell and screamed, of course.

He held the ropes on Roz's wrists while loosening the long rope. When it cleared her head, he shouted at the horse. The animal shied away and the long rope went taut around the screeching Chaney's waist.

With his boot, Carl pushed both girls down so that they lay flat on their backs. A nearby rock became a hammer and he pounded two stakes into the dirt and tied Roz's arms to them.

Chaney, still attached to the long rope and the horse beyond, yelled and screamed as if she were being murdered with a dull knife.

"Really, I have very good news to tell you." Despite her pain and her body's need to throw up, Roz tried to be as earnest as she'd ever been.

"When Jesus died, He took all your sins away."

"Shut up! Stupid slit, ain't never was no Jesus."

She knew what would happen next and it did. He kicked her with his splinted leg. It hurt bad. He fell backwards and landed with a grunt and a curse.

But things grew dark for Roz and she couldn't breathe. She'd knocked the breath out of herself before and knew how to handle this time of no breath. Except it had never hurt this bad; never had she faded all the way.

"Dear Lord," she murmured as the lights went out.

Carl wrestled himself to a vertical position. "There ain't no God!" he yelled.

With her throat constricted and rattling, Roz drew in a little air and the light grew.

"Every bad thing you've done has been paid for by Jesus when he died on the cross." She had to draw a breath. "You have a clean slate if you want it. I'm not kidding."

"I'm not kidding either… you keep it up and I might just shoot you and be done."

"If you'd repent—that means quit doing things you know aren't right—"

Carl growled and stomped over to his horse.

"And tell God you want to make Jesus your Lord—"

He reached in the saddlebag and came out with a roll of duct tape.

"And that you believe he really did come back from the dead the third day after they killed—"

Still growling, Carl stomped back, tore off a piece of tape a little less than six inches long, and though his hands shook, he slammed that piece of tape down on Roz's mouth. He tore off another longer piece and applied it more carefully to her mouth.

"You keep it up and the next piece goes over your nose. Understand?"

Out of options, she nodded.

Lord Jesus, I tried.

Carl went to work on tying down Roz's ankles. She fought him and tried to keep him from tying her legs tightly.

"Be still," he said.

If I could knock him out with a kick…

She tried her best.

"Maybe I'll take my time…maybe you want the treatment you got on the boat." He massaged her calf and knee with shaky hands. "We aims to please." His laugh had a strained quality.

Fear…somehow she knew he was afraid of her. She didn't care whether his hands shook with fear or with Parkinson's, she didn't want him touching her like that. She made noises and shook her head no. Then she lay still.

He laughed and tied her legs to the two stakes he'd hammered into the ground for that purpose.

"That's a good girl." He chuckled. "You ain't my type for lovin'. For killin', yeah, lovin' nah. Too ugly and too blonde. Blondes make me puke."

He wouldn't tell her that tomorrow George would be here and that man had stamina. He'd wear her out. Then if George felt generous, some of his crew would have a go at her—at the other one too.

"I'm tired of messing with you. You done got on my last nerve for the last time."

When they all got through with her, then the ants would enjoy her a while. Didn't really need anything long and drawn out. Couple, three days, that's all.

"Take that black thing off," he told Chaney.

Chaney got the same tie-down treatment as Roz. It took considerably less time because she screamed and cried, but didn't offer even one moment of fight.

"Comfy, ladies?" Carl said with a laugh. "Sleep real good."

Carl used the last of the sunset's glow to find sticks and other woody trash for his fire. Then he did his camp chores. He made the smallest of fires. After that, he patted the horse's neck and put the saddle back on.

"We gonna keep the saddle on this time. Not taking any chances on that gal. She tries to escape, you get to run 'er down, like an old fashioned warhorse."

Chaney screamed, and Carl laughed at her.

"Yeah, you get to flatten her under your hooves, hear her bones crack. Not many horses of today get to feel real blood under their hooves. Now that's a good trade for a little extra saddle time, ain't it?" Rifle in hand, he mounted up.

Chaney screamed and cried. In her useless way, she flailed around, tried to get loose.

He laughed again, put the rifle in his lap and sighed. Soon his head nodded forward and his shoulders followed.

Roz lay absolutely still and watched this strange proceeding. Chaney still cried and tried to twist herself loose. Maybe that was a good thing. If she made noise, then Roz's noise wouldn't be so noticeable.

Getting loose wouldn't be easy. But he hadn't tied her as tightly as he might have. She knew her leg ropes had some play. She'd use that. First she needed to make sure he wasn't playing 'possum, that he really slept. She waited awhile. Let him be deeply asleep.

Please Lord.

Chaney stopped crying and only sniffed a lot. Then finally, she snored that whistle-sigh.

Seventy-five

A hyena's yodel sounded to the east and then another one. If that didn't wake him, Roz decided he must be ocean deep into his alpha rhythm.

Using her feet, she pushed herself upwards. Now she had more slack in the ropes on her arms. She pulled, yanked hard, yet she couldn't get enough play on those ropes. He'd been good at tying her.

Doesn't matter. It wasn't sunrise and he still slept...

She had time, precious time, to use. She pushed upward with her feet and twisted her body to the right to give a little bit more play on that rope. Many times she pulled and then suddenly the stake on her right wrist shot out of the earth, flew up then down, straight into her eye. She barely blinked her eyes closed before that piece of wood hit her.

She yelped—or would have. The tape covering her mouth kept the sound inside.

Thank you for the tape, Lord.

Quiet beyond stealth, Roz reached over and untied her left wrist, then untied the loose rope on her right. She sat up and untied her ankles. While watching for anything that wasn't as it ought to be, she removed the tape from her mouth.

She thought about waking Chaney and having her lob a rock at this thug's head. But no. The girl had gained strength, but she couldn't throw a big rock high enough to do any good. Chaney would be a liability to their escape, no matter what happened.

She thought some more. Maybe if she took a rock and hammered his bad leg.

But no. She didn't want to hurt the man. No matter what he'd done to her, she wouldn't hurt him if she could help it. God wouldn't like it.

Carl still sat on the horse, still slept the sleep of a babe in a warm bed. Still held the rifle loosely across his lap.

And then, she knew exactly what to do.

First, she put her hand over Chaney's mouth and shook her. When the girl woke, Roz kept her hand over the teen's mouth and only removed it when Chaney nodded that she understood. Then Roz untied the ropes that bound Chaney and pointed toward a boulder far enough away for the young teen's safety.

By the light of the fire's embers, Roz's fingers found some soft green plants. She pulled up all she found. Now she'd have the horse's attention and momentary obedience.

While it nibbled at her hand, she approached the horse's side. Her smile had no more joy in it than a hyena's laugh.

Slowly she reached up, grabbed the rifle.

He woke up, but she expected he would.

She danced out of range of his grabbing fists. He still had his revolver. Quick, before he could react, she backed further away. Further into the dark, harder for him to see, to aim.

"Throw the pistol down," she ordered.

"Gal, you think I'm that stupid?"

"You throw the gun down or I'll shoot you."

The words he said had no real meaning, just curses.

Roz responded with a shot, vaguely in Carl's direction, but she didn't intend it to wound him. Just motivate him.

"Throw that gun on the ground. Then we'll talk."

More curses.

Another shot, this one with a little closer aim.

"I don't know how many shots I've got before I run out of bullets." She cocked the rifle again, this time with as much noise as she could coax out of it. "Since I don't know, I'll just have to make the next one count."

His curses seemed less assured.

"The pistol…put it on the ground."

He did nothing.

"Shooting on the count of three. One…"

Nothing

"Two…"

"Awww, here." He threw it at her with the obvious intent of hitting her, thereby causing her to lose focus, or something.

It cartwheeled toward her and landed just in front of her.

"You're very accurate. Did you ever think of taking up pitching? Maybe a sandlot league to start, but you could have a future."

He growled and cursed.

She shouldn't goad him. "That wasn't nice. I apologize, Okay?" She picked up the pistol and tried to figure out how to carry it when she had neither pockets or belt. She needed both hands to work the rifle.

"Chaney, make a big circle around him. Big enough so he can't grab you and come stand by me. I need your help."

Chaney seemed to take forever to reach her.

"Okay?" Chaney said when she finally stood by Roz.

"Hold this pistol. You don't have to aim it, just hold it. At least for now."

"I can't shoot him?"

"We're not taking any pages out of his book. Do you understand me? We're Christians. We don't do things like that—unless he forces us by attacking."

"Okay," Chaney drawled and Roz returned her attention to Carl.

"Now, get off the horse," Roz ordered her prisoner.

More curses.

"I could still shoot you."

He cursed, but dismounted with his good foot in the stirrup and then, when his bad leg reached the ground and he put weight on it, he fell.

He fought his way to a vertical stance. Then Roz noticed that the eastern sky had begun to lighten just a little. Carl faced her; he couldn't see it. They'd need to get out of there before daylight gave him an opportunity for surprises. But how? How could she delay his coming after them?

She didn't want to tie him. There were too many creatures who would like a free meal. She ought to at least give him some leverage.

Seventy-six

But his splinted leg...

"Sit down," she said.

"Awww."

She cut him off. "I mean it. I could try to shoot your other knee. Of course I might miss. I could miss two ways...I might miss your leg entirely, or I might miss and go too high—hit an artery or maybe something you think is equally precious."

"Awww." He sat and spouted unintelligible words.

"Unbuckle your splint."

Cursing, more violent than before.

She raised the rifle. "Maybe I should let Chaney handle you. She's wanted to ever since you beat her so bad when we were on that slave ship you ran. Maybe I'll just tell her to go ahead."

Carl continued his cursing, but unbuckled his splint.

He unbuckled the last buckle.

"Toss it to me."

He pitched it more or less toward the two girls.

"Chaney, give me the pistol and get his splint, please?"

"Can't I shoot his foot first?" She sighted down the barrel. "Just his toe?"

"Please, give me the gun."

"Okay," Chaney drawled. With a sigh, she put the pistol in Roz's hand and stomped over to the splint. Roz carefully put the rifle on the sand and kept the pistol aimed at him.

"Careful, don't get too close to him."

"I'm not." Chaney looked at Roz. "You don't have to be so bossy."

Carl erupted into action and grabbed the younger girl's left ankle.

This time Chaney turned on her attacker. First she screamed, then she bit his ear and hung on to his ear with her teeth while scratching at his face and neck with both hands.

He let her go to protect his eyes.

"Get away, now while you can," Roz said.

For once, Chaney obeyed. She jumped away from him. "Yuck, phooey, yuck." Chaney had Carl's blood all over her face. She spat. "He tastes worse than a snake." She spat again. "Yuck!"

Carl reached up and felt. The he let out an outraged scream. "You bit my ear off."

"Don't be such a baby," Roz said. She couldn't help her grin.

"Scoot back about ten feet," she told Carl.

When he complied, she told Chaney, "Be more careful, grab the splint and come back over here with it."

Chaney did as asked, but with a drawled "Okay."

The sky had definitely lightened.

Roz ordered Carl to move back another ten feet—ten feet further from the horse. She thought she saw God's plan for getting them at least closer to Cairo.

"Chaney, let's blow this place." Roz grabbed the horse's reins. "Think you can climb up into that saddle and scrunch up toward the front so I can climb on behind you?"

Chaney put one foot in the stirrup.

"Be sure to take the splint with you. Please." Chaney went back and picked up the splint, climbed into the saddle.

Carl cursed again.

"Don't worry," she told him. "We're Christians. We wouldn't think of stealing your horse. We're just borrowing him as payment for our pain and suffering. This is in lieu of suing you."

"Okay, I'm ready," Chaney said.

"We'll leave your horse in one of the villages to the north along the Nile trail, say a couple, maybe three days away. We'll take your splint up the trail a little. You'll be able to crawl to it in ten minutes or so. Just follow our trail…we won't try to hide it…that far at least."

"Let's go," Chaney urged.

"But my horse? I can't go anywhere without my horse. I'll die."

"I said we'll leave him up the trail."

"Where?"

"You'll just have to keep looking. Probably have to pay for his keep. But we'll leave him in some village."

"We could shoot him; he isn't gonna stop chasing us. Besides, he's a bad tasting, two-legged snake," Chaney insisted.

"Christians don't go around shooting people."

"But my horse?" Carl bellowed. "I need my horse."

"Guess I'd better tell whoever we give him to that his owner has frizzy red hair. Not many like you in this country. You'll be easy to identify." Roz threw both burkas over Chaney's lap, mounted up and took both the rifle and the revolver with her.

The horse danced as if he would like to run, but Roz held his reins in tight and wouldn't let him.

"One last time, I'm going to tell you God's plan to save you. If you're impolite, and don't listen, I might stop, or I guess I could do a little target shooting. I used to be pretty good. But that was a year ago and I haven't had time to practice lately."

"Awww!"

"Listen to me, it's important. Sin is a fact."

Carl said nothing.

"Sin is doing bad things." She paused, "It's more, but understanding that much will do for now."

"Because of sin we can't be friends with God. And because of sin, bad things happen to us that shouldn't have. Often we don't get the good things that should have happened.

"One thing nobody mentions very much is that we have an eternal spirit. That spirit can't ever die. After these bodies of ours die, our spirit has to go somewhere. If we're God's friends, we get to go to heaven and there we have an eternal life filled with all the enjoyment and all the good things we could ever want.

"But if we aren't God's friends, He won't let us in His perfect heaven. Instead we have to go where God isn't. That's called hell."

Carl mumbled something under his breath.

"But God loves us so, so much that He fixed the whole sin problem. He sent God, the Son to earth as a human…we call him Jesus. Jesus lived for thirty-three years without ever committing even one sin. Then, to pay for our sin, He, the sinless man, died the horrible death of a criminal. He did it so we wouldn't have to. And three days later, as proof that God's judgment was satisfied, God brought Jesus back to life.

"We know God brought Jesus back to life because when Jesus died, soldiers who made their living killing people examined Jesus to make sure He really was dead. Back then, if a criminal got away from the soldiers, the soldiers would be killed. So we know the soldiers wouldn't take chances; Jesus really did die."

Roz knew she talked fast but she couldn't help herself. He had to hear it all.

"At least five hundred people saw Jesus alive again after God brought Him back to life. Then He left the earth and lives with God, the Father in heaven until the time when He will come back to earth to rule it.

"Many of those five hundred people who saw Him alive again, died horrible deaths like being burned alive or pulled apart by horses because they wouldn't say that His coming back to life was a lie. That includes all but one of the eleven men who were closest to Him, the ones we call Apostles. That one Apostle, who didn't die by torture, lived much of a long life in jail.

"All God asks of you is that you repent. Repent means stop doing things you know are wrong and believe that Jesus really did die, but He's alive again and is coming back to earth to be its King when God, the Father says it's time.

"If you would say you believe what I just told you then—"

Grotesque, inhuman sounds came from Carl's throat. He leaped up and tried to reach them by hopping, but fell and then tried to crawl to them.

Roz let the horse move a few yards.

"I told you where I'd leave your splint and your horse." Roz signaled the horse to go but stopped him about a hundred feet away—and dropped the splint.

When the horse had traveled another hundred feet, she said, "I wouldn't leave you without protection," she shouted. "Here's your guns." She tossed the pistol in a clump of grass ten or so feet away. Then she leaned over as close to the ground as she could and dropped the rifle with the barrel up, to keep out as much dirt as possible. Then she gave the horse a little kick and the two girls rode away."

"Ow," Chaney complained. "You're pinching my leg."

Roz sighed and moved further back on the saddle, but her mind began figuring the days to Cairo at the hiking rate of twenty miles a day. If she were somewhere near accurate in her distance estimate, at twenty miles a day, they had about twenty-one days. Twenty-one days of Chaney's griping. Surely a horse could do sixty miles a day. With a horse, they might reach Cairo in as little as a week!

"We're not quite through," she told Chaney and turned the horse back the way they came.

"Wait, why we going back there? We need to go the other way," Chaney protested.

Roz didn't answer her.

The man had already crawled within fifty feet of his splint.

"I've changed my mind. We'll need your horse for about a week, maybe a few days more. That means he'll be waiting for you somewhere close to Cairo.

"Of course, when we get to Cairo, I'll tell every law enforcement officer who'll give me half an ear what you and your gang have done." She paused, tried to think of anything else she should say. Nothing came to mind.Are we ever going to go?" Chaney asked.

"Chaney, just think, in a week or so, you'll be at the embassy eating a hamburger."

Roz gave the horse a gentle kick.

"Cairo, here we come."

Meet

Mona Jean Reed

Mona Jean Reed is a Christian, an optimist and a romantic. She loves to write and to teach. Her hobbies are gardening, history, cooking and having fun—she likes to host parties. She regards life as one big adventure. When things aren't adventurous enough in real life, she has a solution for that—just write someone else's story. Mona Jean gets attached to her characters, so this is probably not the last we'll see of Roz.

VISIT OUR WEBSITE
FOR THE FULL INVENTORY
OF QUALITY BOOKS:

http://www.wings-press.com

*Quality trade paperbacks and downloads
in multiple formats,
in genres ranging from light romantic comedy to general
fiction and horror. Wings has something
for every reader's taste.
Visit the website, then bookmark it.
We add new titles each month!*

Made in the USA
Lexington, KY
20 September 2015